FAR LESS

by

KATHY WOLLENBERG

THE PRESS AT
CAL POLY HUMBOLDT

FAR

LESS

The Press at Cal Poly Humboldt

Cal Poly Humboldt Library

1 Harpst Street

Arcata, California 95521-8299

press@humboldt.edu

press.humboldt.edu

Cover image art by Sarah Whorf

Cover design and layout by Amanda Alster

Layout by Carolyn Delevich & Maximilian Heirich

ISBN: 978-1-947112-33-9

LCCN: 2020931746

To my father, Skip Wollenberg 1933-2010.

Thanks for still standing guard.

Chapter 1

JESSE rolled from under the damp blankets into the duff. He pulled on his shoes and, like a dog after a swim, shook his body to shed any redwood needles and dirt that had accumulated on his clothes during the night. He'd slept in his sweatshirt and jacket but still felt cold. Lizzie looked cold too, huddled in blankets on the ground next to their mother. At least she was asleep. Jesse didn't want to disrupt his sister before he needed to. He checked his watch. There wasn't much time before he had to get her to school. He'd be quick, he thought as he tugged off the hood of his sweatshirt and started running the forest trail to the crest, sluggishly at first, then faster, trying to throw off a lingering dream.

At the top of the hill, Jesse wound his way through a cluster of ferns to the base of a small, familiar redwood. The lowest branch was an easy reach, and from there he climbed the tree, limb after limb, to the spindly crown. It was always a rush, straddling the wispy branches and then making the blind leap to a thick sturdy branch of the massive, neighboring tree.

"Keep three points attached to the tree at all times," Jesse was advised when he first learned to climb. "And don't look down."

Jesse moved up the big tree, climbing hand, foot, hand, through the maze of coarse, barky limbs. He reached the top and wrapped his legs monkey-style around two branches. His mother always warned, "Don't climb all the way up, Jess, it's not safe." He ignored her voice in his head. Why shouldn't he? She ignored him. He was sure that swaying in the wind at the top of a redwood was safer than what she was doing on the ground.

Everything was so clear to him from this lofty precipice, not just the view, which was vast and crisp. His thoughts and dreams seemed clearer—almost attainable—from this vantage. Even the line of fog in the distance seemed defined. Beyond the forest was the small college town of Arcata. Orderly streets and cottage-style houses lined the roads down to the marsh. Beyond the marsh, Humboldt Bay spread out wide and smooth to the blue line of ocean.

From his perch in the tree branches, Jesse liked to imagine walking into any one of those cottages and calling it home. He pictured Lizzie there too, working at a puzzle on the floor. Sometimes he went as far as to imagine furniture. The hardest thing to conjure up was his mom. He could place her in the house somewhere, maybe passed out on a bed or ratty couch. He'd get a glimpse of her making dinner in an imaginary kitchen, but when he zoomed in, there would be a needle or a bottle of booze, or something else, to shatter his vision. This tree was shelter his mother couldn't spoil or take away, the way she'd sabotaged every home they'd had since he was a toddler.

The scratchy tree bark and the musty dirt smell of the forest always sparked memories of climbing with Redwood Jack, Lizzie's dad. He could hear Jack's voice in his head.

"Hold on tight, Jess!'

"Check out this beetle, Jess!"

"Look there, Jess, a red-tailed hawk!"

And then, like the hawk, Jack had vanished, leaving Jesse to climb alone and his mom tired and pregnant with Lizzie. Jesse was seventeen now. In a few months his mom wouldn't have any say in what he did. She didn't really have any say now; she only noticed him when she wasn't high, and lately it seemed like she was high most of the time. If Jack were still around, Jesse might have the nerve to leave his mom and sister, but there was no one else to watch Lizzie when their mom was completely lit or off sleeping with some guy. He couldn't leave. Not without Lizzie, and she still needed their mother, at least for now.

Fog rolled in over the dunes that separated the ocean from the bay, like a foamy ribbon encroaching on the shore. It wouldn't take long for the blanket of air to travel across the bay and up the hill to the crest, where it would settle into the trees—a cold gray mist that could penetrate the fabric of any jacket Jesse owned.

He needed to get Lizzie to school, and then he should probably go to school himself, though he would be late. He started his descent. Maybe he would ditch school and head to the university library, get back to that native plant book he'd been absorbed in. So many of the forest plants were edible, and he'd found some of them around their camp. He'd cooked salal berries in a pot over the fire with a little sugar. Lizzie had eaten most of the gooey mixture, scraping the pot with the spoon and then licking the inside of the cooled vessel.

"You're like a little bear cub," he'd said. She'd smiled, her mouth and cheeks smeared red with salal juice.

Jesse climbed down the tree fast. He had the tree memorized, the branches were so familiar he could have named them: tough, gnarly, bulgy, scrawny. He reached the bottom branch, still thirty feet above ground. This is where he made the traverse to the top of the smaller redwood. He stretched a leg out to a branch on the adjacent tree and, with a quick lunging movement, landed on the smaller tree. Heart thumping, he climbed down, jumping the last several feet into the spongy duff.

***

"Lizzie, wake up." He shook her shoulder gently. She was snuggled against their mother, covered in the mound of damp blankets. "Let's go," he whispered.

He didn't want to wake his mom. She'd pretend they were normal, that she cared about breakfast and school. Jesse put his finger to his lips and pulled Lizzie from the tangle of bedding. She yawned. She was still wearing her tennis shoes and jacket. They had extra clothes in the duffel bag behind the stump, but there wasn't time to change her.

"Hop on," he whispered, as he squatted down. She climbed onto his back and wrapped her little arms around his neck, nuzzling her face against his cheek. Lizzie kicked him lightly with her shoes and he took off galloping, winding his way through the narrow maze of fern-lined trails that led to an open, grassy field and the park below.

"I wanna see Bennie," Lizzie said, pointing to the man sitting on one of the park benches a few yards away, his two dogs lying devotedly at his feet.

"Good morning, goin' to school?" Ben called. He was one of the older homeless guys, someone Jesse trusted. He'd been around for years, not like the younger guys who came and went after a month or two. Ben was a fixture.

"Bennie!" Lizzie beamed. "Put me down, Jess. I wanna pet Toby and Emma."

"No, we're gonna be late."

"Go on now, Lizzie. Get to school." Ben's dog got up and sniffed Jesse's shoes as they passed Ben's bench.

"Can I give them a treat after school?" Lizzie asked.

"Yeah, yeah, sweetheart. Now, scat!" Ben waved his hand.

"Here. Eat one of these," Jesse said, pulling a crumpled granola bar from his pocket, something he'd snagged the day before from the cafeteria. Lizzie grabbed the bar with one hand still holding on like a barnacle to Jesse's back as he loped through the park, darting between the swing sets and slides.

When he reached the road he picked up speed and trotted steadily into town past some of the same homes he'd spotted from the crown of the big tree. Jesse slowed his pace to a walk when a door opened and three kids flooded out to a porch followed by their mom who herded them into a car like an experienced cattle dog. He felt an ache in his stomach and somewhere higher in his chest. It didn't do any good to feel jealous. His mom didn't have those maternal instincts, canine or otherwise. He started running again, fast, towards the school.

***

"Here you are, Chipmunk." Jesse said, depositing Lizzie on the curb.

The principal, Miss Eppers, always out front in the morning directing traffic, walked towards them. "Lizzie, did you get breakfast?" Lizzie held up the half-eaten bar. "That looks good. How about some milk to go with it?"

Lizzie reached for Jesse. He bent down and gave her a kiss on the forehead. Her hair smelled of redwood dirt and something sour, like milk gone bad.

"Have a good day, Lizard. I'll pick you up from aftercare at three-thirty, okay?" He walked backwards, waving.

He knew Miss Eppers would take Lizzie to an aide who would wash her face and hands in the staff bathroom, maybe even check her head for lice and change her into clean clothes. Then, miraculously, Lizzie's own clothes would reappear on her in a couple of days. Jesse wondered if it bothered Lizzie to be pulled aside like that, or if she thought it was normal and all kids were given the same treatment. He had vivid memories of teachers doing the same thing for him when he was young, and he remembered hating being treated differently than the other kids. Still, it was good to know Lizzie was getting cleaned up. It wasn't easy getting a shower for Lizzie or his mom. He could shower at school, and recently he'd found a way to get into the locker room at the university. The university showers were the best—the water was hot enough to thaw out his cold limbs after a night on the forest floor.

He arrived at school twenty minutes late. "Go to the office, Jesse," his math teacher said and pointed at the door. "Actually, just sit down, you've missed enough already."

Jesse squeezed into a seat at the back of the classroom. He liked math. It didn't take him long to figure out what Mr. Harris was explaining on the board. Jesse's problem was homework. It was impossible to get his assignments done in the woods. He tried to go to the university library as much as possible, but usually had to wait until Lizzie and his mom were asleep, and by then it was late. Jesse hated leaving Lizzie alone with their mom anytime, but he rarely left unless they were sleeping. When his mom was conked out, she stayed out of trouble.

"The midterm is next Friday, so I want everyone to review the quizzes and come to me with questions." Mr. Harris was weaving through the aisles handing out review packets. "The last page of the review is a pop quiz. Surprise!" The students groaned.

"Do your best. You can leave class when you're done."

Jesse tore off the back page from the review packet and perused the quiz. It was easy. He finished early and headed for the door. "Jesse," Mr. Harris said in an angry whisper, "I need you to get here on time. I haven't gotten any homework from you in over two weeks. I need it turned in on Monday. No excuses!"

Jesse knew he wouldn't have the math homework done by Monday. There were too many other assignments that were more pressing; besides, he understood this math. As long as he continued to do well on the tests, he would pass.

"Yeah," Jesse said, and went out the door, walking fast

toward the gym. If he hurried, he could take a shower before his next class.

The basketball coach came in as Jesse was fumbling with his locker combination. "Hey, what are you doing in here during class?" Mr. Lewis asked.

"I got out of math early, sir. I was gonna take a quick shower before history."

Mr. Lewis glanced at his watch. "You should only be in here during PE."

"I know, sorry. I went for a run before school and I'm all sweaty."

"Don't let this happen again," Mr. Lewis warned as he turned to leave.

"Thanks, sir," Jesse said. He left his clothes in a heap on the floor and ran to the shower clutching a towel and a bottle of Dollar Store shampoo.

Ms. Nola was already lecturing when Jesse got to history class, his brown, shoulder-length hair still dripping wet. She looked over her shoulder at Jesse and held up two fingers, indicating that he had used up two of the three late arrivals she allowed. She glared at him sternly and went back to delivering her lecture.

At noon, most of the kids left campus to get food in town. Jesse got the free lunch, often having seconds and pocketing as many granola bars and pieces of fruit as he could.

"Here you go." Alma, the kitchen lady, plopped a huge helping of lasagna onto his plate.

Jesse took the tray and sat down in the nearly empty cafeteria. He ate quickly.

"Hey, Jesse," said Finn, a boy Jesse had known since fifth grade, as he walked past the table.

"Hi." Jesse lifted a hand. He liked Finn and some of the other boys he'd known in grade school. They used to shoot hoops at recess, and occasionally he'd been invited to spend the night at one of the boys' houses. But by the time Jesse was in middle school, he'd backed away from the boys. They had started asking questions about his life. Questions Jesse didn't want to answer.

A blonde girl he'd noticed before sat down across from him. "Hi," Jesse said, a little surprised that she'd chosen to sit at his empty table. The girl pulled a sandwich and an apple from her backpack. "Why are you eating in here when you have your own lunch?" Jesse regretted asking the question as soon as the words left his mouth.

"Actually," she said, unwrapping her sandwich, "I got in trouble a couple of weeks ago. I'm not allowed to leave campus until after Christmas break. Can you believe it? Just for drinking a little alcohol on the Ashland trip." She took a bite of her sandwich. "What'd you do?" she asked, her mouth still full.

"Nothing, I just like the fine cuisine," he said, and stabbed a pile of green beans with his fork.

"You stay on campus at lunch, like, voluntarily?"

"Pretty much." Jesse wiped his mouth with a napkin. "I mean, I kinda like it here. It's peaceful." He looked around the barren cafeteria, only a few kids dotting the dozens of tables.

"What's your name?" the girl asked. "I've seen you around."

"Jesse." He smiled. He'd seen her too, but he rarely made an effort to get to know other kids. It always ended in them getting too nosey.

"I'm Raya," she said. "Or just Ray."

"Nice to meet you, Raya, or Ray." Jesse thought the name suited her. She was a bright light in this otherwise drab building. Her hair hung loose around her neck like streams of blond silk. She looked at him from across the table, her eyes the same denim color as her jeans.

"Do you want an apple?" She held out a small, scabby, misshapen piece of fruit.

"That's a funny-looking apple."

Raya tossed it into the air, and Jesse snatched it easily.

"They're from our place down in Briceland. We have an orchard and tons of apples right now. I'm gonna make pies this weekend."

Jesse sank his teeth into the apple. It was sweet and crisp, like a strawberry had mated with an apple and given birth to something succulent and crunchy.

"Good, huh?" Raya asked.

Jesse turned the apple in his hand, examining the mottled skin. "Guess you can't judge an apple by its skin."

"They've always been super sweet." Raya held another deformed fruit and bit into it. Two girls walked towards them from the doorway. "Raya, we got you a brownie from the Co-op, gluten-free!" It was the tall girl Jesse had seen Raya with around campus, and there was a short blonde too. He'd seen them for years but hadn't paid attention to their names. The girls walked over and presented the brownie to Raya. "Now you can't be mad that we deserted you," said the tall girl, glancing at Jesse and narrowing her eyes.

Raya took the brownie without saying thank you. "Nice to meet you, Jesse. Maybe I'll see you tomorrow." She crumpled up her lunch bag and stood.

"Tomorrow's Saturday, so you'll probably be at home making pies." Jesse smiled. "Oh, my God," Raya said, blushing. "Well, maybe I'll see you Monday."

The tall friend pulled Raya by the arm. "Come on, Raya. We gotta get to Spanish. Were you flirting?" she asked, loudly enough for Jesse to hear. "Cuz it looked like you were flirting."

Jesse watched the girls walk away. He wrapped what was left of the apple in a napkin, tucking it into his backpack. He wanted Lizzie to taste the sweet, crunchy fruit sealed up under that mottled skin.

As soon as Jesse's last class ended he took off running toward Lizzie's school. It was only a mile away, but Lizzie got out twenty minutes before he did. When he reached Coastal Elementary he was sweaty and out of breath. Even though

Jesse always told Lizzie to go to aftercare, she rarely did. He sprinted around the last corner to the school. She wasn't on the grass playing with the other kids. He scanned the school fence line, searching for her, when he heard a distinctive clucking. He looked up into the big laurel tree in the corner of the school grounds; there, nestled into the yellowing leaves, was Lizzie, cawing like a baby raven.

"Whatcha doin', Chipmunk?" Jesse asked from the base of the tree. He'd taught her to imitate birds they heard in the forest, and her raven call had gotten pretty good. He held his arms up, and Lizzie scooted off the branch and fell into Jesse's embrace. He swung her around to his back where she settled onto the lump of his pack. "Hold on tight," he said, as he took off running.

"Wait!" called Miss Eppers, coming toward them. "Jesse, a woman offering free backpacks came by today. Even shoes and a set of clothes. I helped Lizzie pick out some things. They're in this pack." Miss Eppers held up a pale pink backpack with a yellow hibiscus print. Lizzie reached for the pack.

"The lady was so nice, Jess!" Lizzie tapped her finger on Jesse's shoulder to emphasize her point. "And she says we can call her if we need more stuff. Even stuff for you."

"I'm fine, Liz." Jesse shifted his weight from side to side, he could feel the muscles in his jaw tighten. "We'd better get home. Thanks, Miss Eppers."

"Sure, Jesse, tell your mom to come by and talk to me."

"Uh, she's been sick, got bad bronchitis right now, but I'll tell her. Ready, Liz? Here we go." Jesse started a slow run towards camp.

***

"Mama, wake up. Look what I got!" Lizzie slid off Jesse's back and ran to the lump of blankets that covered their mother. It was four o'clock in the afternoon.

"What is it, baby?" Carla's voice was thin and raspy.

"Look…" Lizzie pulled new shoes and clothes out of the backpack. "I got flash shoes!" She hammered the shoes on the redwood duff, and the heels flashed a series of red blinks. "This is my favorite." Lizzie held up a green T-shirt with a grey kitten silk-screened on the front. "Isn't it cute?" she exclaimed, hugging the shirt.

"Cute," Carla agreed. "Who hooked you up?"

"A really nice lady. She said she could get stuff for Jess, too."

"I don't need shoes or a backpack, Liz. I already got 'em," Jesse said, lifting his tennis-shoed foot. He sat next to their little fire ring coaxing the coals that had been smoldering since morning.

"Jess, if she offers you stuff, take it—we can always trade it for something." Carla sat up and pushed the mat of dark, greasy hair from her face.

"Yeah, we can always trade a backpack for a couple hits of something for you, Mom," he stabbed at the coals with a short stick.

"Don't say that shit in front of Lizzie." Carla got up and stumbled to the bushes where she squatted to pee.

"Yeah, like you never do stuff in front of her," Jesse mumbled. He didn't want to hurt Lizzie, but sometimes his anger at his mom erupted like a volcano gone suddenly active, spewing lava.

Lizzie was still contentedly digging through her new pack. "Look Mama, bars!" Lizzie held up a Zip-lock bag full of protein bars. "Can I eat one now? It could be like an after-school snack, like Hana has when she gets home from school."

"Hana probably doesn't eat bars for her snack," Jesse said.

"Jess, don't ruin it for her. Of course you can, sweetie," Carla said, sitting down cross-legged by the fire. "Come here, I'll have a bite." Carla patted the ground next to her.

Watching his mom take food from his sister was more than he could stand. Carla was supposed to be providing for them, not mooching off of Lizzie's private stash of bars. "This is bullshit, Mom!" Jesse stood. "I'm gonna get firewood," he mumbled.

"Hmmm, it's good, Jess. Have a bite," Carla said, holding a half-eaten bar toward him.

"I'm not hungry," he lied, and headed away from camp, deeper into the woods.

Breathe, he thought, *just breathe and you'll feel better.*

He started running uphill through the maze of redwood trunks, brushing past massive ferns the size of small cars and old-growth tree stumps covered with huckleberry. He kept running up, up, up. It felt good to breathe hard, so hard he couldn't think about anything but the air filling his lungs and the steady pumping of his legs. When he reached the ridge he stopped and leaned over, hands on his knees, while he caught his breath. His head felt clear. That suffocating feeling he got around his mother had subsided. He focused on finding the big tree on the ridge that he wanted to climb. It took a while to locate the tree, but when he saw it he knew it was the one he'd spotted from the perch of a smaller tree near camp. This tree stood out. Not only was it the tallest on the ridge, but its girth and crown were thicker and more developed than those of the surrounding trees.

Jesse walked to the base of the tree and stared up into the mass of branches. He couldn't see the top; surrounding trees blocked his view. There was no small tree from which Jesse could launch onto a low limb of the big redwood but there was a tall old-growth stump. Maybe he could jump from the top of the stump and grab onto a bottom limb of the big tree.

There were fissures in the silver flanks of the weathered stump and Jesse shimmied up the side until he reached a crack big enough to squeeze into the interior of the hollowed trunk. The inside was sloped and slippery with moss and small ferns growing from dark crevasses. Jesse continued his slow shimmy upward. He pulled himself onto the slivered top and straddled the jagged edge of the stump. This ledge was way up, maybe forty feet above the ground. It was a precarious perch with nothing to hold onto, but Jesse had good balance and no real fear of heights. He squatted on the mossy lip of the stump and stood up slowly. He looked across the open space to one of the branches on the big tree. It was a stretch. It might be the farthest he'd ever jumped. He thought he could hear his mother in his head, yelling, "Jesse noooo…"

"You never listen to me!" his mother's voice followed him, as he leapt into the open space, aiming for the low branch.

If he didn't grab it, it would be bad. He would free-fall forty feet down onto the forest floor. He'd probably survive but he'd definitely break something and that was the last thing he needed right now. Broken bones were hard enough to deal with when he had been couch surfing; a broken bone while living in the redwoods would be almost impossible to deal with. He knew first-hand because he'd broken a bone in his calf when he was seven, doing a crazy maneuver off the top of a climbing structure at school. He'd landed badly, and they couldn't track down his mom anywhere. The principal had to take him to the emergency room and stay with him while they set his leg in a cast. The pain had been awful, the slightest movement sending splintering sensations through his entire leg. It was something he didn't want to repeat.

He caught hold of the low limb on the big tree and dug his nails into the wood as he swung back and forth. His heart was beating fast. He did a pull-up, lifting his body onto the branch. Then he rested against the trunk until his heart stopped racing. He peered up through the tangle of branches, planning his route through the maze toward the top. He started his ascent, feeling himself calm down and focus as he climbed.

More than halfway up, the tree divided into two distinctive trunks. This was what he'd seen from a distance; the widening of the tree and the mass of greenery where the trunk split. Jesse climbed into the crotch between the splayed trunks. There was a thick spongy build-up of decaying redwood needles and moss. With his legs curled up to his chin, Jesse fit into the tree nest. It felt safe to be tucked into the branches, sitting on the soft duff. There were small ferns he recognized as bracken and thick green moss that stretched up the shaded trunks like gaudy green ladies' gloves. Jesse breathed in the heavy smell of redwood bark and decaying needles. The scent was like a drug that made him forget everything else. He closed his eyes and let Carla and Lizzie and his whole shitty life fall away.

He dreamed he was little, three or four, sitting on his mom's lap in a garden somewhere, in the sun. She played with his hair and smiled at him with clear, bright eyes.

"The itsy bitsy spider crawled up the water spout…" Her fingers walked up his pudgy little arm as she sang the familiar song.

"Mama, that tickles!" he squealed.

Jesse woke to the sound of his own voice, but he wasn't a little boy in his mother's arms. He was himself and he knew his mother was herself, not the sweet doting mother from the dream. He wondered if the dream were a memory, if his mom had ever looked at him like that when he was little. His arm still tickled. He brushed the back of his forearm and felt a smooth wet bulge. He flicked at the spot, thinking it was a banana slug, though he'd never seen one way up in a tree before. He flicked the thing again and it went flying into the piled up duff where the two trunks converged.

It was a pale yellow salamander with small black spots on its back. It had the large triangular head and the splayed feet for climbing that he'd seen on other male arboreal, or tree, salamanders. But the spots on the yellow body were unusual. Jesse was pretty sure he hadn't seen this particular species before. Whenever he found an amphibian in the woods he would memorize its features and try to key them out later in the library with one of the herpetology guides. He reached down and gently picked the stunned amphibian out of the duff. The creature let out an alarmed squeaking sound, which Jesse knew was to be expected from a scared salamander.

Jesse and his mom had lived at the base of Redwood Jack's tree-sit for a year when Jesse was eleven. He and his mom had the task of delivering supplies and hoisting them up to the tree-sit platform on a rope. In return, Jack would lower money for food and a five-gallon bucket full of feces. Jesse's mom had stayed drug-free most of that year, then the bad weather set in and Jack's tree sitting came to an end. Jesse had thought they'd follow Jack to his next gig, some protest three-hundred-miles south in San Francisco. Instead, they woke up one morning with hail pelting the tarp that covered their camp and all of Jack's stuff gone. That same day a group of tree sitters showed up and the airy fort that had been their home for a year was stripped away from the two-hundred-foot tree. Jack was gone, leaving Jesse with tree climbing skills and an impulse to observe. But the most important thing he left behind was the seed he'd planted in Carla that would become Jesse's sister.

Redwood Jack had taught Jesse about edible plants and the names of most of the birds in the forest. Jesse had taken it seriously when Jack said it was important to learn as much about his environment as possible.

"Learn the names of everything," Jack had said. "Someday all those names will make sense and the forest will be like a best friend, someone you understand and trust."

That's what Jesse had done, memorized the names of everything he found and could identify. He sneaked plants, insects, and occasionally amphibians, into the library to compare them to the photos and drawings in the books. After six years of observing and looking things up, there wasn't much he hadn't already seen in the forest at least a dozen times. He didn't have a university library card, but he tracked down the same stack of books every time he visited the library. The notebook he kept in his backpack at all times contained details written in his small, neat print about salamanders, plants, birds and insects—anything he saw in the forest.

But this pale yellow guy wasn't in his notes. He'd have to

remember the markings. The salamander stopped squeaking and skittered out of his hand and onto a mossy branch. The sun was getting low in the sky and Jesse needed to make sure Lizzie had something to eat besides a power bar, and that their camp was set up for the night. He climbed down quickly still trying to commit the spots on the yellow salamander to memory.

When he reached the bottom branch he didn't hesitate, he leapt out to the neighboring stump and slid down the cracks in the smooth trunk, jumping to the forest floor. It was always easier if he was moving fast, not thinking about the distance or the risk. It was better to think of it as forest free-running, one crazy fluid movement following another.

It was dusk when he reached camp. Hazy light filtered through the trees and the sparrows were chirping and rustling, settling in before dark. Lizzie poked at the coals of the fire. A pot of water set on a grate above the flames was starting to boil. Carla was opening pouches of ramen.

"Hey, Chipmunk," Jesse said, ruffling Lizzie's hair. "Way to get the fire going!"

"Mommy did it. I'm just watching, so it stays lit."

Jesse glanced briefly at his mom, who raised her eyebrows and smiled.

Mom's back for now, Jesse thought. He didn't know whether to be grateful or pissed off. He hated how forgiving Lizzie was with their mother. She never held a grudge; she just kept loving Carla no matter what stupid shit happened. Jesse knew better. He knew their mother would stay clean for a day or a week and then she'd break down, get high, and disappear into that listless, drugged state he'd come to recognize and loathe.

"Ramen for dinner, Jesse. How's that sound?" Carla asked.

Jesse didn't respond.

"Jess, Mama asked you a question! Please don't ignore her," Lizzie scolded, sounding more like a stern mother than a six-year-old.

"She ignores me," Jesse mumbled.

Carla stood up, disregarding Jesse's comment. "I'm gonna collect some more sticks for the fire." She wandered off into the dusky forest.

"Only when she's sick. She can't help it if she gets sick," Lizzie whispered to Jesse.

"Most people don't get sick as often as Mom," Jesse said. "It's not normal, just so you know."

"It's good to be different, that's what Mama says."

"You shouldn't listen to everything Mom says." Jesse stretched and sat next to his sister.

Carla came back down the trail with an armload of broken branches. "Hey gang, have you put the ramen in?" Carla added branches to the fire.

"No, Mama, we're waiting for you to make dinner. Jesse made dinner the whole time you were sick."

Carla crouched and poured the packets of ramen noodles and powder into the boiling water, stirring the mixture with a big spoon from their canvas cooking bag.

"Thanks for taking such good care of me," Carla said, looking across the fire at Jesse. "You know how much I love you both, don't you?" Carla eyes were pleading.

Lizzie nodded. "Yeah, Mama, we know."

"If you really loved us you'd go to Sempervirens and get clean, really clean, like for good. Not all this up and down roller-coaster stuff," Jesse said, waving his arm in illustration of Carla's vacillating moods.

"I'm trying, Jesse. I don't want to leave you and Lizzie alone for long. If the state finds out and puts you in foster care, you and Lizzie could be separated. I'd be cooped up in rehab not able to do anything about it."

"I wouldn't let that happen, Mom. If you got clean, you could get a job. Maybe we could get an apartment." Jesse looked at Carla as if he'd had a realization. "I've only got one more year of school. I can get a job after that."

"You don't need to stay with us after you finish school. You should go to college somewhere. You've always been smart, Jess. Your teachers all say you are."

"When was the last time you met with one of my teachers? Like seventh grade?" Jesse asked. "I'm not going to leave you alone with Lizzie. Not unless you move in with your sister or something."

"I told you not to talk about her! You know what she is. We need to stay as far away from her as possible."

"She's not an alien, Mom! Why do you always say that? What did she ever do to you?"

"I've seen the truth about her, Jess, a side you haven't seen. She's not human. We can't trust her."

"And she should trust you after all the shit you've pulled?" Jesse asked.

"At least I'm not a creature from another planet inhabiting some innocent girl's body!" Carla's eyes were wide and sincere.

"Oh, my God! Do you know how crazy you sound? You were probably just tripping and hallucinated this whole crazy theory of yours." Jesse had the urge to run, to take off into the woods again, or go to the library where he could look up that yellow salamander. He needed to get away from his mother and go to a place where things made sense.

Both the forest and the library provided him with a sense of order that made him feel safe. He wanted to be in the logical realm of kingdom, phylum, class, order, family, genus, and species. That was something he could relate to. There was no way for him to organize his mother's sudden bouts of delusion. He didn't know how to describe them or look them up. She wasn't something that he could identify. Jesse had scanned a row of books on mental disorders in the library but nothing had really matched his mom's long list of dysfunctions. He wondered if she had all of the disorders bundled into one giant disorder, almost like a super power gone wrong. In any case she was impossible for Jesse to label. She was some kind of rogue mutant. Maybe *she* was the alien!

Chapter 2

IN his favorite corner on the third floor of the library, Jesse leafed through *Peterson's Field Guide to Western Reptiles and Amphibians*, looking at photos of local salamanders. Most of the species were dark brown or copper colored. Some exhibited black spots, but he couldn't find any examples of salamanders that were pale yellow with black spots. He'd looked through the book dozens of times. His salamander simply wasn't there. He'd have to ask the librarian if there were any recent papers on amphibians in Northern California. Maybe this yellow guy just hadn't made it into the guidebooks yet.

Jesse stuffed his notebook into his backpack and put the stack of books he'd gotten off the shelves on the return rack. He hadn't realized how late it was, almost 11:30 p.m. He needed to get back and check on Ben, who'd promised to camp near Lizzie and his mom so Jesse could spend time in the library. He'd told Ben that he had a paper to write for history. But instead of doing history, he'd spent two hours searching through herpetology books trying to find that damn, elusive salamander. His mystery amphibian looked a little like an inverted California Tiger salamander, which was mostly black with a few yellow spots. Maybe Jesse's salamander was some weird anomaly of the California Tiger.

Tomorrow he'd try to bring Lizzie with him to the library. They could hang out in the kids' corner where she loved to sit on the floor among the low stacks of children's books. He'd get his favorite herpetology books off the shelves on the third floor and set up at one of the tables in the kids' area by the big windows. They could stay there all day if Lizzie was up for it. He needed to figure out a topic for his history paper and he could talk to the librarian about recent herpetology publications. He'd been thinking about writing his history paper on logging in Humboldt County. There were picture books on the subject in the library showing photos of loggers standing next to trees as wide as houses. The pictures haunted him at night when he slept at the base of big second-growth redwoods. These trees were his home; he couldn't imagine them being chopped down by men with giant handsaws. There were old-growth stumps throughout the forest, mostly charred to a grey polished sheen from fires, but nothing like the massive trees getting chopped down in the old black-and-white photos. Ben had discovered one of these stumps with an opening at the base that you could climb through on hands and knees to arrive in a room-sized sanctuary. The interior of the stump was dark except for a round beam of light coming from the opening thirty feet up. It was cold and musty until Ben made a fire, and then the space would heat up like a sauna.

Jesse sped down the library steps two at a time to the first floor, where he made a last stop at the bathroom. It was usually empty at this time of night. He pulled out a plastic bag that held a worn washcloth, a toothbrush, and toothpaste. He let the hot water run until there was steam erupting. Then he ran his washcloth under the water and dabbed on soap from the dispenser on the wall. He took the soapy cloth into one of the stalls and washed his face, then his armpits and finally his crotch. He zipped up his pants and went back out to the sink, where he rinsed the cloth and splashed warm water on his face. Jesse brushed his teeth thoroughly and reminded himself that he needed to get floss at the Dollar Store sometime during the weekend. He tried to get Lizzie to floss at least a couple of times a week. It was a waste of time urging his mom to floss anymore. Her once-perfect smile was rapidly eroding like cliffs sloughing away at the beach. She'd get a toothache and then put off having it looked at for so long that the tooth would have to be pulled. All that was available to them was the local dental clinic. They only did the basics, and the basics meant extracting teeth.

It was almost midnight when Jesse walked out of the library into the brisk fall night. There were a few college kids making their way through campus back to the dorms. Jesse walked up the steps between the music and art buildings. It was cold. He started running, up the path to the geology department and down the wooded steps past the gym, then up the steep road to the social sciences building. From there it was an easy coast downhill to the park entrance and the forest. Running felt good and a half-moon lighted his way.

He tried to imagine the life those college kids had, leisurely walking back to warm dormitories with cozy beds made with sheets and comforters provided by doting mothers who lived hundreds of miles away. He'd watched the kids in the university food court mindlessly swiping their meal cards like it was a birthright, having access to all that food. He overheard them whining about the bad food or having to do their own laundry. It was bullshit; they had no idea what it was like to be out on their own. They didn't recognize the cord that tied them to their parents every time they ran that meal card through the register. Jesse slept inches away from his mother every night, yet he knew more about being on his own than any of these college kids ever would.

In the morning he'd buy Lizzie a hot cocoa at the library café, and maybe they could split a day-old scone. He had a little money stashed in his wallet from last month's welfare deposit. His mom got six hundred dollars a month, automatically, on a debit card. She treated the beginning of every month like a party. They'd take the bus over to the row of shabby hotels and get a room. The hotel cost fifty dollars a night, and they usually stayed for two or three nights. After showers and a long nap, Carla would take them to the Mexican place across the street. They'd sit in a booth eating chips and salsa, sipping the root beers Carla insisted on buying. They'd laugh and tell stories about their day. Even Lizzie seemed to understand that they were acting, pretending to be a normal family out for dinner. She'd sit up straight and laugh louder than usual, and then she'd look around to see who was watching.

Jesse didn't mind; he indulged his family on those days at the hotel. He wanted Carla to see how happy and functional they could be in the real world. He wanted her to get a taste of normal and to want it. Jesse wanted to get a job, something part-time after school. But he needed to be able to pick up Lizzie, get dinner together, and watch over his mom. He was barely getting his homework done as it was. Besides every application he'd looked at required an address and that was something he didn't have.

After a few nights, they'd agree that they needed to save the rest of the money for other things. They'd go to the Dollar Store and stock up on food, shampoo, and toothpaste. They couldn't buy too much, because everything had to fit into their backpacks and a couple of duffel bags. They'd take the bus back to the park and silently walk past the playground and into the woods.

It was always depressing going back to camp. That was how Jesse felt now as he entered the forest and walked quickly up the dark trail. Their camp was a good hundred yards from the main trail and hidden by a massive huckleberry laden stump.

One of Ben's dogs let out a low growl. Jesse relaxed, knowing that Ben and the dogs were still there watching over his family.

"Shh," Jesse whispered to the dog. Emma's tail thumped the ground in recognition. Then both dogs were up and plodding over to Jesse, sniffing his pants, taking a smell inventory of all the people he'd come in contact with at the library. "Good girl, Emma. Hi, Toby." Jesse squatted to greet the dogs. Ben stirred, and then rolled back into his pile of blankets. Lizzie and Carla had already pulled Jesse's blankets out and spread them next to where Lizzie lay sleeping.

It was cold. Jesse pulled the hood of his sweatshirt up tight around his head and face. He kept his jacket on and crawled under the blankets next to his sister. Then he began his ritual of tucking his body into his clothes. He pulled his sleeves down and retracted his fingers to keep them warm. He always went to sleep with his shoes on, but by morning he had usually kicked them off. Jesse snuggled in close to Lizzie and breathed in the familiar scent of decomposed redwood needles.

In the morning, he woke up to the smell of smoke and onions. Lizzie was still asleep, curled next to him like a compact heater. He rolled on his side toward the fire where Ben was scratching away at a pan full of scrambled eggs and onions. "Ben, you really know how to live it up! Eggs... I'm impressed."

"I like to buy eggs on Friday afternoon so I can cook up a real meal for Saturday morning. That's what we always did when I was a kid. My mom scrambled up a dozen eggs every Saturday. That was the best part of my whole week, still is."

"Where did you grow up?" Jesse asked, sitting up and pulling his blanket around him like a cape.

"All over. My dad was military, so we were moving all the time."

"Are your parents alive?" Jesse thought Ben looked too old to have living parents, but people on the street aged fast. It was easy to misjudge someone's age by a decade or more.

"Nah," Ben said, dishing a serving of steaming eggs into a beat-up plastic bowl and handing it to Jesse. "They died a long time ago. They were living in Rhode Island. I have a brother out there, but I haven't talked to him in years."

"What happened?" Jesse asked, digging into the eggs with a fork. "How'd you end up on the street?"

"It's a long story, Jess. I don't think you wanna hear it."

"Yeah, I do, Ben. You're not all drugged up, you're not psycho. You could be working, maybe as a chef." Jesse smiled and took another bite.

Ben looked up from his plate. "I'm not as good a guy as you think, Jesse. I've done shit you wouldn't like. You're a decent kid, and smart as hell from what I can see, the way you're always writing things down in those notebooks. It's too late for me. I've screwed everything up. I'm just trying to stay out of people's way and, ya know, not hurt anyone else."

Jesse swallowed a bite of the hot eggs. "What do you mean, Ben? You're the best guy I know. You've never been anything but nice to us, and everybody else as far as I can tell."

"Let me put it this way, Jesse: if you knew the things I've done you wouldn't like me. At all."

***

In the early afternoon, Jesse was in the university library looking at a familiar stack of forest field guides and a big pile of books on the history of logging. Lizzie was on the floor by the window, surrounded by picture books. She was reading the story in one book aloud to a character in another. Jesse thought it was a little odd, but he was always impressed with how Lizzie managed to find creative ways to keep herself entertained.

They'd shared a chai and a day-old burrito from the café, so Jesse was content to stay as long as Lizzie was willing.

"Listen, little girl," Lizzie spoke softly to the image of the girl in the picture book. "This story will make you happy.

I like your worn-out dress and your bare feet. I might get you shoes like mine someday." Lizzie banged her heel on the floor to demonstrate her flash shoes for the faded girl in the book.

Jesse noticed that Lizzie's new shoes were already streaked with dirt from the forest trail.

"Now listen, little girl, I'm gonna keep reading and cheer you up."

Jesse put his fingers to his lips to remind Lizzie that they needed to be quiet in the library. Lizzie smiled at him and began mumbling softly to herself.

The librarian had helped Jesse search for recent herpetology publications, but they'd found none that addressed his yellow salamander. He'd set the salamander books aside and was taking notes for his history paper.

"Hey, kiddos!" The voice startled Jesse. It was Carla coming toward them, talking way too loud. "Want some lunch? That girl who hands out dog food gave me a loaf of bread and a block of cheese. I guess she's started caring about more than just the dogs." Carla laughed and began pulling the food out of her backpack.

"Mom," Jesse hissed, "you need to be quiet. We can't eat here, we're in a library." Jesse's eyes darted around the nearby tables to see who had been disturbed by his mother's loud voice. A guy on a couch continued staring at a thick chemistry book, but a woman at one of the round tables was looking right at them, in fascination or irritation—Jesse couldn't tell which. It didn't matter why she was scrutinizing them; Jesse hated being stared at.

"Let's just go, come on, Liz," Jesse stacked his books neatly in the center of the table, hoping they might still be there later if he managed to sneak back.

"I don't wanna go, I gotta finish reading this story to the Blue Girl," Lizzie said, pointing to the girl in the story with the faded dress.

"We don't have to go, Jesse, no one will notice us eating,"

Carla said, sprawling on a chair by the window. She looked washed-out and sunken sitting in all that sunlight. Jesse was used to seeing her in the dark haze of the forest where her disintegrating face was veiled by tree-filtered light and mist. In the library she looked old and skinny and out of place. The woman at the round table stared at Carla. Jesse figured she was probably a psych major going through a mental checklist of drug-addiction symptoms. Jesse didn't know whether to scream at his mom or at the staring woman.

"We're going," Jesse said coldly, grabbing Lizzie's small, warm hand.

"Ok, we can eat outside, it's a sunny day," Carla said, carelessly trailing after her children.

They never got back to the library. Jesse figured he'd give up on the salamander for now and write his history paper tomorrow. After lunch Carla had talked them into doing laundry in town and going to the community pool for showers. Then they had taken the bus to the Dollar Store for supplies.

"Mama, let's stay inside tonight. I wanna sleep in the bed with the fuzzy blankets!" Lizzie said wiping her nose on her sleeve and pointing across the street to the row of run-down hotels.

"No, hon, can't afford it. But after Halloween we will; we'll stay for three whole nights if you want." Carla put her palm on Lizzie's flushed cheek.

"We should spread the hotel nights out, Mom, instead of doing them all at once. Then we'd have something to look forward to," Jesse said, pushing the cart with Lizzie toward the canned-food section of the Dollar Store.

"We run out of money too fast, Jesse. You know that," Carla said.

Jesse pushed the cart faster. "It's the same amount of money, Mom, three nights at the beginning of the month or three nights spread out, there's no difference."

"It's just better to do it at the beginning when we know

we'll have the money," Carla said, stopping in front of some canned soup.

"It just means saving," Jesse said, reaching for cans of chicken noodle and hearty chili.

"We never have enough later. We always end up spending it on something," Carla argued.

"Like meth or coke," Jesse said, tossing the heavy cans into the cart.

"Stop!" Carla stared at him. Her blue eyes appeared dead and flat.

"Whatever, you'll never change, not even for Lizzie." Jesse slammed another can into the cart and stormed off to look for batteries.

It was almost dark by the time they got back to camp with all of their laundry and supplies. They had taken the bus from the Dollar Store and walked from the center of town back to the forest.

"Come on, Liz, let's collect wood while Mom unloads stuff." Jesse squatted for Lizzie to climb onto his back.

"I'm too tired, I can't," Lizzie curled up in the duff and closed her eyes.

"We're all tired, Liz, but we gotta get wood and we gotta eat." Jesse grabbed Lizzie's hands to pull her onto her feet.

"Nooo," Lizzie's protest turned into a sob. Jesse sat down and pulled her into his lap.

"Mom, Lizzie's really warm. I think she's got a fever." He held his palm to Lizzie's cheek.

Carla stopped rummaging through their bags and looked at Jesse. "You mean just warm? Or hot, warm?" Carla asked.

"I don't know. Hot, I guess. You're the mom, you tell me!"

Carla knelt to feel Lizzie's forehead and neck with the back of her hand. "She's pretty warm. Let's see if we still have Tylenol." Carla scrounged through her backpack and came up with a bottle of ibuprofen. "This is all I've got," Carla shook the blue plastic bottle.

"You're not supposed to give kids that, it has to be acet-aminophen." Jesse shifted Lizzie in his arms, allowing her to snuggle into his chest. "We should have gotten some at the Dollar Store."

"Yeah, well, we didn't know, did we?" Carla snapped.

"I could run down to town and get some at Safeway, it's not that far," Jesse offered.

"We can't afford it. That shit's expensive at Safeway. She'll be fine. Let's get her to bed; all she needs is rest."

***

Jesse woke to Lizzie's feet kicking at his legs. "Stop, Liz," he mumbled. Lizzie let out a weak moan and he remembered the fever. He scooted next to her and put his hand on her face. She was burning up, attempting to throw off her covers.

"Mom! Lizzie's still hot, wake up."

Carla had walked down the trail to the park in search of Tylenol earlier in the evening but no one had any. Jesse suspected that she'd scored a dose of something else because she'd come back looking way too relaxed. Maybe someone had given her a couple of Vicoden or Xanax. The hippie crowd down by the park's edge seemed to have prescription meds.

"Mom, wake up! We need to do something to cool her down."

"Don' hassle me now." Carla groaned, rolled over and went back to sleep.

"Shit," he said, recognizing his mother's signature drug-in-duced lack of interest. She wasn't getting up anytime soon. Jesse felt Lizzie's forehead and neck again. It was like holding his hand in front of a stoked fire. He grabbed his backpack, scooped Lizzie in his arms and started towards the park, not bothering to ask any of the homeless folks for help. He knew they wouldn't have what he needed and, besides, he was wor-ried Lizzie's condition had gone past needing a simple pill for a cure. She moaned as he carried her across the grassy park to the road, but she didn't talk or open her eyes. It wasn't easy carrying her in his arms, but he didn't know if she could hang onto his back.

"It's okay, Liz, you're gonna be okay." Jesse picked up speed when he reached the road. Adrenaline fueled his arms and legs. It was twenty minutes before he reached his aunt's house in the lower part of town. He was hesitant about knocking. It was the middle of the night; he wasn't even sure what time it was. He didn't want to put Lizzie down until he was inside, so he kicked at the door with his foot, cringing in anticipation of his aunt's reaction.

He'd met his aunt Ellen only a handful of times, but it always ended with his mother freaking out and telling Jesse to run fast to get away from "the alien." He had spent a couple of nights at her house when he was six or seven. It was a blurry memory because, like Lizzie, he'd been sick. He wasn't even sure how he'd gotten to Ellen's house that time, but he assumed his mother had been desperate just as he was now.

He could hear a dog barking inside and the sound of footsteps. The curtain at the porch window was swept aside briefly and he thought he saw the alien looking out at them. Then the door opened and there she was, only a few inches away, staring at Jesse and his sister, limp in his arms.

"Bring her in, Jesse, put her on the couch." Ellen said his name in a calm familiar way as if they saw each other every day. His aunt ushered them towards the couch, her dog following, sniffing at their clothes. Jesse set Lizzie down gently, placing a blue floral pillow under her head. Ellen kneeled next to Lizzie, feeling her face and neck. "She's running really hot. You were right to bring her, Jesse. Go to the bathroom and get me a wet washcloth. I'll crush some acetaminophen into juice and see if we can get her to drink a little." Ellen went off in her bathrobe and stocking feet, the grizzled chocolate Lab trailing behind her.

Jesse didn't want to leave Lizzie alone, even for a minute,

but Ellen had said to get a wet cloth. He found the bathroom down the hall and turned on the tap. It was impossible to avoid his image in the big mirror above the sink. He was surprised at how young he still looked, brown-haired with dark eyes. He avoided mirrors in general, afraid they would reflect the truth about his situation. He didn't want to see how homeless he looked to other people. He'd overheard girls at school talking about how mysterious he was. Keeping his situation a mystery to everyone else was so much work. Tonight, he thought he'd somehow look older than the boy reflected in the mirror. He thought he'd look more grown-up, more like how he felt.

He wrung out the cloth and went back to the living room. Ellen was kneeling beside Lizzie, trying to spoon a syrupy liquid into her mouth. The old dog had curled up on a blanket by the wall heater.

"I found some liquid Tylenol. This should help bring down the fever if we can get her to take it."

For an instant Jesse hesitated, thinking he'd made a mistake coming here. What if this woman was an alien trying to poison his sister? But he looked around the living room at the nice furniture and the photos of people on the wall. This woman wasn't crazy or from outer space. It was his mom who'd poisoned him and Lizzie with delusional ideas about Ellen.

"Come on, Jesse, help me prop her up so we can spoon this in." Jesse squeezed in behind his sister on the couch.

"Liz, you've gotta drink this; it'll make you feel better."

***

Jesse woke to the sound of NPR news and the smell of coffee. He was in a twin bed with a purple comforter and his head resting on a matching purple pillow. The bed felt amazing, soft, supportive and warm, better than any hotel bed he'd ever slept in. There were band posters on the wall and lots of photos of teenage girls posing and smiling for the camera. There was a blonde girl in the photos who looked familiar. He got out of bed, pulled on his jeans, and went to examine one of the pictures more closely. The girl was beautiful with big blue eyes and a quirky off-kilter smile that was mesmerizing. Was this girl Ellen's daughter—his cousin? Or was she just some girl who'd graduated a few years ago, a girl he'd seen around town?

Out in the living room, Jesse found Lizzie still asleep on the couch with a down comforter pulled up to her chin. Ellen leaned back in a chair next to the couch, sipping coffee and reading the newspaper. When he walked into the room his aunt looked up and held a finger to her lips.

"She's just gone back to sleep," Ellen whispered. "There's coffee and cereal in the kitchen."

It felt good to be shushed by an adult. Jesse was always the one telling his mom and Lizzie to be quiet, be respectful. Having someone shush him made him relax, like someone else had taken the helm for a while.

In the kitchen, he poured coffee and cereal and then went quietly back to the living room to sit near Lizzie. Ellen smiled when he came into the room and then went back to reading her paper. It was another twenty minutes before she put the paper down and motioned for Jesse to follow her to the kitchen. She poured them each another cup of coffee.

"I can't believe I'm pushing caffeine on a teenager," she said, smiling and handing him his cup. "But it was a rough night and I'm guessing caffeine is the least of your worries."

"I'm already six feet tall, so don't worry about stunting my growth." Jesse added milk and sugar to his cup, and took a sip. "This is so good," he said, not sure if it was the taste of the milky coffee or cradling the warm mug in his aunt's kitchen, that he liked more. "So is she gonna be okay, or do we need to take her to a doctor?"

"She'll be fine, but that thought did cross my mind when I took her temperature at four in the morning and the thermometer read a hundred and three. If it'd gone any higher I would have taken her to the Emergency Room. She's still running a hundred and one, but that's okay. She's burning out whatever nasty bug she caught."

"Thanks, Ellen." Jesse realized it was probably the first time he'd used her name. "My mom's not going to be happy if she finds out we came here, but I didn't know what to do."

"I'm not going to tell your mom, Jesse. She won't talk to me anyway. But she might come looking for you." Ellen leaned against the kitchen counter and stared at him.

"We'll go back today," Jesse said, fiddling with the lid to the cereal box. "We can't stay. My mom won't..."

"I know how your mom thinks, Jesse. You don't have to skirt around it. She's been like this most of her life."

Jesse set his coffee cup on the counter. "You mean she was like she is now, even when she was little?"

"Well, she's been battling mental illness for as long as I can remember and it's gone untreated for decades. I'm four years older than your mom, so I've seen her ups and downs for a long time." Jesse looked at his aunt closely, noticing for the first time her vibrant blue eyes, graying blonde hair, and clear skin.

"You don't look four years older; you look a lot younger," Jesse observed.

"You mean healthier? Jesse, your mom has been using drugs since she was in junior high. That takes a toll." Jesse swallowed hard. He'd never thought of his mom as a young drug addict. He swore he had memories, like his dream in the tree, of a healthy mom.

As if she'd read his mind, Ellen said, "There were good times too. When you were little, she got better for a few years. Pregnancy was like a cure for her. The overload of hormones seemed to satiate her need for drugs. Some women are horrible when they're pregnant, but it put your mom at ease, like she finally got a chance to be unfettered—to be herself. At other times, she'd do almost anything to escape herself. I'm guessing that hasn't changed."

"When did she start... thinking you were—"

"An alien?" Ellen smiled, and then shook her head. "It was before you were born. She overdosed and my parents had her hospitalized for a couple of months. I'm the one who found her and I guess what she saw in her drug-induced state was pretty horrific, because she's never let it go. Believe me, I've tried everything." Ellen wiped at tears. "It was never easy being your mom's sister, but after the overdose I lost her completely."

"She's pretty certain that you're the bad guy."

"Jesse," Ellen said, putting a hand on his arm, "I've offered, I mean, I've tried to get her to let me raise you and Lizzie. But you can imagine how that offer has been received."

Jesse knew what his mom would threaten. She might even follow through with one of her threats if Ellen tried to take him and Lizzie away. Jesse had heard Carla babble on after they'd run into Ellen in town. She'd say things like, "If that creature takes you, Jesse, I'll kill myself. I won't be able to live knowing the alien has you."

"Jesse, Jess..." Lizzie called from the living room. He set his coffee down and ran to his sister.

"I'm right here, Liz," he pushed a sweaty lock of Lizzie's hair from her eyes.

"Jess, Mama got us a room." Lizzie smiled and stared at the white ceiling. Jesse looked out the window, and for the first time that morning, noticed the wind and rain. The thick walls of the house and the well-sealed roof kept them so insulated from the elements that Jesse had lost sight of something that was usually in the forefront of his mind—the weather.

"Yeah, we're in a room. Here, drink a little." Jesse propped Lizzie's head up with a pillow and held a glass of water to her chapped lips. "Try to drink a little." Lizzie took a couple of weak sips, then collapsed back into the pillows and closed her eyes. "There you go. Go back to sleep."

***

They stayed for two days. Ellen called both kids' schools to say that they would miss class on Monday. Ellen took Jesse to the library and checked out the books he needed for his history paper. He couldn't help but envy the casual way his aunt whisked her university library card out of her wallet to check out the books. They spent the days lazing around the house, taking turns spoon-feeding broth and tea to Lizzie.

Jesse thought he could get used to this very quickly: the endless supply of food in the fridge and cupboards, the twenty-four-hour access to a bathroom and shower. He used Ellen's computer to hunt for any work published on the yellow salamander. He didn't find anything, but he spent hours studying other species on the California Herp website.

By Monday evening Lizzie was sitting up, talking, and sneaking bites of her toast to Ellen's dog, Sweet. Ellen ran Lizzie a bath, and Jesse could hear Ellen and Lizzie chatting away about Lizzie's teacher and the kids in her class. After the bath the three of them sat on the couch watching a Star Trek movie. Lizzie fell asleep with her head on Ellen's lap, Ellen absentmindedly running her fingers through Lizzie's pale honey-colored hair.

"So, that's your daughter, right?" Jesse asked, pointing toward a photo of a smiling blonde girl standing on a beach, hands on her hips.

"Yep, that's Carlie, your first cousin. Sort of named after your mom, actually. She's in her second year at UC Santa Cruz."

"Did she... I mean does she know about us?"

"Yes. She knows who you are. She went to the charter school so you probably didn't see her at your campus but she saw you around town. We thought it'd be harder if she reached out to you. She wants to though. It's just difficult because of your mom—and there's also your uncle."

"You and Mom have a brother?" Jesse asked.

"No." Ellen shook her head. "I have a husband, and he's not exactly supportive of your mom. She's put us through a lot of stuff over the years and he's done giving her second chances. He'd be pretty upset to find you and Lizzie here."

"We can leave." Jesse jumped off the couch. "I don't want to make trouble for you."

"You're not trouble. I want you here. All the time, if I could. Frank works for Caltrans, so he's gone a lot. He won't be back until Wednesday evening. There's nothing to worry about."

Jesse looked at the dark windows, streaked with rain. It had been raining for two days, and he had started to worry about his mom. If she were high, she wouldn't be thinking straight, wouldn't take the precautions necessary to keep herself or their stuff dry. Maybe Ben had let her stay with him and the dogs in the protected stump. But Ben would be less inclined to help Carla if Jesse and Lizzie weren't around.

"I think Lizzie will be good to go tomorrow. We can head back to my mom after school," Jesse said.

"Stay one more day; let Lizzie rest. Frank won't be back until Wednesday. If this storm hasn't let up by then maybe I can get you a hotel for a couple of nights."

"It's not a big deal. We're used to camping and we can get a hotel in about a week, when my mom's money comes in." Jesse had twinges of concern for Carla, but he knew Lizzie still needed rest.

"Promise me you'll stay until tomorrow, just to let Lizzie really heal."

"Okay, we'll leave Wednesday morning."

"Great! I really like having you both here. I know Frank would love it too... he's just not ready yet. Sit back down. Let's finish this movie."

Chapter 3

"WAKE up!" Lizzie shook Jesse's arm. "We're making waffles. Ellen's showing me how. There's gonna be syrup and strawberries!"

"Just a minute…" Jesse was torn between the idea of lolling in the deliciously warm bed or getting up to eat a hot breakfast in the comfort of a warm house. He wondered why normal teenagers complained so much about their lives. To sleep in or to eat a hot breakfast, it all sounded pretty deluxe.

"Look," Lizzie said when Jesse joined them. "I know how to fold napkins and which side to put the fork on." She held up her small left hand. "Not the hand I write with, but my other hand."

"Good to know," Jesse smiled, hoping his sister might actually get the chance to use her new table-setting skills in the future.

They were sitting like that, sipping tea and eating waffles drenched in syrup, when Frank came in. At first he had a mischievous smile like he was excited to have surprised Ellen. He even had a small bouquet of flowers in one hand. Sweet left her spot under the table to greet Frank at the door.

"Who's here?" he'd asked, still grinning and absentmindedly petting the dog.

Ellen stood up and walked over to give her husband a hug. "You're home so early," Ellen said, with an edge of trepidation in her voice.

"Yeah, the storm got so bad they closed the highway. Don't need me till next week." Frank stole glances at Jesse and Lizzie. "Who are our guests?" he asked, narrowing his eyes at Jesse.

"You know Jesse and you've seen Lizzie before, our niece and nephew. Carla's kids. It's been a few years, they've both grown a lot," Ellen said, squeezing Frank's hand.

Frank launched into a tirade. He yelled at Ellen and pointed at the door. "What the hell, Ellen! I told you I don't want anything to do with Carla or her kids. If they're here, she'll show up—guaranteed! I thought we agreed on this!"

Ellen looked at Frank with pleading eyes. "Please Frank. We're having breakfast." Ellen gestured at the table set for three, and the platter of waffles letting off a vague wisp of steam.

Jesse got up and quickly gathered the few articles of clothing he and Lizzie had scattered around the house and stuffed them into his pack.

"Come on, Liz," he said. "Put on your jacket, we gotta check on Mom."

"But I wanna finish my waffle," Lizzie pointed at her half-eaten breakfast.

"Put it in a napkin. Now!"

"It's okay, you guys can stay until tomorrow, really," Ellen said, her eyes darting back and forth from Frank to Jesse.

"Yeah, you stay," Frank said, in a low grumble. "I obviously came home too early. Maybe next time I should call first and see if it's a good time to come home to my own house!" Frank flung the bouquet of flowers onto the dining table and stomped out the door.

"Frank, they were just here because Lizzie got sick," Ellen yelled, following Frank to his truck.

"Come on, wrap up your waffle. We're going back to Mom." Lizzie sat silently in the window seat of the dining nook. The fever haze Lizzie had come out of had been happily met with a cheerful Ellen, ready to embrace Lizzie and show her how to make waffles. It wasn't surprising to Jesse that all of that domestic rapture had unraveled so quickly. He was sure that as far as Frank was concerned, he and Lizzie were the conduit that inevitably led to the chaos that was their mother.

Jesse looked out the open door to the wall of rain. "Jacket! Now! Come on." Lizzie quickly wrapped her waffle in a napkin, walked over to Jesse, and put on her jacket. Jesse swung Lizzie up onto his back and walked out the door, into the hard rain.

***

They took refuge from the downpour under the pagoda next to the tennis courts. Jesse needed to rest. He'd run the whole way from Ellen's house without stopping. Lizzie sat on one of the sheltered benches, picking pieces of soggy napkin off of her waffle. They were drenched. Neither of their jackets was waterproof. Jesse wondered if there was such a thing as a completely waterproof jacket. This kind of rain was so hard and unyielding he doubted any special weave of fabric could keep out the wet.

There was a group of high school kids playing tennis in the rain. Jesse watched them laughing and hitting the puddles of water that had formed on the courts. The kids didn't seem to care that they were soaking wet, probably because all they had to do was punch in some numbers on their cell phones and within minutes doting parents would pull up in cars with heaters blasting, ready to cart their teenagers home for warm showers. Jesse recognized one of the girls—she was the one who passed out the bags of food, the same girl his mom had gotten the bread and cheese from only a few days ago. He hoped she didn't notice him now. He hated that she knew he was homeless. He never saw her at school, so he assumed she and this group of kids went to the charter high school his cousin had attended. A silver van pulled into the parking lot, probably one of the moms coming to rescue the wet teenagers. A woman in a green raincoat got out of the van and walked through the downpour to the pagoda, maybe to wait for the kids out of the rain, Jesse thought. She reached the pagoda and pulled off the hood of her coat. It was Ellen, looking tear-smudged and distraught.

"Jesse, I'm so sorry." Ellen's voice shook. "I had to talk to Frank, he was… He wants to call Child Protective Services. He thinks you guys should be in foster care. He thinks it's the only way your mom will get her act together. And he wants you and Lizzie to be safe."

Jesse kicked at the concrete floor of the pagoda with the heel of his shoe. "We're not going into foster care," he said coolly, "that's one thing my mom and I agree on." He looked past Ellen to the tennis courts where the kids were gathering up their wet sweatshirts and backpacks.

"I don't want you in foster care either, Jess, and I won't call CPS. I couldn't do that to my sister or to you. If they took you and Lizzie from her, she'd probably…" Ellen looked over at Lizzie, nibbling on her soggy waffle. "I don't want to think about what she might do."

The kids were funneling out of the courts, running toward the pagoda. Some of the girls were screaming and laughing, shaking their hands in the air. Ellen didn't seem to have noticed the pod of teenagers; she looked surprised when they swarmed in and around them. "Oh, I… wow!" Ellen said.

"Oh my God, my shirt is totally see-through," one of the tennis girls said, pulling at her thin, wet shirt. The chatty girls were standing only ten feet away from where Jesse, Lizzie, and Ellen were hashing out things like foster care and CPS.

"I know, mine too," said another girl. The boys were smirking and trying unsuccessfully to avert their eyes.

"I might have something dry in my pack." It was the dark-haired girl who knew Jesse. He watched her dig through her backpack. "Here," she said, pulling out a long-sleeved shirt and tossing it to one of the girls. "It's still dry." As the dark-haired girl stood up, her eyes met Jesse's and he thought she nodded slightly. He hoped that they had an understanding, that she wouldn't rat him out to her friends. That was his worst fear; more than almost anything else, he wanted to remain anonymous.

"Let's just go to your car," Jesse said to Ellen, grabbing his backpack. "Come on, Liz, let's go with Ellen for a minute." Jesse wanted out of that gazebo. The dark-haired girl was the only one who had noticed them, but he didn't want these carefree kids overhearing their conversation. Ellen and Lizzie trotted behind him to the car. It was only a hundred yards, but the rain was coming down so hard they were drenched instantly. Ellen unlocked the doors and they piled into the musty van.

Lizzie and Jesse got in the back seat and Ellen twisted around in the driver's seat to talk to them.

"Look, you guys, I'm not going to let you camp out in those woods with the rain coming down like this."

"This is how we live, Ellen. It's nothing new."

Ellen shook her head. "No, Lizzie's still recuperating. I'm getting you a hotel room until this storm passes."

Jesse leaned towards Ellen. "I need to get back to Mom. She's probably freaking out that we're still gone. And when she freaks," his voice lowered to a whisper, "she does stupid shit."

"Mom's not stupid," Lizzie said, drops of water plopping onto her nose from the hood of her coat.

"I'm taking you to a hotel. I'll stay with Lizzie while you get your mom. Lizzie needs to stay warm." Ellen started the engine and blasted the heat.

Jesse pulled Lizzie's wet hood from her head. "Mom's not gonna want anything to do with you," he said.

Ellen craned her neck so she could look Jesse in the eyes. "Just call the room from the front desk before you bring her up. I'll leave before she can see me. I promise."

Jesse looked down at his wet lap. "She's gonna suspect it's you behind all this. I was gonna tell her we'd been at the hospital," he said.

Lizzie kicked her legs against the seat, making her flash-shoes erupt with strobes of red light. "You shouldn't lie to Mama; it's not good to lie."

"In this case, we need to lie to Mom. Trust me. Don't say a word about Ellen." Jesse sounded stern.

"Your brother's right, Lizzie. Talking about me will only make your mom feel sick, and we want your mama feeling good. Right, Sweetie?"

"Yeah, but Mama likes me to tell the truth, it makes me a good person," Lizzie answered matter-of-factly.

Ellen reached back and cupped Lizzie's small, cold hands between her own palms. "Your mom's right about that, but you're going to have to trust Jesse and me on this. Telling your mom about staying with me will make things worse, not better. We don't want that."

"But I wanna tell Mama about my bath and making breakfast."

"You can tell her those things, sweetie," Ellen said, "but you need to tell her that they happened at the hospital and that a nurse named Alice did those things with you."

"Why do I have to say Alice?" Lizzie asked.

"You can call her anything, just not Ellen. Okay?" Jesse said impatiently.

"Okay," Lizzie sighed, and leaned back in her seat. She closed her eyes and shuddered a little, despite the wave of heat coming from the vents.

Ellen pulled into the Hampton Inn and Suites parking lot.

"Wow," Jesse said, "we never stay here. There are cheaper places down the road."

"They're cheap for a reason," Ellen said. "Besides, I'll earn mileage on my credit card. Let's check in."

*** *** ***

"Oooooh… This room is sooo pretty!" Lizzie said, running to the bed by the window. "Can I have this bed, Jess?"

"Whichever one you want," Jesse tossed his backpack on a table in the corner and sat down on the end of the other bed. "This is really nice, Ellen, thanks." He patted the white duvet cover and leaned back on one of the oversized pillows.

"I wish I could do more than three nights, but it'll get you to Friday, and hopefully by then the storm will have passed," Ellen said.

Jesse put his hands on his knees and looked at the floor. "I guess I should go get Mom. I'll call you from the desk when I get back."

Ellen jingled the car keys. "I'd offer you the van, but your mom would recognize it."

"Yeah, and there's the fact that I don't have my license," Jesse said.

"Oh, right." Ellen seemed embarrassed to have made the assumption that he could drive.

"It's better for the environment," he said, trying to diffuse the awkward silence. "When we did the 'track your carbon footprint' assignment in science class, ours was so low I had to invent stuff to make us look like normal people." Ellen laughed and then sighed.

"Okay, I'll be back in a while." Jesse stood up and grabbed Lizzie's flash shoes and wiggled them from her feet. "No shoes on the nice beds, Liz," he said, tossing the shoes onto the floor.

Ellen got up from a chair by the rain-streaked window and held her arms open to Jesse. He let her hold him in a tight hug while he stood stiffly, waiting to be released. When she finally let her arms drop and stepped back, he could see that she was crying. He wished he'd hugged her back. Maybe then she wouldn't have cried. But it was probably better this way. Better not to get attached to someone who couldn't be a part of his real life.

It didn't take long for Jesse to run from the bus stop in town through the web of roads to the forest. It was still raining hard and he was soaked through. Once he was on the path in the woods, the rain turned quickly from pelting deluge to a light mist. The dense tree canopy acted like a towering green filter, dispersing the heavy rain. There was no sign of the regular hippie homeless crowd in the park. Maybe the weather had driven them deeper into the woods. Jesse hurried up the trail, feeling suddenly anxious to get to his mother; he hoped that what he found wouldn't be too horrible. He figured she'd be strung out on something by now. She'd probably used up the last of their monthly cash on whatever substance was being sold down in the park.

Picking up speed on the trail, Jesse kept picturing his mom still asleep under the green tarp next to the mossy stump. What if she'd caught Lizzie's flu and had been lying there burning up with a fever for days? Rounding the bend in the trail to camp, he stopped, and stared, stricken. There was no green tarp, no pile of garbage bags protecting their bedding. Even the fire ring that he and Lizzie had labored over, hauling carefully selected rocks up from the creek bed, was gone.

He looked around, noting landmarks like the stump, the distinctive ring of redwoods, and the location of the sword ferns that dotted the camp. Even Lizzie's wool fairy people were missing from the little ledges of moss that she referred to as fairyland.

"What the hell!" Jesse shouted, falling on his knees and pounding the soggy duff. "What the fucking hell!" He slowly felt himself start to yield, to open a crack in the door that had held back how he really felt about his life. That door had been bolted shut for a long time; there wasn't time or a place to feel the sorrow piled up behind that barrier. But now, even his shitty mom and his crummy, so-called "home" had been swept away. He heard himself muffle a cry, and then finally let the door swing wide, and all of his burdens came tumbling out—burying him in anger, rage, and frustration.

***

Jesse opened his eyes. He didn't know how long he'd been crying, but his chest shuddered from the force of facing all of that calamity. He tilted his head up to the dark mass of interwoven branches, which were obscuring the grey clouds. Drops of rain fell onto his face, and he heard the lonely song of a hermit thrush.

The path to Ben's stump looked unusually packed down. Jesse had a last small hope that he'd find Carla secure and dry inside the stump with all of their belongings. But after finding their camp swept clean, he was taking in the forest scene with new eyes. The place was really empty. None of the hippie homeless were there, and Ben and the dogs probably weren't either.

It was wet and soggy on the ground by the hole to Ben's hideout. Jesse called Ben's name a couple of times but heard no reply. On his stomach, he scooted into the hole, poking his head into the hollow cavity. It took his eyes a minute to adjust. He felt a wet lick on his nose and exhaled with relief.

"Emma, Toby, you're here. Good thing Ben trained you to be quiet and stay," he said.

He pulled himself into the hollow of the stump and sat on his knees patting the dogs. "Where's Ben, huh? Where's Ben?" he asked the eager dogs. Their tails flapped against the stump wall. Ben wasn't there but hot coals still glowed orange in the fire pit.

"That feels good, huh, guys," he said, warming his hands over the dying fire. Adding small sticks to the coals, he watched them smolder and ignite into yellow darting flames. The dogs curled up on either side of Jesse, groaned, and closed their eyes.

It was dusk-like in the stump, but he could make out the numbers on his watch. It was only two in the afternoon. He would wait for an hour and see if Ben turned up. If not, he'd head back into town and start asking people about his mom. The fire was mesmerizing. He leaned on his elbows and stared at the burning coals. His eyes felt heavy, and he let himself fall back and rest, warmed by the dogs.

***

"Wake up." Ben said, gently tapping Jesse's shoulder. "Time to get up, buddy." Ben sat cross-legged, poking the fire with a stick. Jesse stretched and sat up across from him, yawning.

"So what the hell happened, Ben? Our camp? Everything's gone?"

Ben continued stirring the fire with his long charred stick. "The park rangers did a full sweep, took everything. Thank God I had the dogs with me. Most of my stuff was already in here, so I tried to get what I could of yours, Jess, but I came in the middle of the operation, and most of the stuff had already been hauled off to a garbage truck."

"I can't believe it," Jesse said. "I've heard about sweeps, but I didn't think they'd actually take our blankets and clothes. And damn, what about my notebooks?"

Ben shook his head, "No, I asked about them, Jess, but once stuff was in the truck they wouldn't look for it. This is all I got." Ben reached behind him for a plastic shopping bag and handed it to Jesse. Jesse tentatively looked in the bag and pulled out four of Lizzie's fairy people, soggy and deformed from rain and handling.

"That's it?" Jesse asked, defeated.

"I'm sorry, Jess."

"Well," Jesse said, trying to straighten out one of the fairies. "At least Lizzie will have these."

"Yeah," Ben said, "It's something."

"Any idea where my mom is?" Jesse tried not to sound too anxious.

"She's okay. She freaked when she came back to camp yesterday and saw everything gone. A whole group of folks went down to join the Occupy at City Hall. Pretty sure your mom's staying with Leo."

"Who's Leo?" Jesse asked, lowering his voice.

"He's one of the head guys down at the Occupy. He's okay. He's not gonna hurt her. It's a good place to get back on your feet, Jess. People are dropping off sleeping bags, tents, food, jackets. Every day there's more stuff."

"I've seen people there. It's just so crowded and... I'm glad she's safe... but shit... " Jesse dug his fingers into his hair and let out a low groan. "Arrgg... I can't believe they took our stuff. My notebooks... man, that's years of notes."

"Yeah, I'm sorry about that." Ben continued raking the stick through the coals. "But most of that stuff is locked in your head. You write it down, but I never see you lookin' through those old notebooks. Maybe you already have it," Ben tapped his finger on his head, "in here."

***

The rain had let up, and Jesse walked toward town trying to avoid the deep puddles that had formed on sidewalks and streets. It was dark by the time he got to City Hall where the Occupy had taken up residence. The sloped lawn in front of the building was covered with compact tents and lawn chairs. From the sidewalk, Jesse watched as the tents lit up like oversized Chinese lanterns. Dusk was fading rapidly into night and Occupiers were settling down to sleep. There was no one Jesse recognized, so he approached a big man in a lawn chair, wearing a ball cap with glow-in-the-dark writing that said, "We are the 99%!"

"Excuse me," Jesse asked, "Do you know a guy named

Leo?" The man shifted his weight, causing the metal joints of his chair to squeak.

"Everybody knows Leo," the man said, squinting in the near dark.

"I mean..." Jesse shifted his feet back and forth and shoved his hands deep into his sweatshirt pockets. "Like, which tent is he in 'cause... my mom is staying with him."

"Shit! You're Carla's kid. She's been making a big stink over you and your sister. She had one of Leo's guys go to the hospital and ask about you."

"We're fine, now..." Jesse rocked from one foot to the other.

The 99% man looked at Jesse like he might not believe him, and then pointed. "Leo's tent's the big dome at the top of the hill. Hey, don't worry, he's cool. He'll be glad to know your mom's not psycho, making up all this shit about you and your sister."

Jesse couldn't help but leak out a little laugh. "Nah, we're for real, but she *is* psycho." Even in the dark, Jesse could see the man's teeth form a genuine smile.

"Psycho or not, you and your sister are all she talks about." Jesse's heart beat a little faster at the thought of his mother fretting about them.

"Thanks." Jesse raised a hand in farewell and walked up the hill to the illuminated dome tent. He stood silently for a minute, listening for conversation inside the tent. It was quiet except for the rustling of nylon. "Um, hello, it's Jesse. Is Carla in there?" He bit down on his lip waiting for a reply.

"Carla, wake up. It's your boy," a man's voice said.

He heard his mom mumbling incoherently.

"Get up, Carla!" It sounded like the man was shaking her awake.

"Stop! I'm getting up," Carla protested. The tent zipper opened and a big man with a mass of dark curls emerged from inside.

"You must be Jesse. Nice to meet you." Leo held out his hand. Jesse hesitated and then shook the man's hand. "Your mom's been pretty shook up about losing track of you and your sister." Leo was wearing a headlamp that illuminated portions of his face, making his features look ghoulish. His voice was kind, though, and Jesse noticed that his own racing heart had settled back to a normal rhythm.

"Yeah, my sister got sick and I took her to the doctor." Jesse shoved his hands into his pants pockets to avoid letting the lie fly out in the form of some awkward gesture.

"We actually called the hospital." Leo raised his thick eyebrows; they merged with the band of the headlamp, forming a wide unibrow.

"Yeah, they have to keep it confidential," Jesse said, hoping this second lie would suffice.

"Baby, you're here!" Carla crawled out of the tent with a blanket wrapped around her shoulders. She stood up and embraced Jesse, wrapping her blanketed arms around him, enfolding him like bat wings. For a moment he remained stiff like he had when Ellen hugged him, but Carla only wrapped her arms around him more tightly until Jesse relented and dissolved in her embrace. "Jesse, Jesse, Jesse," Carla said, "I've been so worried. Where's Lizzie?" Carla asked, pulling away from Jesse and looking into his eyes. "Is she okay? That fever?"

"It's fine; she's fine now, Mom."

Carla exhaled. "Thank God, but where is she? Is she still at the…"

Jesse cut her off quickly. "She's safe, at a hotel. The… hospital paid for us to stay in a hotel for a few days until she's better."

"But did you leave her there alone? I've told you never to leave…" Carla's right eye began to twitch and she placed her finger at her temple to try to calm it.

Jesse put his hands firmly on his mother's shoulders. "She's safe. There's a nurse with her until we get back."

Carla's eyes welled with tears. "Have you been up to the forest yet? We, uh…" She covered her eyes with her hands and sobbed.

"Yeah, I went… I saw Ben."

Leo put a hand on Carla's shoulder. "That was a tough break, guys. We're gathering stuff for your family. We have two sleeping bags and a tent. And there are bags of clothes you can look through in the morning."

"Thanks," Jesse said, thinking of their perfectly good stuff thrown into a garbage truck and hauled off to the dump. "Mom, we need to get back to Lizzie so the... nurse can leave."

Carla ran shaky hands through her greasy hair. "You go back. I need to stay here and gather more supplies so we can set up camp again."

Jesse kicked at the grass with his toe. "But Mom, what about Lizzie... don't you wanna see her?"

"Of course I do. Tomorrow I'll come visit. It's just... Leo's been so sweet and helpful." Carla put her arm around Leo's shoulder and gave his neck a little massage. "This Occupy movement is really important. I mean people are losing their homes all around the country."

"Yeah, Mom, that's a big problem, but it's not our problem. We don't even have a home." Jesse's eyes were like darts, and Carla looked nervously at her bare feet. "I'm pretty sure you're our problem, and I don't think the Occupy movement can fix you." Jesse turned and marched away, fuming at the idea of returning to Lizzie without their mother.

What did she owe that guy Leo after knowing him for two days? It was like as soon as she met a new guy she'd just forget who she was and take on all of the guy's causes like they were her own. What about her causes? What about him and Lizzie?

It was dark and cold, with a light mist falling. The bus depot was only a couple of blocks from City Hall and Jesse reached the bus stop in a matter of minutes. A few people were standing around looking stiff and cold in the mist-diffused light of a street lamp. Carla was probably back in the big dome tent by now with her legs curled around Leo.

"The bus is running late," said a tall man wearing a puffy orange jacket.

"I hope we didn't miss it," said a thin woman with an umbrella. The thought of waiting around for a bus that might not turn up was more than Jesse could stand. He exhaled his frustration and took off running. He ran north past campus and down the long row of student housing until the road dead-ended in a cul-de-sac. It was drizzling again, and his jacket was damp on the inside. It had been wet since his run earlier in the day to the tennis courts with Lizzie. He couldn't believe this was the same day. It felt like a week ago that Frank had come home to Ellen's and screwed everything up.

There was a trail, a shortcut that zig-zagged down the hill, past the freeway, and through the cow fields. The light of the street lamps faded behind him as he walked fast down the darkening trail into the brush. At the bottom of the hill he lost the trail, but it didn't matter; he just ran across the field in the direction of the hotels. There was a big dilapidated barn on his right. He picked up speed, wanting to avoid any contact with humans or cows. It felt good to be moving fast, making his way over the lumpy soil. The hazy light of hotel row glowed in the distance. He ran faster, thinking of Ellen and Lizzie waiting patiently for him to return with Carla. They'd be disappointed, but not surprised. Not Ellen anyway—she probably already guessed he was having trouble tracking Carla down and reeling her in. But Lizzie always thought their mom was doing her best. How old had Jesse been when he'd stopped assuming the best of Carla? When had that bubble of hope burst and the reality of his mother settled in?

A low fence that bordered the freeway interchange hemmed in the pasture. There wasn't much traffic, so Jesse hopped the fence and darted across the four lanes of freeway. Running had calmed him, but now he was tired, and he wanted to stop thinking about his mom and their camp and his damn, precious notebooks. The whole day made him feel sick. Jesse walked across a wet field toward a cluster of tract homes that was only a few blocks away from the hotel.

***

He opened the door to their room quietly, not wanting to wake Lizzie and not in the mood to explain why his mom wasn't with him. A dim table lamp gave the room a snug hue. Lizzie was sprawled out under the covers with Ellen curled up next to her. It didn't make sense to wake Ellen and explain, so he pulled a blanket out of the closet and spread it carefully over her.

Jesse turned off the table lamp, peeled off his wet jacket and pants, and slipped into the clean, neat bed. He should have taken a shower and brushed his teeth, but he didn't want to go into the bathroom and see the image of a boy whose life was so bleak and wrong. A picture of his mom with her arms around Leo, who she hardly knew, kept popping into his head. He tried to think about running through the cow pasture in the dark, avoiding rocks and big clumps of dirt. If he kept moving, maybe he could forget everything. He fell asleep quickly, like a dog, his legs twitching as he ran.

Chapter 4

"HEY, stranger. I'm glad to see you're back," Alma said. "We've got enchiladas and flan today."

"Pretty good timing, coming back just in time for my favorite foods," Jesse said, taking the plate she handed him.

"Where you been?" Alma asked. "I haven't seen you in over a week."

Jesse set the plate on his tray and reached for a bowl of flan. "Yeah, I caught a bug from my sister. I've been in bed, burning up, for two days."

Alma put her hands on her hips and frowned. "You been gone longer than two days, or maybe you just stopped liking my cooking."

"You know I love your cooking," Jesse said, giving Alma a big smile. "I had to take care of my sister before I got sick. She caught the flu first."

"Well, go on an' eat and don' be missin' any more school,

you hear?" Alma stared at him sternly and then shooed him away.

The cafeteria was almost empty. Jesse found a seat by himself at one of the long tables dotted with kids. He took a tentative bite of enchilada. It was warm and spicy and the first real meal he'd eaten in days.

***

The three nights in the hotel had been a delirious blur. When he'd finally woken up from the fever, Ellen was there dabbing his forehead with a damp cloth.

"I'd better get to school," he said, looking out the window at the midday sun. "I must have slept in. Where's Lizzie?"

"She's fine. She's back in school. And don't bother getting up," Ellen said, sitting down on the edge of the bed. "I've already called the school; you might as well rest until it's time to pick up Lizzie."

He'd slept on and off for two days with Ellen urging him to take sips of water and 7UP. By Friday he was feeling well enough to get up and walk around. But anxiety about his mother kept creeping in. "I need to go check on my mom," he told Ellen. "See if she's still hanging out at the Occupy."

"She's back in the forest," Ellen said bluntly. "I had a friend of mine ask around at the Occupy. A couple of folks were helping your mom set up a new camp."

Climbing out of bed felt like trying to swim out of a whirl-pool. The room swirled around him and he teetered for a moment before walking to the bathroom.

"Look, Jess. Frank and I are going down to Santa Cruz tomorrow to help Carlie move into an apartment."

Jesse held onto the frame of the bathroom door. "It's fine, Ellen. You've done enough, really. Thanks." Jesse went into the bathroom and shut the door. He stood in the shower for ages, letting the warm water wash away the grunge of fever sweat.

When he came out of the shower he found a note on the table by the window.

Jesse,

    Frank and I will be in Santa Cruz until next Wednesday. Please take Lizzie and stay in the house while we're gone. There's plenty of food in the fridge. There's a wind chime made of old spoons and keys hanging off the back porch, and the key decorated with the purple beads is for the house. It slips easily off the wind chime. Stay safe, Jesse, and always come to me in an emergency.

Love, Ellen

There was a knock at the door. When it swung open, two cleaning ladies stood ready to push in their cart of supplies.

"Excuse me, sir, checkout was at 11:00 and it's almost 1:30."

"Sorry," Jesse said, quickly stuffing his few belongings into his backpack. "I was just leaving."

***

In the cafeteria, Jesse took another bite of the enchilada. He'd lost weight with the fever and he hated the idea of getting too skinny.

"Hey, you're back." It was Raya, the apple girl, standing two tables away holding her tray.

"Oh, hi." Jesse waved her over.

"You know," Raya, said, sitting down across the table from him. "I carried around a piece of apple pie for you for days last week, but you never showed."

"That was nice of you." Jesse smiled. "My sister and I caught the flu. It was pretty bad," he said, running a hand through his hair.

"Oh, bummer. I've heard there's a bug going around."

"I guess the pie's probably gone bad by now, huh?" Jesse raised an eyebrow and gave Raya a half-smile.

"Uh, definitely. I threw it away, cuz people started wrinkling their noses at my backpack." Raya smiled broadly, revealing two rows of beautiful, straight teeth.

"So, how've you been?" Jesse asked. "Still have to hang here while your friends go off campus for lunch?"

"Yep, it's been lonely," she said, looking around the nearly empty cafeteria.

"The food's not bad, though," Jesse said, taking another bite of enchilada.

"Look, a bunch of us are gonna hang out on Halloween if you wanna come," Raya said, setting down her fork.

"Halloween?" Jesse said, "When is that? I've lost track of the date, getting sick and all."

Raya twirled her fork through the cheese and sauce pooling on her untouched plate. "Well, it sucks cause it's on a Monday this year, but it should be fun. We're just gonna meet on the plaza at dark and walk around."

"That's cool. I'll try," Jesse said, thinking of past Halloweens when he and his mom and sister would tear down their camp. They moved more deeply into the woods to avoid contact with the teenagers who tromped through the forest on haunted hikes at Halloween.

"What are you gonna be?" Jesse asked. "For Halloween?"

"Oh, it'll be a surprise," Raya said, getting up from the table. "I gotta go, but I'll look for you at lunch tomorrow, unless you're planning on vanishing again."

"Nah," Jesse said with a laugh. "I should be here all week. I've got a lotta homework to make up."

***

The tent Carla scored from the Occupy was a brand-new four-person from K-Mart. It was set up next to the stump where they used to sleep under the green tarp. The tent took up so much space, they'd had to dig out a new spot for their fire ring. They had tried to set up camp deeper in the forest but there was no other flat spot big enough for their new colossal shelter. In a way it felt good to re-inhabit their old camp. Word in the park was that after a sweep like the one they'd experienced, there'd be no one snooping around for quite a while. He'd thought about Ellen's invitation to stay in her house while she was gone, but he couldn't take his mom, and there was work to do setting up their new place. Jesse poked around in the ferns and salal looking for rocks that had been tossed aside during the sweep. He and Lizzie found most of the rocks from the old fire ring, and Lizzie tried to replace them in their original order.

"This green one was next to that one with all the white squiggly things," she said, thoughtfully arranging the rocks.

"We can go pick out new ones too, if you want, down at the creek." Jesse said.

"Yeah, yeah, let's go to the creek. We can take one of the fairies down for a drink. Mama!" Lizzie said, running over to the mossy ledges of the stump. "We're gonna take Fairy Ann down to the creek and get rocks."

"Okay," Carla said, and she went back to humming a cheery tune and organizing their belongings. Jesse had the urge to tell his mom to stop nesting, stop settling into a tent that was too visible even in these dark woods. If no one was there to guard it, it might just get torn down and thrown away. But Carla looked content setting up the sleeping bags Leo had gotten them and making tidy little piles of the new clothes she'd collected for them at the Occupy.

Lizzie's new backpack had vanished with the rest of their old stuff. But Lizzie hadn't really cared about the pack. She'd had it for only a few days. Her stuffies were another story. She'd cried for hours when she found out that Rabbit and Jay Jay, her stuffed blue jay were gone. After hours of her convulsive sobbing, Jesse had finally told Lizzie that Rabbit and Jay Jay might come back someday. He hated to lie to her but she wouldn't calm down, and he thought eventually she'd let go or maybe just forget.

Jesse took Lizzie's hand as they started down the spongy path to the creek. When they were out of earshot of camp, Jesse squeezed Lizzie's hand. "Mom likes the new tent, huh?" Jesse glanced at Lizzie.

"Yeah, it's like a little house." Lizzie smiled, making Fairy Ann dance along the tops of fern fronds bordering the creek trail.

"So, let's remember not to bring up Ellen, okay?" Jesse stopped walking and looked Lizzie in the eyes.

"I haven't told Mama about nice Ellen. I just call her the nurse." Lizzie looked concerned, like she'd already done something wrong.

"That's good," Jesse said firmly. "Pretty soon you won't have to bring her up at all cuz it'll just be a memory, right?"

"But won't we get to see Ellen?" Lizzie asked.

"Maybe, someday," Jesse said, squeezing Lizzie's hand. "But not soon. So just try to forget about it and don't bring her up to Mom, whatever you do. Mom seems kinda happy right now, don't you think?"

"Mama likes Leo," Lizzie said, in a near whisper, looking over her shoulder as if she thought Carla might be loping down the trail after them.

"We'll see how long that lasts," Jesse said. He swung Lizzie onto his back and galloped through the oversized ferns toward the rushing creek.

***

It felt good to be up in the tree, away from all of life's hassles. It was Saturday, so he didn't have to rush or worry about getting Lizzie to school. Between getting sick and setting up camp, almost two weeks had passed since he'd last climbed a tree. Leo actually seemed okay, but watching his mom swoon over the guy's every move was nauseating. She'd been backing off the drugs, which was good, but it bothered Jesse that she would get healthy for Leo but couldn't give up her addictions for her own kids. There was a chill in the air. The warm glow of late summer seemed to be giving way to fall. He climbed up, up, up, enjoying the scratchy bark rubbing against his hands and brushing his arms. He reached the notch in the tree where he'd seen the salamander last and climbed into the nest of decomposed needles and bark.

"Ahh..." he sighed, surprising himself with the sound of his own voice. He settled into the protected notch and looked up through the interlacing weave of branches to the blue sky and the white puffs of clouds whizzing by. It felt as if he and the trees were the ones moving swiftly, like vertical trains racing past docile, stationary clouds.

A slight movement in the branches caught his attention. His eyes searched the tree limbs while he kept his body rigid. Then he saw it: a vole, frozen in place, looking right at him. He'd seen voles in the redwoods, but never this high up. This unusual cache of soil seemed to lure all kinds of creatures.

Jesse studied the rest of the surrounding branches, hoping to catch another glimpse of the yellow salamander. He searched the limbs thoroughly while the vole scampered off and out of sight. The wind was picking up, and the tree branches squeaked and cracked against the waving limbs of neighboring trees. A raven cawed and soared by. Jesse could hear the flap of its wings and the rush of air as it flew past.

He wished he could transport Lizzie into the protected notch. He wanted her to know the feeling he got up in a tree like this. The feeling that nothing could go wrong, and that even though everything was changing and uncertain down on the ground, the tree would be there, growing up through the misty fog towards the sun.

Jesse could feel the sway of the trunk increasing. He should climb down and help Lizzie and his mom make a fire for cooking the hot dogs he'd gotten earlier at Safeway. He started his descent, enjoying the blast of cold air on his face and arms. He stayed close to the trunk following the branches down like he was descending a spiral staircase.

Ten feet below the tree nest, he saw a flash of pale yellow on the trunk by his foot. He climbed down to the spot where he'd glimpsed the salamander. There was nothing there, just a few pill bugs navigating the grooves of silver-reddish bark. Slowly, he began to circle the tree, scanning every surface for signs of the salamander or some other pale yellow creature. He continued circumnavigating the tree, hand, foot, hand—and there it was, on a branch, inches from his foot. The salamander was frozen in place, probably hoping Jesse hadn't noticed it poised there. Again Jesse tried to memorize the pale yellow color and the small black spots that dotted its back. Was it the same one he'd seen the last time? There was no way of knowing. It looked the same size but he hadn't measured it before. He should have brought a ruler or a measuring tape, neither of which he owned. Maybe he'd ask Leo if he could borrow a measuring tape for a school project.

He needed to get more precise about his observations, or what good were they? Then again, why bother? He remembered his lost notebooks. Why even write anything down when it could so easily be swept away? He stared intently at the salamander, trying to memorize the pattern of spots, the webbed toes, the spacing of the bulging eyes. It was safer to keep it all locked away in his mind. The swoosh of bird wings drew Jesse's attention, and he saw a red-tailed hawk soar past. He looked back to the salamander, but it had fled up the trunk towards the safety of a notch.

By the time Jesse reached camp it was dusk. Lizzie was squatting, holding a hot-dog-laden stick over the yellow flames of the fire.

"Jess, I already picked you out a stick!" Lizzie said, pointing at a neat pile of de-barked skewers. "I have them for Mama and Leo, too," she added.

"Leo?" Jesse said. "Is he coming for dinner?"

"He's already here," Lizzie whispered, glancing towards the tent. "Mama and him are having alone time."

Jesse let out a long stream of air. "How long has he been here?" Jesse asked quietly.

"I don't know... a while," Lizzie said, holding up a long slim stick for Jesse's hot dog. Jesse smiled and reached for the stick. "And here's a hot dog," she said, reaching into a gooey package.

"Thanks." Jesse took the hot dog and carefully skewered it. "That's perfect," he said, holding the meat over the flames.

"The sticks I have for Ma and Leo aren't as good," she whispered. Jesse smiled across the fire at her.

The rustling and groaning in the tent was getting louder and Lizzie kept turning toward the noise, looking concerned.

"Do you think Mama is okay?" Lizzie asked, sounding scared.

"Yeah," Jesse said. "Leo's probably just massaging her back."

"Oh," Lizzie, turned back to check the progress of her hot dog.

"Hey, wanna take dinner down to the park and eat on the swings?" Jesse asked, trying to sound excited.

"Yeah! Let's take the ketchup."

"Okay," Jesse, said, giving his hot dog one last twirl through the fire.

"Mama, we're going to the park to eat," Lizzie yelled at the rustling tent. Carla didn't respond but her moans were getting louder. Jesse scooped Lizzie up in his free arm and started down the trail towards the park.

They sat on the swings eating their hot dogs. Lizzie had eaten down to the bare stick and was licking the last bits of meat off of the wood.

"I'm still hungry," Lizzie said, pumping her legs back and forth.

"Me too. Let me push you for a while, then we'll go back."

"I wanna go back now. It's dark and I'm cold."

"I know," Jesse said, "look up at the sky and I'll push you while you look for stars." The clouds were moving fast past the first bright stars erupting in the evening sky. Jesse stationed himself behind Lizzie's swing, pulled back on the chains and let go, launching her into the wind-blown dark.

***

When Jesse and Lizzie got back to camp, Leo was sitting by the fire roasting a hot dog.

"Your mom's passed out in the tent," Leo said, looking across the fire at the kids.

"Bad word choice," Jesse said, raising an eyebrow at Leo.

"I mean she's sleeping... soundly," Leo stammered.

"I'm tired too," Lizzie said, yawning.

"I thought you were hungry," Jesse poked Lizzie in the belly with his finger.

"I wanna go sleep with Mama." Lizzie's voice was high and fatigued.

"Okay," Jesse said, putting his hands on his hips, "let's get your teeth brushed." After tucking Lizzie next to Carla, Jesse sat across the fire from Leo.

"So, how's it going living out here?" Leo asked.

Jesse's eyes narrowed, "What do you mean?"

"I'm not trying to pry, kid, I'm just wondering how you're holding up living in the woods, watching over your mom and sister."

Jesse laughed and then shook his head in disbelief. "You fuck my mom while my sister and I are sitting here cooking our dinner and then you ask how it's going!" Jesse stood up and grabbed his backpack. "Everything's peachy, Leo. Just great! I have homework to do," Jesse said. He had a serious urge to bolt and let Leo deal with taking care of Carla and Lizzie. But he forced himself to ask, "Can you hang out while I go to the library?"

"Sorry, kid, I didn't mean to offend you. I wanna help, if I can." Leo ran a hand nervously through his thick hair. "If you wanna help, stay here until I get back from the library." Jesse said, gruffly, looking at the ground. Leo stood up and held a tentative hand out to Jesse. "Sure thing, I'll stay. You get your homework done."

"I'll be back in a couple of hours." Jesse ignored Leo's outstretched hand, and walked down the trail.

It was already nine-thirty by the time he reached the university library. There were still lots of college kids tucked into cream-colored cubicles, immersed in elaborate diagrams and graphs in chemistry and biology texts. There were people reading history and literature, but Jesse liked to fantasize about the luxury of studying a biology textbook all day. He'd heard kids complaining to one another about having to cram for this or that test. What these kids whined about was always his idea of paradise. They had textbooks with clear, concrete explanations to problems, unlimited access to food and, at the end of every day, a bed to sleep in. *Heaven*, he thought, as he turned down the row with the herpetology books. Jesse scanned the bindings, fingers poised to pluck his selection of regulars off the shelf. *California Herpetology* wasn't there. He searched the titles more carefully, looking for the familiar blue binding.

"Shit," he said under his breath and shifted down the row to look for another herpetology text. After searching the stacks for another fifteen minutes and not locating any of his preferred reference books, he gave up, exasperated. Running his fingers idly along the colored bindings, he walked down the row of books, resigning himself to doing his homework. Jesse turned and walked along an outer row toward his favorite table. As he passed a return-to-stack cart, his eye was drawn to a collection of familiar bindings. There they were: all six of his favorite books piled up together.

"Weird," he said aloud. He took the books and walked to his table. As he leafed through the familiar pages of *California*

Herpetology, he found small pieces of paper marking the pages. It was nice to think about someone else on the lookout for a certain salamander. *Maybe one of these college girls,* he thought, glancing down the row of shelves to the figure of a pretty girl pulling books off a shelf. But he didn't have time to stare at random girls. That was a luxury for normal teenage boys.

Twenty minutes passed, and he forced himself to put the stack of books back on the return cart and get down to all the homework he had to finish. He was making quick work of an assignment on *The Grapes of Wrath.* The task was for the students to put themselves in the place of the characters and write a fictional response as if they too were living in those devastating circumstances. It was easy writing for Jesse. He just transported his own family back in time and made his mom sick instead of an addict. It felt good to express what was going on in his life, even in the form of time-machine fiction. But he couldn't stop thinking about the stack of books and how odd it was that they were the exact six that he always plucked off the shelves. Then again, it did kind of make sense—they were the best books for looking up local herps, insects, and flora. He went back to his story and created a young blonde woman who resembled Raya from the cafeteria. He had the mother die of consumption and felt the prick of a tear forming as he described her last gasping breath. It was easy writing but he didn't enjoy it. He'd much rather be looking up salamanders or pounding out math problems. Anything with a concrete answer. He'd had enough amorphous emotional crap in his own history for several lifetimes.

It was past midnight when he got back to camp. Leo was still sitting by the fire.

"Hey, you can go now," Jesse said, then hesitated. "Thanks for sticking around while I studied."

Leo stood up and looked at Jesse in the dim light of the fire. "No problem. I know this shit ain't easy for you," Leo gestured at the tent and the rest of their camp. "We'll keep collecting stuff for you. If there's anything you need let me know."

"A measuring tape would be great," Jesse said, bluntly.

"A measuring tape?"

"Yeah, for school. I need one for science class." Jesse lied, looking at Leo through the fire-glow.

"I'll see what I can do."

"Thanks, see you later," Jesse said, escorting Leo toward the trail down to the park. He wanted Leo gone.

***

Carla and Lizzie were curled up together in one sleeping bag. The other new bag was still folded in the corner of the tent. Quietly he unrolled the bag and climbed into the new crinkly nylon and sighed. There was nothing like a sleeping bag to keep you really warm. It gave Jesse comfort knowing they had two new bags going into fall and winter. He snuggled down and reached a hand into the dark, intending to grasp Lizzie's small pudgy hand. Instead, he felt Carla's bony fingers. He hesitated, then, hearing her even-breathing, he closed his hand around his mother's.

He fell asleep thinking about *The Grapes of Wrath* and how grateful he was for clinics and antibiotics. Then he was climbing, dreaming of a lofty redwood, chasing a yellow salamander through lichen-covered limbs to a glittering, sun-drenched redwood crown.

***

At school everyone was talking about college applications. Jesse could feel the buzz of information passing from kid to kid: the schools they were applying to, the packets they were receiving from different universities. He tried to block out all the talk. He wasn't planning to apply anywhere. Why should he? He couldn't leave his mom and Lizzie. Applying to Humboldt State was an option he'd thought about, but nobody talked about Humboldt. It was considered a back-up school for most of the kids.

At lunch Jesse sat next to Raya and teased, "So tell me what you're gonna be for Halloween." He nudged her with his shoulder.

"Nooo!" she giggled, "I told you you're going to have to find me in the crowd." She laughed again. "It's a test."

"A test? I'm pretty good at tests."

"We'll see how you do on this one," Raya said. Jesse gave her a knowing half-smile. "So have you started applying to schools?" Raya asked, looking curious.

"I don't think I wanna go to school right away." Jesse scanned her face, searching for any sign of disapproval.

"That's cool," she said with a shrug. "Are you gonna travel?" she asked, sounding hopeful. The idea of traveling had never really occurred to him. Staying in one secure spot was the goal, not purposely moving from place to place.

"I think I'm gonna work, save money for a while," Jesse said.

"That's a good idea, then go to college after a year or so?"

"Maybe, I don't know," Jesse shook his head. "What about you?" he asked. "Where do you want to go?"

"Well, I'm applying to the UC's. Of course I'd go to Berkeley if I got in, but I think I'll probably only get into Santa Cruz. I'm also applying to Lewis and Clark and Puget Sound and Humboldt just in case. If I get into a UC I'll probably go there, just 'cause it's cheaper than a private school."

"Wow, sounds like you have it all figured out," Jesse said, and took a bite of Alma's macaroni casserole.

"You should at least apply to Humboldt," Raya said. "They have an early acceptance thing for local kids."

"I'll think about it," Jesse said, scooping the last bite of macaroni onto his fork.

"I think you have to have your application in by next week. You could talk to the school counselor."

Jesse smiled. He liked how pushy Raya was being about this college stuff. But his plan was to work and save enough to get Lizzie and Carla and him into an apartment.

"Why are you smiling like that?" Raya asked. "I know you're smart. One of my friends had you in a math class. She said you always got the highest scores on the tests."

"I was just lucky," Jesse said, wondering what being lucky really meant. Was he lucky that math came easily to him? It was a revelation to think that something came more easily to him than to other kids. "I'll talk to the counselor," he said. "You happy now?"

"Yes!" Raya said, and took a bite of macaroni. "What's your story anyway?" Raya asked, squinting her eyes. "Why are you so mysterious?"

"Mysterious? I don't know, do girls like mysterious guys?" Jesse gave another half-smile.

"I guess they do," she said, and grinned, looking down at her plate. "I'm excited about Halloween," she said, loading her dishes onto a tray.

"Talk about mysterious. You still haven't told me what you're gonna be," Jesse said, and laughed.

Raya's friends appeared in the doorway. "We have treats for you, Ray," the tall one yelled across the nearly empty room.

"I guess I'll see you tomorrow," Raya said, sounding suddenly shy.

"Yeah," Jesse said. "Can't beat Café Alma."

***

On his way to history Jesse noticed a table set up in the quad by some military recruiters. He didn't have time to stop and talk to them, but he wanted to. There were rumors flying around campus that if you signed up for two years of service they'd pay for four years of college. Other kids said that was bogus, that the military didn't deliver when it came down to it. And that was if you even survived. Anyway, he wanted to talk to the recruiters and see if they offered housing for families while you served.

At the end of the day, the uniformed recruiters and their

table of pamphlets were gone. Maybe it was just as well. Jesse needed to pick up Lizzie and get something cheap for them to eat for dinner. He still had a full belly from Alma's macaroni, but that feeling could go away fast, and they were down to their last few dollars for the month.

***

Lizzie opened cans of tuna while Jesse held a plastic bag for her to drain the fishy liquid into. They were set up at one of the park picnic tables making dinner. It was better to keep strong food smells away from camp so they didn't attract raccoons or bears. Carla and Leo were taking their time in the tent. Jesse tried to convince himself that he didn't care what they did as long as Carla wasn't getting high.

"I'm making the biggest sandwich for you," Lizzie said, holding up two slices of day-old sourdough.

"Thanks, that's sweet, make a big one for you too!"

"Oh, I will," she said, and grinned.

After dinner Lizzie was on one of the swings pumping her legs hard in order to, as she said, "Catch the big air!" Jesse had cleaned up the mess from their sandwich assembly and helped Lizzie wash the fishy smell from her hands in the park water fountain. Lizzie insisted that they set aside two sandwiches, ready-made, for Carla and Leo. Jesse kept catching himself glancing up the hill at the trail leading into the woods, hoping to see Leo or his mom ambling towards them. But they didn't materialize.

"How's the evening treating you?" It was Ben, with Toby and Emma in tow on old frayed ropes. The dogs beat their tails back and forth in friendly greeting.

"Ben, you want a sandwich?" Jesse offered, holding up one of the sandwiches Lizzie had carefully wrapped in a paper napkin for Carla.

"Sure, if you got an extra."

"We already ate," Jesse said, giving the trail from camp a last cursory scan.

"Ben, look, I'm touching the sky!" Lizzie hollered from her high arc on the swing.

"Point your toes, and you'll touch that sliver of moon up there." Ben pointed at the thin slice of moon rising above the dark border of trees.

Lizzie let out a string of bubbly laughs and stretched her toes up and out as she pumped the swing into the dusky air.

"Ben... uh... you were in the military, right?" Jesse asked, still watching Lizzie's progress.

"Vietnam, way before you were born."

"Sounds like a pretty crazy war," Jesse said, shaking his head.

"All wars are crazy." Ben sounded suddenly stern.

"I guess, but it seems like the military might be a way out... you know, of this." Jesse gestured towards the nearly vacant park and the fading light.

"It's a way out, that's for sure, but not from this. Look at me. I'm here, just trying to stay clear of everyone, trying not to screw up any more lives than I already have."

Jesse narrowed his eyes at Ben. "But if you wanted to live in a house you could, like in military housing, right?"

"Nah, they'll promise you the moon, but they won't do shit. They'll send you over to some country and tell you to shoot the crap out of innocent people and then... shit, you'll never sleep through another night of your life without getting drunk or high." Ben tore off chunks of the sandwich and hand-fed bites to Emma and Toby.

"What about a free ride to college and housing? Did you get that?"

"Hell, it doesn't matter what they offer you, once you get back from whatever tiny country they send you to, you'll be too fucked up to function anymore."

"You function. You're the most together guy out here," Jesse said, nodding his head at the park.

Ben stopped feeding the dogs and looked at Jesse. "Yeah, I'm here. I'm not in a house. I left my family, I left everything, so I wouldn't keep hurting people and screwing things up. Like I said before, if I told you the things I've done to innocent people... you wouldn't like me."

Jesse stared down at his hands, trying to imagine what Ben had done that was so bad. When he glanced up, Ben was looking at him like he was daring him to ask what the big secret was. "But I need a way out of this for all of us," Jesse said, pointing to Lizzie's silhouette swinging through the dark.

Ben stood up and kicked at a pile of wood chips. "The military is not your way out. It's a death sentence. Whether you die out there or not, you come back as good as dead."

"I wanna come down!" Lizzie called from the swing. She had stopped pumping her legs but was still swinging in high arcs.

"Coming!" Jesse walked over to the swing set and reached out to Lizzie. "Jump," he said, holding out his arms.

"Catch me!" She leapt out of the swing and into Jesse's strong embrace.

It was dark by the time they headed up the trail towards camp. Ben followed silently behind with the dogs. When they reached camp, Carla was climbing out of the tent, her shirt unbuttoned. Leo was standing by the fire-pit zipping his pants.

"Here's a sandwich, Mom. It's tuna, so you should probably take it down to the park to eat," Jesse said, coolly. He was embarrassed to have Ben witnessing Carla's unbuttoned shirt and Leo's gaping pants.

"Thanks, I'll be back in half an hour, promise." Carla looped her arm through Leo's and led him down the trail.

"Mama," Lizzie called out. "I wanna come."

"No, I'll be right back. Get yourself to bed and I'll come and read to you."

"But Mama..." Lizzie whined, tears streaming down her face as Jesse held her hand tightly.

Carla ignored Lizzie's cries and continued down the dark path.

"It's okay, let's get ready for bed. I'll read you a story till Mom gets back," Jesse said. Lizzie's cries turned to a quiet heaving of her small chest. She leaned her head on Jesse's leg and shuddered against him.

"Night, kids," Ben said with a wave.

"Night, Ben," Jesse said. Lizzie waved meekly with a half-raised hand.

"Oh, and Jess," Ben turned and looked toward them in the dusky light. "If you ever join the military, I'll track you down and shoot you... in the foot. So, don't bother joining up. A shattered foot would be a real bummer." Ben turned and walked slowly away, with the dogs padding behind him, leaving Jesse and Lizzie huddled together.

"Why does Ben wanna shoot you?" Lizzie asked, intermittent shudders still intruding on her speech.

"Maybe so I can't ever leave you."

Lizzie took Jesse's face in her small pudgy hands. "You'd never leave me or Mama," she whispered.

Jesse sighed and looked into his sister's watery blue eyes. "Nope."

Chapter 5

THE weather changed overnight. The air had a crisp, cold edge, and Jesse noticed frost on the park grass in the morning on his way to school. It was a relief to know they had the sleeping bags and tent. Still, if it got really cold they'd have to consider sleeping in one of the church shelters. Jesse hated the shelters. Not because they were bad, but because people volunteered there; he might run into someone from school and then word could spread about him being homeless. Sometimes he helped in the kitchens of the shelters so people would think he was just another volunteer, a volunteer who stayed all night.

It was dark out by the time he reached town. Streetlights illuminated the sidewalks, which were getting crowded as he neared the town plaza. He walked past a tall, thin woman dressed in a blue Lycra bodysuit with a matching headdress. She batted her eyes at Jesse as he walked by and her eyelids flashed a silver pewter color. He continued down the street past a clown and an Egyptian princess. When he reached the town square, he lowered the Spider-Man mask that he'd bought at the Dollar Store.

The plaza was crowded with costumed teenagers as well as the regular crowd of hippie-homeless and their dogs. Jesse scrutinized the mob of teens, looking for Raya and her friends. He had no idea who was who. Almost everyone wore masks. He weaved cautiously through the crowd, listening for the sound of Raya's voice. There was a very tall girl dressed as a flamenco dancer standing next to a short girl dressed as a witch. They could be Raya's friends, but he didn't see anyone who looked or sounded like Raya.

Jesse inched closer to the witch and the flamenco dancer so he could hear their voices. It was hard to know if Raya would recognize him. He wore his black beanie pulled down low on his head and the Spider-Man mask covered most of his face. But his clothes were just street clothes and he was sure his sweatshirt was infused with his distinctive smell of wood smoke and redwood needles. Even if Raya recognized him, she wouldn't approach him; that was his job. She'd called it a test, and when it came to tests he liked to do well. *Use your Spidey senses*, he thought, smiling to himself.

He looked around the plaza with fresh eyes, watching the body language of all of the girls congregating around the statue of McKinley. No one looked quite right; none of the girls had that slow, easy grace that Raya had when she walked away from him in the cafeteria. "Just close your eyes," he said to himself, "and listen." With his eyes closed the voices seemed louder and more distinctive. There was a lot of flirting and teasing going on. Some of the voices sounded recognizable, but none of them had Raya's sweet, familiar tone.

"Shit," he said, under his breath. Deciding that he'd just have to ask around for her, he opened his eyes to the blur of colorful costumes. When his vision adjusted to the dim light, he scanned the crowd for the flamenco dancer, hoping to cor-

ner her and ask if she was indeed Raya's friend. "Think tall,"
he thought, as he turned in a circle hunting for the statuesque
girl. His slow rotation came to an abrupt halt when he set eyes
on the sleek figure of a girl dressed in a black cat costume. She
was perched alone on a bench on the far side of the plaza, her
hands mindlessly stroking her own silky black tail. She was far
away and, with the exception of her mouth and eyes, she was
completely covered in shiny black fabric. The sight of her with
her long thin legs curled under her lithe body, and the slow
graceful turning of her neck as she scanned the crowd, was
alarming and familiar. Even if she wasn't Raya, Jesse thought
he might have fallen instantly for this elusive, graceful Cat-Girl.

He turned and walked the perimeter of the plaza so he
could approach the girl from behind. There was a lump forming
in his throat and his hands shook a little. What was it about this
girl, he wondered, thinking, *It better be Raya*. There was a tree
behind the bench where the Cat-Girl sat curled. Jesse crouched
behind the tree and watched her glancing at the crowd. Finally
she rested her head on her knee. Jesse left the dark shadows of
the tree and approached her. He was reaching out to tap her
silky black shoulder when she turned slowly and faced him. She
didn't yelp or look alarmed, but she didn't smile either. She just
stared at him with intense blue eyes that looked a deep shade
of indigo in the fading light.

"Raya?" Jesse asked, feeling fairly certain, but wanting
confirmation that it really was her. The Cat-Girl didn't respond,
but uncurled herself from the bench and walked silently around
to face Jesse. In the body-hugging cat suit, the girl looked like
some kind of curvy black goddess. Jesse gasped slightly as she
approached.

"Spider-Man," was all she said, in a low, husky, only slightly
recognizable voice.

"Raya?" he asked again, looking into her eyes, feeling almost
certain it was her.

"No, Cat-Woman." she said, wrapping her arms around him

and inhaling the scent of his neck. "You smell really good," she said, and he didn't care anymore if it was Raya or someone else. He leaned down and gently kissed the Cat-Girl on her warm lips. The girl kissed him back with an eagerness that surprised him, and he was floating and they were turning in circles across the grass as they kissed in the hazy light of the plaza.

The Cat-Girl laughed and he thought he recognized Raya's familiar giggle.

"God," he said, "I really hope you're who I think you are." Then, he leaned down to kiss the girl's warm lips again.

"Why," she asked in a low, sultry voice, "what's wrong with kissing Cat-Woman?"

"Nothing…" Jesse said, running his hands over the silky arch of her back. "It's just that I don't want to fail… you know, the…"

"The test?' she finished his sentence. "Don't worry," she said, pulling gently at the hair under his beanie. "You got an A." She smiled, revealing the perfect white teeth that Jesse recognized from his lunches in the cafeteria.

"Oh, man," Jesse sighed. "I really like it when I do well on a test." Then he leaned down, eager to resume the kissing that seemed to levitate them off the ground and suspend them in some sort of bliss-cloud that he'd never inhabited before.

"Get a room!" the short witch-friend snapped. "Come on, Ray, we're all walking up to the park. We're gonna do that spooky tromp through the woods." The short one walked closer to Raya, and Jesse realized he was actually holding Raya off the ground. Reluctantly, he set her down and instantly felt heavy and sluggish.

"I'm gonna scream and reach for Nick like I'm super scared, come on!" the short witch demanded.

"Which park?" Jesse asked, coming out of his kiss-stupor.

"Redwood Park, you know, behind campus."

"We'll come along," Raya said, squeezing Jesse's hand.

"Actually," Jesse, said, dropping her hand, "I need to run

home really quick and get something… then I'll meet up with you at the park."

"Okay… I guess I'll see you there…" It was definitely Raya in the cat suit. The Cat-Woman with the low husky voice had given way to a teenaged girl with a nervous giggle.

"Promise I'll find you," Jesse said. "I'll be quick."

"That's fine," Raya sounded unconvinced. Jesse leaned down and kissed her lightly on the lips. She hesitated and then kissed him back with her original Cat-Girl passion.

"Okay," Jesse said, reluctantly pulling away. "I'll meet you in the park in about a half hour." He turned and took off at a steady trot. As soon as he was out of sight of Raya and her friends, he accelerated into a sprint towards the woods. He felt weird and blissful, like his body was a motor humming along at optimal speed. He'd kissed other girls, but it had never felt like that. He could still feel the heat from her lips burning on his. He smiled as he ran fast towards camp.

***

Leo and his Occupy posse had offered to help Carla take down the tent. Teens inevitably came to the park on Halloween and Carla didn't want to risk getting the new tent slashed or set on fire. She told Jesse to go ahead and meet his friends, like she was a real mom letting him out of his chores for a special occasion. But real moms didn't have to take their houses down on Halloween—or any other night for that matter. Jesse left Carla and Lizzie reluctantly, not trusting that Leo would show up.

Jesse had to be sure that his mom and Lizzle and their camp were tucked away somewhere safe. When he reached the park entrance, the wind had picked up enough to make the swings sway eerily in the dark. He saw a group of people milling around at the forest trailhead. Probably kids gathering their courage before entering Mother Nature's haunted house.

When he reached the group, Jesse hung back at the edge,

not wanting to be noticed. It was a pack of teenagers from the high school. The kids were listening to some guy talk about respecting people and privacy. Suddenly it dawned on Jesse that the guy's voice belonged to Leo. Jesse pushed through the shadowy crowd of kids. It was dark, but some of the kids had flashlights, which sporadically illuminated Leo's wide face and curly dark hair.

"People live back here," Leo was saying. "You gotta be respectful of people and their stuff." Leo squatted and picked up a handful of dirt. "This belongs to all of us. We own this place together." Some of the kids in the front squatted so they were eye level with Leo. "If you're going back there to commune with nature, that's cool." Leo let some of the dirt sift out through his fingers. The kids were being so quiet Jesse could hear bits of dirt sprinkle onto the ground. "Imagine," Leo continued, "if you lived in those woods, would you want a bunch of rowdy kids coming through and trashing your scene?" Leo made eye contact with the kids who were kneeling. Jesse was surprised they were so attentive. It was like he had them in some sort of trance.

"These people don't have homes or cars or even food some of the time. Can you guys imagine what that would be like?" Leo scanned the kids with his big brooding eyes, and when his eyes met Jesse's he lingered for a moment and then moved on, making eye contact with each of the kids. "Respect," Leo said, firmly. "If you decide you need to go back there because it's Halloween... that's cool. Just remember you might be walking through someone's bedroom while they're sleeping. So, walk through quietly the way your mom would if you were asleep."

Leo stood up still clutching some of the dirt in his fist.

"Okay," he said, softly, "do what you need to do." Leo looked at Jesse, turned and walked up the trail.

"That guy is hot," said a girl dressed as a rock star with an electric guitar strapped over her shoulder.

"I know," said a pirate girl, "I've seen him at the Occupy. He's like one of the main guys."

"He's old," said a boy with a ghoulish mask pulled up onto his forehead so his still-innocent features were revealed.

"He's only like thirty," said the pirate girl. "Not that old." She and the rock star girl giggled and jabbed elbows.

"His voice was like totally soothing," said a girl sitting on the grass.

"Are we gonna go up there or what?" asked a boy with no apparent costume.

"I don't think we should," said the pirate girl. "I feel like he was telling us not to without telling us not to, which is so cool." She giggled and reached her arms up so the costume-less boy could pull her onto her feet.

"I know," agreed the girl with the guitar, which she was strumming absentmindedly. "He has some kind of calming powers."

"Totally," said a clown girl, "like his super power is to calm people with his voice."

Jesse was surprised at all the Leo adoration. He hadn't noticed anything special about the guy, but apparently his mom had. At least he was putting his "powers," to good use. It was tempting to follow Leo back to camp, but Jesse didn't want the other kids to think he was instigating a haunted hike. The group seemed to have lost the motivation to go into the woods anyway.

"I wanna play on the jungle gym," said the pirate girl.

"What about my guitar?" the rock star complained.

"I can hold it," said the boy with the ghoul mask. The rock star girl lifted the guitar over her shoulder, handed it to the ghoul and then took off running for the climbing structure. The ghoul plucked at the guitar and then started tuning it.

A pack of kids was walking from the road towards the swings and Jesse thought he saw a sleek, black cat-girl in the crowd. Was Leo going to magically appear at the trailhead each time a group tried to enter the forest? Jesse wondered where his mom and Lizzie were. The plan had been for Leo to help them tear down camp and then take them to the Occupy. Jesse had decided to sleep in the stump with Ben and the dogs. But Leo was there to protect something. He wouldn't hang around all night to protect an empty camp.

Jesse felt his shoulders relax at the thought of Leo standing guard over his tent and family.

The cat-girl had split off from the group and was walking across the grass towards Jesse.

"Hey, Spider-Man," she said. She walked up to Jesse and pushed a loose strand of hair out of his eyes. "Where's your mask?"

"Oh, shit," Jesse felt the top of his head for the mask. "I guess it fell off when I was running."

"You must live nearby," Raya, said. "I thought we'd beat you here since you had to go home."

"Yeah, I do live nearby," Jesse wrapped Raya in his arms and smiled to himself, glad that he hadn't had to lie, yet, about where he lived.

He reached behind Raya's neck and gently pulled the cat mask off of her head. A mane of auburn hair fell down around her shoulders, and Jesse stopped. He looked closely at her features. Her large, oval blue eyes and her straight, white teeth, even the light sprinkling of freckles across her nose, were Raya's, but Raya's hair was blonde, not auburn.

Raya laughed, and her blue eyes crinkled with her smile. "Don't worry, it's me. I just dyed my hair."

Jesse took a silky strand of hair and rubbed it between his fingers.

"It feels nice," he said in a low voice.

"You like it?" she asked.

"Yeah," he said, and then looked into her eyes, which appeared dark in the inky light. "I think I'd like it any color," he said, leaning down to kiss her smiling lips.

***

It wasn't easy getting up the next morning, but Jesse was relieved to be in the dry tent at camp with his mom and Lizzie. He had to admit that if it weren't for Leo, Jesse and his family would have had to move down to the Occupy. Just the thought of pitching their tent on the Town Hall lawn made him recoil; it was too exposed, like the penguin enclosure at the zoo. If it had come to that and they'd had to move their tent to town he'd probably have taken a sleeping bag and walked deeper into the woods or slept with Ben and the dogs in the stump. Leo had really helped out by acting like a sentry at the trailhead.

When Jesse had finally returned from walking Raya to her house it was late, but Leo was still up, sitting by the fire strumming quietly on a battered ukulele. Jesse had wanted to sit down and listen to Leo plunk out Jack Johnson tunes, but something made him hold back; maybe it was pride, or maybe anger.

"Thanks," was all he'd managed to say.

Leo stopped playing the ukulele and looked at Jesse. "Those kids don't know you live out here, do they?"

"No… not really. I gotta go to bed," Jesse said, pretending to look for something in the dirt. "School in the morning," he mumbled.

"No problem," Leo said. "I'm gonna stick around for a while 'til the fire burns down."

"Fine," Jesse said, and walked to the far side of camp. As he brushed his teeth, he thought about Leo and how he had protected Carla and Lizzie from the hordes of rowdy teenagers. He wanted to hate the guy, but he couldn't help but soften a little towards him.

***

Jesse might not have bothered going to his first class if he didn't need to get Lizzie to school. There was something sweet gnawing away at him as he tried to wake up and climb out of his sleep haze. He remembered Raya and their kiss on the plaza. And her cat suit—he couldn't get that suit out of his head. He opened his eyes and stared at the grey seam in the tent cloth and tried to recall his dream. He knew it was something about Raya. They'd been high in a tree looking for his salamander. She'd had the cat suit on and climbed up the tree fast with real claws. She saw the salamander first, and he was scared that she might kill it with her claws, the way a cat would. But she'd picked it up gently and handed it to Jesse. He couldn't remember anything else from the dream, but it was enough to get him up and out of the dew-dampened tent.

On their way to school Lizzie rattled on about Leo and how he'd gotten her lavender fairy wings and a butterfly mask at the Dollar Store. "And Mama took me tricker treating on the plaza." She reached into the pocket of her grungy pink coat and pulled out a mini chocolate bar. "Mama has my candy but I snuck this one for you," she said, handing Jesse the small smooshed bar.

"You have it."

"No," she said, sounding serious. "I snuck it for you."

Jesse took the bar and peeled off the foil wrapper. He broke the small bar in half and popped a piece into his mouth. "Mmmm..." he said. "That is good. I have so much energy now, I think I need to run." He scooped her onto his back and handed Lizzie the other half. "Now you try, I think that's a special-powers bar." Lizzie laughed and nibbled while Jesse picked up speed, galloping towards school.

It was hard sitting through class until lunch. It felt like Christmas with a special package waiting for him in the cafeteria. When the bell rang he ran-walked to lunch and scanned the room for Raya. He was disappointed that she wasn't there yet. Deflated, he went through the food line alone and let Alma dish him up a hefty portion of sausage and potatoes. He was really hungry and the sausage smelled so good he almost forgot about finding Raya. He started to sit down when he noticed her turn around and wave from a few tables in front of him.

"Hey." He smiled, taking his tray and walking to her. "I forgot about your new hair. I was looking for blonde and probably stared right at your back."

Raya giggled. Jesse set down his tray across from her and sat. "So, how's your day going?" he asked, grinning at her.

"Fine," she said, sounding evasive.

"Is something wrong?" Jesse hoped he hadn't offended her in some way.

"No, nothing," she said, "it's just... I got you this online." She held up a stapled sheath of papers.

"What is it?" Jesse was worried. Like she was holding up some kind of evidence that he was homeless and camping illegally.

"It's an application," she said, "to HSU... if you want. It's just that early applications for local kids are due this week and I thought you'd want to... you know... turn one in." Raya looked like she'd stepped over an invisible threshold. "I don't want to be acting like some pushy girlfriend, when we're just starting to go..." Raya stopped herself and poked at a bowl of vanilla pudding with her spoon.

Jesse laughed and reached across the table for her hand. "What?" he said, "finish what you were going to say."

"No, I shouldn't have said that, I'm just tired from last night and all..."

"Shouldn't have said what?" Jesse teased. "That we're going out? Cuz you're right, I haven't asked you out yet." He smiled mischievously.

"I know, that was stupid of me... it's just that last night was... I don't know."

"I do know," Jesse said, standing up.

"Don't go," Raya pleaded. "I can be so stupid and controlling. You don't have to apply to college if you don't want to."

Jesse walked around the table so he was standing behind her. He reached over her shoulder for the application and leaned down so that his lips were brushing her ear. "Raya, will you go out with me?" he asked, in a soft voice. Raya let out a sigh and turned her head so she was looking into Jesse's eyes.

"Sure," she said, and her whole face smiled.

***

After school Jesse went to the counselor's office to ask about some of the questions on the application.

"I was wondering," Jesse asked, "if I could put your name and the school as my return address?"

Miss Meyer looked at Jesse for a moment before answering. "Well, that would be unconventional, but I suppose so. Is there a problem at home, Jesse? Are you being discouraged from attending college?"

"Not exactly... I'd rather hear if I get in and then tell my family."

"That's reasonable. The other thing we need to get done is the SAT. There's a test in early November and you'll need to take that."

"I'll keep that in mind. I'd better go. My sister's waiting for me."

"Come see me tomorrow about signing up for that test," Miss Meyer pressed.

"Yeah," Jesse said, standing up to leave.

It was late and he needed to pick up Lizzie. Running down the hill from school he heard his name and turned to see Raya trying to catch up with him.

"Hey," she said, out of breath when she reached him. "I was looking all over for you after school."

"Oh, sorry, I went to talk to Miss Meyer about that application and now I'm really late getting my sister."

"It's just that it's hard to reach you cuz you don't have a phone and all..."

"Sorry, my mom's… uh… anti-cell-phone. She thinks they give you brain tumors."

"Can I come with you… to pick up your sister?"

"If you want," Jesse said with a smile. Raya reached for his hand and instead of rushing they walked lazily, their fingers intertwined, towards Lizzie's school.

When they reached the campus the lawn was empty of kids. Only a few stray cars were parked in the lot.

"Shit, I must be really late." Jesse let go of Raya's hand and ran his fingers through his hair. "I better go check the office."

"I'm not in the office. He, he, he…" giggled a small voice.

Jesse laughed with relief. "Of course you're not. Climb down, Lizard, and meet my friend." Lizzie stared down at Jesse and Raya from the flimsy top limbs of the laurel tree.

"You're a good climber!" Raya said, looking up through the branches of yellowing leaves. "Wouldn't catch me climbing that high."

"You should climb with Jesse," Lizzie said, as she dropped easily to a low branch.

"Why?" Raya smiled up at Lizzie. "I'm sure he can't climb as high as you." Lizzie giggled and swung from the branch.

"Catch me, Jess." Lizzie launched off the branch and into Jesse's arms.

"Oh, man," he whispered into Lizzie's ear, "you reek of pee. Did you pee your pants today?"

"I tried not to, but we had a substitute and he didn't notice my hand."

"What an asshole," Jesse said, neglecting to whisper, and forgetting that Raya was standing behind him.

"Mama says don't swear!" Lizzie scolded.

"Mom says a lotta things."

Raya tapped Jesse on the back and he turned to face her, still holding Lizzie in his arms.

"Are you going to introduce me?" Raya asked, shyly.

"Sorry. Raya, this is Lizzie, my chipmunk sister." Lizzie smiled and then buried her face in Jesse's chest.

"Are you gonna be shy?" Jesse set Lizzie on the ground and reached out for her hand. "Let's walk Raya to her house."

Raya reached for Lizzie's free hand, but Lizzie moved to the other side of Jesse and took his hand.

"Hey, don't be rude. Raya is being nice."

Lizzie tugged at Jesse's shirt until he squatted down at eye level with his sister. "What's up Chipmunk, why so shy?" Lizzie put her mouth up to Jesse's ear and whispered.

"You said I smell bad."

"Don't worry about that. I'll take you to the pool later for a shower," Jesse whispered almost inaudibly into Lizzie's ear.

"It's not nice to tell secrets," Raya teased.

"You're right," Jesse said, taking Raya's hand. "Let's walk you home."

When they reached Raya's house, Jesse fought the urge to wrap his arms around Raya and try to recreate the kiss they'd had the night before on the plaza. It wasn't going to happen with Lizzie there clinging to him, smelling of urine.

"Wanna study tonight… at the university library?" Jesse asked. "I could meet you somewhere on the third floor at around eight."

"Yeah, I have tons of homework and my college essays to work on."

They smiled awkwardly, and then Raya turned and went through the gate to her house.

"I'm hungry." Lizzie tugged on Jesse's arm.

"Me too," Jesse said, looking longingly at the winding garden path to Raya's house.

***

They met at the library every night that week, and when Jesse walked Raya home he was rewarded with cat-girl kisses. He'd never felt this way about a girl. He thought about doing things with her that he guessed neither of them was really ready to do. He wondered if this was how Leo felt about Jesse's mom. But why Carla? She was at least five years older than Leo, and Jesse didn't think she looked very good. She had been beautiful when he was younger. He remembered her soft smooth skin and clear blue eyes that had since gone hazy and bloodshot. Maybe Leo still saw a glimmer of the old Carla, who Jesse thought they'd lost a long time ago. Since Halloween, Jesse had softened towards Leo. It seemed like the guy honestly wanted to help out. Hell, he'd stayed with Carla and Lizzie all week while Jesse had been off at the library "studying" with Raya. He'd even brought Jesse that tape measure that Jesse had lied about needing for science class.

***

Jesse and Raya spent more time playing hide and seek in the book stacks, blatantly annoying some of the serious library goers, than really studying. It was next to impossible to concentrate with Raya sitting across from him, her blue eyes darting between her notebook and Jesse's steady gaze.

One night, when it was getting late and they had books and papers strewn all over one of the round tables on the third floor of the library, Jesse hooked his foot around Raya's under the table. "I'm not getting anything done," he said.

Raya leaned her head to the side, letting her hair fall seductively across one arched eyebrow. "I know. I started writing about you in my college essay and I'm pretty sure that's a bad idea."

Jesse was thinking that his story, if she knew it, was actually the perfect college essay. A struggling homeless boy gets his shit together to apply to college. "Yeah, don't write about me... talk about boring," he tried to sound upbeat.

"Wanna play hide and seek?" Raya asked, using her sultry cat-woman voice. Jesse loved that voice.

"You mean cat and mouse?" he asked, and grinned.

"I'll be the mouse," she said.

"I thought you were the cat?" he teased.

"Okay, let's play cat and dog," she said, trying to keep a straight face.

"I'll sniff you out." He forgot to whisper and a serious-looking girl at a neighboring table glared at him. Raya giggled and slunk off to the stacks.

After a few minutes of sitting at the table glancing apologetically at the serious girl, Jesse headed into the rows between the stacks. Usually he was the solemn one in the library, wondering how people found time to goof off. But with Raya it was different. He didn't really care what anyone thought; he just wanted to be near her.

There weren't any good hiding places in the tall rows of books, he thought, as he walked through the corridor glancing down each aisle in search of Raya or even a glimpse of the light blue scarf she'd wound loosely around her neck. He reached the end of the corridor without finding her. "Maybe under a table or chair?" he muttered, and began meandering through the stacks, peering under the round tables and cream-colored cubicles.

Jesse was back at their table with no sign of Raya. A grey-haired man was placing a stack of books on the return cart as Jesse approached his own table strewn with binders of abandoned homework. He glanced at the man's pile of books and noted something familiar. They were his books. Almost all the same six or seven that he plucked off the shelves during each library visit.

"Wait!" Jesse said, loudly. But the grey-haired man had turned the corner and was already out of sight. The studious girl glared at him as if to say, "Really, you're going to be loud again!" Jesse fought the urge to run but instead walked quickly around the corner after the man. At the stairwell he finally caught up, and almost shouted, "Excuse me."

"Yes?" The man turned toward Jesse, his eyes big and magnified behind thick round glasses.

Jesse stuttered, "Those books you put back... are you studying salamanders or something?"

The man smiled like he suddenly recognized Jesse. "Are you the one who's always pulling those books off the shelf?" the man asked, holding out his hand. "Henry Pelsinski, or just Henry."

"Jesse." He shook the man's hand.

"So, what's of so much interest to you in those books?"

"I climb a lot of trees, and I come here to identify some of the stuff I see."

Henry was nodding his head as if he agreed with Jesse's need to climb and identify things. "What kinds of things are you finding?" Pelsinski asked.

Jesse felt suddenly sheepish and amateur. This guy was older and so well kept. Jesse was sure the man was expecting Jesse to say something profound. "Just ferns, moss, some salamanders, insects, lots of birds," Jesse replied.

"I noticed that you dog-eared all of the herp books on the pages with the arboreal salamanders. Have you found those salamanders up in the trees?" Henry asked, sounding serious.

"No," Jesse raked his fingers through his hair. "I've found one like that, but it's more of a pale yellow color with black spots. It has a lot of the other features of an arboreal salamander, but I haven't actually been able to key it out yet."

"Really? That's interesting. I'd like to hear more about your description of the salamander. Could you come to my office?"

"Jesse, there you are! I've been hiding on a shelf for like fifteen minutes," Raya sounded stern.

"Sorry, Kay, I ran into Henry... Mr. Pelsinski here and we started talking about..."

Pelsinski smiled at Jesse and Raya. "Look, I've got to get going, but I'd love to talk to you more about that salamander. Come by my office tomorrow at noon. I'm in Science B-305."

Jesse shook his head. "I'm in school then. I don't think I can get away till later. Maybe like four?"

"Four will work," Pelsinski said. "I'll see you then." He raised a hand in farewell and headed down the stairs.

"How do you know that guy?" Raya asked, lacing her fingers through Jesse's.

"I don't, actually. I mean I just met him now. I was looking for you," he squeezed her hand, "and he had my books."

"Your books?" Raya scrunched her eyebrows together.

Jesse rubbed his thumb over her knuckle. "He had this specific stack of books that I always get when I come here to look stuff up that I've found in the redwoods. I saw him putting them back on the shelf, so I went after him to find out who he is."

"That's cool that you look stuff up. He sounds pretty interested."

"I'm curious what he's after," Jesse said, and raised his eyebrows. "But what I really want to know is where you were hiding. I looked all over for you."

Raya turned and led him back towards the stacks. "Follow me," she said, letting him trail behind her, their fingers threaded loosely together.

Chapter 6

"I CAN'T believe this view!" Jesse had coaxed Raya up a not-so-tall tree. It was on the ridge and tall enough for them to have a clear view of the bay and the ocean beyond.

"Pretty great, huh?"

"I had no idea you did this, Jess. It's amazing." She stared down at him with a look of open joy. Raya was perched on a branch above him. He had stayed right below her the whole time. If she slipped he wanted to be able to stop her fall. She'd seemed nervous at first, and tentative, but as they neared the crown he saw her relax into the hand-foot-hand rhythm of real tree climbing.

"You have so much crap in your hair." She plucked a piece of tree bark off his head and let it drop into the airy abyss.

"I'm trying not to look down," she added. "It really freaks me out."

"Don't look down," he said, laughing.

"I can't help it." She pulled a redwood needle out of Jesse's tangled hair. "You're down there, so I keep looking down."

"Okay," he said, pulling himself into a nest of branches next to her. "How's that?" he asked.

"Better, but I'd like it more if you had your arm around me."

"What did I say, before we started up, about points of contact?"

"What about points of contact with each other instead of the tree?" Raya joked.

"Look, I can keep two hands on the tree," Jesse said, sliding one foot onto the branch by Raya's feet. "And still have a point of contact left for you," he said, leaned in and gently kissed her on the lips.

Raya pulled out of the kiss and let out a big sigh. "This just makes me want to break all the tree-climbing rules," she said.

"I know what you mean. I wouldn't mind making at least ten points of contact with you right now."

"Ten. That sounds tempting. But show me what you look for, what you're studying that's so interesting to that professor guy."

The air was crisp, the sun still high in the noon sky. It was getting more difficult to climb after school. By the time he picked up Lizzie and got back to camp with something for dinner, the sun was usually starting its evening display of mandarin pink streaks across the horizon. It was finally the weekend and Jesse had been itching to climb. He'd met with Pelsinski a week ago and they'd talked for two hours about the yellow salamander. They hadn't found it in any of Pelsinski's reference books. Henry encouraged Jesse to climb as often as he could and check back if he spotted any more of the yellow salamanders.

A light breeze blew through the high branches of the tree and Raya reached for Jesse's arm. "Whoa, we're moving," she said, looking alarmed.

"It's just a little wind. These trees really rock when it howls. It can get scary."

"What exactly are you looking for up here?"

"Everything. I mean all of it, I guess." He pointed out to

the bay and swept his hand through the air indicating his interest in everything between the bay and the tree they were sitting in. "I'm into the salamanders, sure, but I'm just as into checking out the birds or the insects, even plants." He pointed to a patch of green moss blanketing the north side of the tree.

"Find one of the yellow salamanders for me. I'd love to see one."

"I don't know if they hang out in these smaller trees. I've only seen them in the really big one. The one with the pile of soil."

"Next time take me up a big tree. I wanna see what you see up there," she said, pointing into the crown of a nearby tree.

"It's not easy getting up to where the limbs start on those tall trees."

"It's so beautiful up here. I can see why you climb. It's like another planet... up high and away from all the struggles down below."

"It's a different perspective, for sure."

"Have you been in that tree?" Raya pointed to a tall neighboring redwood.

"No, actually, not yet. I usually climb a couple of the big trees a little to the south of us." He laid his arm over Raya's shoulder and pointed towards a clump of tall trees.

"But if you wanted to climb that tree right there, how would you get up? Ropes?" Raya asked.

"I don't actually own any ropes. I usually find a big tree with a smaller tree next to it. And then I do some kind of traverse, if the trees aren't too far apart."

"What do you mean by traverse? You mean you jump?" Raya asked, sounding scared and a little bit excited.

"Kind of. I like to think of it as reaching for a nearby branch."

"That sounds totally dangerous. I mean what if you fell?" she said, looking down through the overlapping branches to the ground.

"It always seems to work out," he said, remembering the time he almost hadn't made the leap to a branch. His blood pumped faster just thinking about it. "I think I could do this," he said, climbing below Raya.

"No Jess, don't even think about it… I wasn't trying to encourage you…"

But it was too late. Jesse had his eye on a branch jutting out of the big tree. It was close but the angle wasn't perfect. Still, if he just aimed for it, he always seemed to get there.

Raya's "Nooooo!" wove in and around his "Whooo hooo," as he leapt for the branch of the big tree. He kept his eyes focused on the limb and he was there, slamming into a fan of needles as he grabbed for the branch.

"Shit, Jesse, are you okay? Oh my God. I can't believe you did that." Raya's voice was shaking like she might cry or laugh, in a crazy way.

"I'm okay," he said, and pulled himself up onto a few close limbs so he could sit and let his breathing slow. "How about you?" Jesse looked through the dense tangle of needles to where Raya stood gripping the tree with both hands.

"I liked it better when you were over here," she said, sounding scared. "How will you get back?"

"Don't worry, it's actually easier going that way, because the branches are so close together, there's more to grab onto." Jesse wanted to sound reassuring, but it was also true; he always had an easier time descending a tree. Crossing over to a big tree was sketchy. There were only so many branches. You couldn't make any mistakes. "You okay there for a couple of minutes while I climb up and look around?"

"I guess." Raya sounded hesitant.

"I won't be long. Listen for me at the top. I'll whistle like this, 'thew oot, thew oot'." Jesse whistled so Raya would recognize the sound.

Raya let out a nervous laugh. "This is so crazy," she said. "And scary and beautiful!"

"Glad you think it's beautiful. I won't be long." He tried to make eye contact with her through the mass of greenery. And then he was climbing up fast through the spiraling branches of the big tree. It was always exciting, climbing a new tree: like hiking up a mountain you'd never summited before. Sure there was a lot of the same in every tree but each one was also completely unique. The bark varied slightly in color, and trunks split and splayed in different configurations. Even the light varied, depending on the location and aspect of the tree.

He moved quickly toward the top, not wanting to leave Raya for too long. He had to admit that it felt good to be alone and moving easily up and around the tree. It was usually the one place he didn't have to worry about someone else. But he'd wanted her to see it, to feel the height and serenity. He was nearing the crown, and the branches were thick and lush. There was no split trunk but some of the branches had shoots growing straight up like miniature aerial forests.

At the top, he sat only briefly to whistle and absorb the panoramic view of the bay and the miles of forest blanketing the hills to the east. Climbing down, he took time to note a few small beetles navigating the grooves of the redwood bark. There were large ants circling the trunk, which for them must have felt like an edible vertical moonscape. He would have liked to show Raya some of the insects and birds that seemed more inclined to inhabit the big trees than their smaller, flanking neighbors, but he couldn't risk a dangerous approach with her, like the one he'd just made.

He was close to Raya's tree when he spotted the pair of yellow salamanders. "Raya!" he called, too loudly, "They're here in this tree… the salamanders." They were like the one he'd seen in the big tree with the over-sized notch, pale yellow with blackish grey spots.

"You saw them?" Raya called back, sounding excited.

"I'm seeing them right now!" he said. "There are two of them on the trunk only a foot away from me."

"I wish I could see them," she said. "You don't have a phone; shit, do you have a camera in your pack?"

"No," he said, thinking about how he had to use his eyes and memory as a camera. Maybe that was why tests were easy for him. Maybe he was using a part of the brain that other kids had stopped accessing years ago when they got their first cell phones.

"I could throw you my phone!" Raya called out.

"Nah, I've got them in my head. I'll draw you a picture." The salamanders stayed frozen to the trunk of the tree. One looked like a three-inch adult and the other was about two and a half inches long and smaller all over, probably a juvenile. He reached out, hoping to turn one over and inspect its belly, maybe even determine the sex, but both skittered around the trunk and away.

"They're gone. I'm coming back," Jesse said into the cluster of limbs separating him from Raya.

"Be careful," she called out.

He sailed toward the smaller tree, grabbing at whatever he could.

"Oh my God, Jess, shit, shit, are you okay?" Raya looked down at Jesse through the sheaf of branches.

"Fine," he said clinging to two tree limbs. He climbed up towards Raya breathing hard, sweating, and wearing a big grin. "I'm fine!"

***

"Who's this girl Lizzie keeps talking about, Jess?" Carla was squatting next to their morning fire, with just enough wood to heat up water for oatmeal.

"You mean Raya?" Jesse kept his voice flat and lifeless, not wanting to give anything away. But it wasn't easy sounding indifferent when saying her name. The curving *R* and the happy *a* at the end of her name sounded like sunlight on a cold morning.

"She's just a friend." He narrowed his eyes at Lizzie in warning.

Lizzie giggled and squeezed onto her mother's lap. "He says goodbye to her like this." Lizzie kissed her mom on the lips. Carla tickled Lizzie and they both squealed.

"She sounds like a nice friend. Bring her by. I'd like to meet her."

"Bring her by?" Jesse said, gesturing at the fire and tent. "Bring her by and show her what? Our tent? Maybe I'll get really lucky and bring her by on a day that you're passed out cold in the dirt. She can help me roll you over so you don't choke on your vomit!" His heart was beating fast and he wanted to get away.

"Stop it! That's not fair. I've been clean for over a month. Leo's helped me get off of everything, and…" Carla lowered her head onto Lizzie's back and her voice began to shake. "I'm trying. I'm trying to be a good mom and you haven't even noticed. I want to be there for you and Liz. I want to meet Raya and talk to you about safe sex and birth control. I want to do all that." Carla looked up at Jesse with pleading watery eyes.

"I don't want to talk to you about any of that, Carla." He knew it hurt her when he called her by her name. He couldn't help staring as her eyelid began to twitch. "Maybe if we had a house and beds and a table to eat at and a place to do homework. Maybe if I came home to someplace for a whole year and never once found you high or passed out… then I might risk bringing someone over. But until then, don't ask me to bring a friend to visit. And don't talk to me about safe sex. You don't even know what that means."

Jesse threw down the cup of oatmeal that Carla had handed him and tramped up the path into the damp woods. Damn her, he thought, as he walked up the muddy trail past salal and huckleberry bushes that were now barren of fruit. It was mid-November and the temperature dropped a little each night. The big trees acted like a blanket protecting their camp from the thick frost that formed in the open part of the park, but soon, they'd have to find somewhere else to stay. In the past, they'd tried some of the temporary housing situations but had been kicked out because Carla always broke the drug-free rules. She was clean now, but Jesse didn't trust her. He'd never seen her stick it out for more than a couple of months. If Leo got a house, something small that they could all live in together, Jesse might actually believe in his mom. But Carla was probably a temporary obsession for Leo. His real passion was the Occupy and Jesse didn't trust Leo to drop all of that for a homeless woman and her kids.

There was no sun streaming through the canopy of big trees, just a dull grey layer of clouds threatening to drizzle. Jesse came around a corner and realized he was at Ben's stump. No wisp of smoke swirled from the top of the hollow tree. Jesse assumed that Ben and the dogs had already headed to the park or town in search of morning coffee. Jesse heard rustling at the base of the stump and saw Toby's head poking out of the dark opening.

"What's up?" Jess knelt to scratch Toby's ears but the dog pulled away and disappeared back into the tree. "Hey, Ben, you up yet?" Jesse called into the dark. There was no reply. It was unlike Ben to leave the dogs in the stump during the day. On his hands and knees, Jesse crawled through the wet redwood needles into the dimness of the cavity. There was only a narrow band of light coming from the small opening at the top of the tree. Toby and Emma wagged their tails and nuzzled Jesse in greeting and then laid down next to Ben, who was wrapped up tightly in a dirt-colored army blanket. Jesse crawled to Ben and placed a hand on the older man's back. He was shivering and Jesse could hear a deep rattling coming from his chest with each rough exhalation.

"Ben," Jesse shook his friend's shoulder. "Wake up. I think you need to go to the clinic." Ben coughed. Jesse put a hand on Ben's cheek. "Shit, Ben, you're totally burning up." The dogs thumped their tails on the dirt floor and looked attentively at Jesse. "Ben, I gotta get you to the clinic. Maybe I can get some-

one to come here or bring you back antibiotics or something."
Ben was unresponsive and seemed to be in some kind of fever
coma, not comprehending anything. There was a thin blanket
next to a pack and Jesse spread it over Ben's shuddering body.
He found the remnants of a bag of dog food and divided it
between Toby and Emma. Jesse scooted back out of the stump
and ran down the trail to camp, arriving flustered and out of
breath. Leo was there, helping Carla take down the tent.

"What's going on?" Jesse asked. Before Carla or Leo could
answer he cut them off and blurted, "Ben's really sick. Boiling
hot and he won't wake up. Maybe I should call the hospital or
get someone from the clinic."

"It's Sunday, the clinic is closed," Leo said, matter of factly.

"If you get an ambulance out here," Carla warned, "they'll
shut the whole place down."

Jesse ran his hands through his hair. "Why are you taking
down the tent?" he asked again.

"It was freezing last night, Jess. The church on Eleventh
Street has opened up for nighttime sleeping. Leo thinks we
should stay there until it warms up."

"But what about Ben!" Jesse almost screamed. "We can't
just leave him here. They never take dogs in those places."

"You can't take on all of Ben's problems," Carla said. "He'll
probably sleep for a couple of days and wake up feeling fine."

Jesse stomped his foot. "You don't understand, Carla,"
Jesse said, enunciating his mother's name. "Ben is my friend.
He's probably the best guy I know. And he's been more of a
parent than you have. You didn't do shit when Lizzie got sick.
I guess you didn't want to take on all of our problems." Jesse
was shouting.

"That's not fair. I looked all over for you and I was crazy
worried about both of you."

"Well you didn't look that hard," Jesse, said, squinting his
eyes at Carla. "We were at your sister's house. Did you ever
think of looking there? Or are you too scared that she's a

human-eating alien?" Jesse felt sick as he heard the angry words leap out of his mouth, but he couldn't stop them. And part of him was oddly satisfied to see Carla's eyes brim with tears. "You didn't. I've told you to never..." Carla put her hands to her face and clawed at her eyes with her long dirty nails. Leo tried to embrace her but she shrugged him off.

Leo lifted his hands and quietly muttered, "You have a sister?"

"Oh, fuck, I don't have time for this shit, Mom. Your sister is not an alien and she probably saved Lizzie's life. So get over it!"

Jesse ran down the trail to the park past the pods of homeless people huddled around their dogs tethered with frayed ropes. At first he headed towards the clinic, but then he remembered Leo saying that it was Sunday. He ran past the plaza, littered with a handful of weekend shoppers and more homeless folks with their dogs. It was cold even as he ran fast through the bare tree-lined streets.

It surprised Jesse to find himself on Ellen's porch knocking on her front door and calling out her name. Ellen looked equally surprised to find Jesse standing there, breathing hard from his run.

"Is he here?" Jesse looked into the house nervously checking for the whereabouts of his uncle.

"No, he's on a trip, Jesse. Where's Lizzie? Is she okay?"

"Lizzie is fine. It's Ben, my friend. I think he might be really sick. I don't know what to do."

Ellen inhaled through her teeth. "Jesse, really, he probably needs to go to the Emergency Room. You need to call 911 and report his whereabouts."

Jesse leaned against the white siding of the house and ran his fingers through his hair. "I can't. He'd hate me. They all would. We already got wiped out a month ago. People are just settling back in. Look, could you just get me some antibiotics or tell me what to do?" Jesse's voice was hushed and desperate.

"Come inside. It's freezing out here." Ellen ushered Jesse

into the warm house and made him sit by the fire while she went to the kitchen. "Can you put another log in the wood-stove?" Ellen called from the kitchen. "I made some onion soup yesterday that you could take to your friend, and I think I have some amoxicillin that Frank refused to finish off last year when he had that sinus infection."

"Thanks, Ellen." Jesse's voice was low and hesitant. "I didn't know what to do. I just kind of ended up here."

"It's okay. I'm glad Frank's not here. He comes back sometime tonight or I'd have you and Lizzie come for dinner."

"It's fine. Liz and my mom are going to sleep at a church tonight anyway."

"Oh good!" Ellen sounded relieved. "How is Lizzie… and your mom?"

Jesse shrugged. "Fine. Lizzie likes her teacher this year and my mom has a boyfriend, so she's been clean for a while."

Ellen's eyebrows arched in surprise. "That's great." She sounded hopeful but Jesse knew Ellen didn't trust the news, and neither did he.

"Yeah, it's good for now," Jesse said.

"This friend of yours… is he your age?"

"No." Jesse sighed. "He's a Vietnam vet. He's older… I don't really know. He's been really good to Lizzie and me. Kind of like a…" Jesse felt his throat catch and he stopped talking. He could see into the kitchen where Ellen was heating up the soup and adding what looked like fresh garlic to the day-old mixture.

"This is going to take a few minutes. Why don't you take a hot shower while I put this together? You know where the towels are." Part of him wanted to refuse. It was too much—this warm house, the smell of soup heating, the shower standing empty down the hallway. And then there was Ben shivering in his tree-stump.

"Go on Jesse. I mean it."

Jesse opened the woodstove, enjoying the wave of heat on his face as he carefully placed pieces of wood onto the smoldering fire. "Hey, where's your dog?" Jesse asked, suddenly noticing the empty space by the fire where the dog bed had been.

"We had to put Sweet down a couple of weeks ago. She had some kind of seizure and became paralyzed. It was an awful shock. I'm looking for her around the house all the time."

"I'm so sorry." Jesse never thought about Ellen having problems or heartache of her own. He had forgotten that having a house and food didn't make you immune to tragedy. He shut the woodstove, stood up, and concentrated on watching Ellen cut bread with efficient knife strokes.

"She had a good life. Go take that shower!"

***

An hour later, Jesse was running back towards the park, a thermos of hot soup sloshing around in his backpack. He breathed the cold air in short, even puffs. When he reached camp his mom and Lizzie were gone, along with the tent. There was a smudged piece of paper hanging from a bare huckleberry branch. Jesse tore the paper from the bush.

We've gone to the Occupy with Leo. We'll be at the church shelter tonight. See you there.

Mom and Liz

Jesse crumpled the paper and stuffed it into his pocket. He walked around the back of the stump and found that the tent and a few supplies had been tucked under a threadbare tarp. The sleeping bags were gone, but there was a dirty fleece blanket that he grabbed before hurrying up the trail to Ben's place.

Emma and Toby were curled outside the stump like a couple of security guards. Their tails thumped the ground at the sight of Jesse.

"Good dogs," he said, as he crawled into the dark hole. Ben's face was glossy with fever and his chest rattled as he breathed. Ellen had packed the thermos of soup and a canning jar with tea that was still warm. She'd told Jesse to get the antibiotics into Ben as quickly as possible. Jesse sat down and pulled the big man by the armpits into his own lap. Ben moaned and protested, but finally settled limply against Jesse's chest.

"You gotta cooperate, or I'll call an ambulance."

"Noo…" Ben moaned. "No cops."

"Not the cops, the hospital. You're really sick." Jesse unscrewed the lid of the Mason jar of tea and brought it to Ben's mouth. "Drink!" he ordered, "or I go get help."

Ben allowed Jesse to tip the warm liquid into his mouth and he let out a grateful sigh after drinking. "Good. Now you gotta swallow some pills." Jesse opened the bottle of antibiotics and poured two pills into his hand. Ben raised an arm to resist as Jesse pushed the pills into his mouth, but relaxed and swallowed when Jesse offered more of the honey-sweetened tea. "That's gonna help. Now how about some soup?" Jesse opened the thermos and poured some of the soup into the lid. Jesse tried spooning broth into Ben's mouth, but it just dribbled down his chin and onto his jacket. Ben's shallow breaths were louder now and Jesse realized his friend had fallen into a fitful sleep. Emma crawled into the stump and curled up at Ben's feet. Jesse moved a backpack under Ben's head to keep it elevated.

"Let's get some firewood," Jesse said to Emma. He looked at Ben's flushed face and thought the heat made the man look younger, like a boy with rosy cheeks. On hands and knees, Jesse crawled out of the stump. It was a relief to breathe in the forest air and be out of what felt like a cramped sickroom.

"Come on, let's go to the creek for a drink and firewood." Toby followed Jesse down the hill toward the drainage, but nothing could persuade Emma to leave her post.

***

Skipping school wasn't something Jesse liked to do often, but he didn't dare leave Ben alone. It was still cold, and someone had to keep a fire going and make sure Ben took the pills. Jesse ran into town each day to meet Ellen near the high school where she'd hand over more soup, which he'd swap her for an empty thermos. She usually included sandwiches and fruit for Jesse, which meant he didn't have to waste time scrounging for his own food.

The afternoon meetings with Ellen were also an opportunity to see Raya. Jesse tried to squeeze in a shower at the community pool before the rendezvous. He needed some part of himself to be clean. His clothes were saturated with the smell of wood smoke from the fire he'd been constantly nursing in the stump. There hadn't been time for laundry or homework.

"When do you think you'll come back to school?" Raya was standing with him on the street corner waiting for Ellen to show up with fresh supplies.

"I don't know. Probably another couple of days. Hey, you're shivering." Jesse pulled Raya against his chest and kissed her neck.

"I love that smell," Raya murmured, sounding half-drugged.

Jesse pulled away, suddenly alarmed. "What smell?"

Raya reached for him. "The campfire smell. You always remind me of summer and camping. Even when it's freezing and dreary like this," she said, nuzzling into him. "You make me think of lying on warm rocks by the river and fires under the stars."

Jesse relaxed into Raya's embrace. "I need to go to the laundromat. I just haven't had time, with taking care of my uncle and all…"

"You don't have a washer and dryer at home?" Raya asked, sounding surprised.

"No, like I said, my mom doesn't like technology or… machinery… There's a lot of regular stuff we don't have." It felt good to be telling some portion of the truth. He wanted

Raya to know who he really was, even though he could never tell her the whole story.

"I still don't understand why you got stuck taking care of your uncle. I mean why can't your mom or aunt do it? You've missed almost a week of school."

"My mom and Lizzie are out of town and my aunt has to work. I'm really the only one who can be there." Lizzie and Carla were just a few blocks away at the church, but it felt like they were out of town. He hadn't seen them in days. He hoped Carla was getting Lizzie to school on time, or at all, for that matter. Jesse buried his nose in Raya's hair and inhaled the fruity shampoo scent.

"Jess," Ellen had pulled up without Jesse noticing and was leaning out of her car window.

"Oh! Ellen." Jesse pulled out of Raya's arms but kept his fingers laced through hers.

"I made a thicker soup today. I think he can start eating some solid food now. How are those antibiotics holding up?"

"There's still half a bottle," Jesse said, letting go of Raya's hand and opening Ellen's car door to retrieve the food bag. "This is Raya, my friend…"

"Nice to meet you. I'd get out of the car but I'm on my way to work and running late." Raya smiled and reached out to shake Ellen's hand through the half-opened window.

"Nice to meet you, too," Raya said, sounding shy.

"So, Jesse, you seeing improvement? Is he getting up at all?"

"Definitely, he's eating and drinking, thanks to you." Jess held up the bag of food in demonstration. "And he gets up now and then. Not for very long though. But the cough is bad… it never stops."

"Don't quit those antibiotics until they're gone. I'm getting you more, and there's cough syrup in the bag. I really gotta go. See you tomorrow."

Jesse took Ellen's hand through the window and squeezed hard. "Thank you."

"She seems nice." Raya said to Jesse as they watched Ellen's car disappear around the corner.

"She's amazing, actually."

"Do you have time to come over later and do a little homework at my house? You could bring your laundry if you want... kill two birds with one stone."

Jesse put a hand on the curve of Raya's hip. "Won't your mom think it's weird that I'm doing laundry?"

"She doesn't care. She has yoga tonight. She's usually gone for a couple of hours."

"I guess I can get Ben... my uncle... settled in. He might even fall asleep early now that I have cough syrup."

"Okay then," Raya reached up and ran her fingers through Jesse's hair, which was still damp from his shower at the pool.

"I'll see you later," Raya said, pulling away. But Jesse drew her back and kissed her, first softly and then more eagerly, until she laughed and pulled away.

"Seven," he said, breathing hard from the kiss.

"Yeah," Raya said in a whisper.

***

Ben did seem a little stronger and more alert each day. That first night, Jesse had thought his old friend might not make it. But after four doses of the antibiotics Jesse could see the illness loosening its grip.

"Where'd you get all this stuff?" was the first thing Ben had said after two days of Jesse tipping tea and spooning soup into his mouth.

"My aunt Ellen," Jess had said, looking at Ben cautiously. "You said not to call 911, so I didn't know what else to do."

"Nice aunt..." Ben said, sounding grateful but listless. Jesse liked seeing him coming back to life, inquiring about details, even looking a little paranoid about Ellen's efforts to help a stranger.

"Your buddies down at the park keep sending up dog food."
Jess held up a Zip-Lock bag of kibble.

Ben smiled. "That's from the girl... you know, who brings
the bags of food."

"Well they didn't hand over the bread and cheese, but at
least they're sharing this." Jesse divided the bag between Toby
and Emma who waited politely, wagging their tails until Jesse
gave the okay to chow down.

"Does that girl go to your school, Jess?"

"Nah, she goes to the charter, but I kind of know her."

"She seems like a sweetie, doesn't she?" Ben asked, patting
Emma on the back.

"Yeah, she's nice." Jesse couldn't help but consider the girl
a threat. She was the only high schooler who knew that Jesse
lived out here. He didn't get the feeling that she was a gossip.
Still, she knew, and there was danger in that.

"You're looking better..." Jesse said, handing Ben the bottle of cough syrup. "I'm thinking of going to the church this
evening, to check on my mom and Lizzie. Then I might go to
a friend's house to study for a couple of hours."

"Good. I'm fine; you can stop pampering me. Really, you
need to go back to school, back to your life." Ben sat up by the
fire, trying to look strong.

"I'm not leaving you the whole night. I'll be back in a few
hours."

Ben grimaced from the effort it took to sit upright and
let himself slump back against the mound of backpacks and
blankets that Jesse had piled up for him to lean against.

The fire was well stoked, sending up a clean line of smoke
through the hole in the top of the stump. Jesse made a neat pile
of wood near Ben so it would be easy to feed the fire.

"Here's the soup," Jesse pointed to the thermos next to
Ben. "And there's bread in the bag if you feel up to eating."

Before Jesse could move to the hole in the stump, Ben

placed a hand on Jesse's arm and looked at him with glazed eyes. "I'd be compost by now if you hadn't come by that first day." "You've saved my neck dozens of times. I still owe you." Jesse squirmed out of the stump into the hazy evening light and headed toward town.

***

"Look what I found," Lizzie pulled an etched silver locket from under her puffy jacket.

"Wow, where'd you get that?" Jesse tried not to sound concerned.

"And look," Lizzie ignored his question, "it opens." She faced Jesse as her pudgy fingers worked at unfastening the locket. "There," she opened the delicate halves of the heart. One side held a photo of an older man with kind, smiling eyes, and the other side had a picture of a dog, all golden and fluffy. "It's Grandpa," Lizzie said, in a hushed tone. She looked around the room warily like someone might contradict her. "And that's Heart." She pointed to the yellow dog.

"Okay." Jesse touched the etched metal. "I just wonder if someone might be missing this." Jesse glanced around the church cafeteria lined with tables filled with homeless people eating cheesy casserole.

"I didn't find it in here." Lizzie sounded cold and unlike herself. "It was outside in the dirt. Look, it's been smashed." Lizzie turned the locket over, revealing a dent in the silver.

"It's just that someone might still care about it. You know... the man and the dog..."

"I care." Lizzie looked down at the locket and then carefully closed it. "They're mine, now. Grandpa and Heart." She tucked the locket back into the pink folds of her jacket.

Jesse sighed and reached for her hand. "How's it been sleeping here, Chipmunk? It feel good to be toasty warm?"

"We get cots. Mama and I sleep in one together, and they have special blankets so we don't need any of our stuff from camp."

"Do you guys wanna play cards?" a boy interrupted. He looked several years older than Lizzie, maybe ten or eleven. Jesse smelled something rank wafting off of the boy. It was probably just dirty clothes. Jesse couldn't resist sniffing his jacket to be sure the smell wasn't emanating from his own clothes.

"Yeah!" Lizzie said. "Let's play Crazy Eights!" The boy sat across from Lizzie and began shuffling a worn deck. He looked up at Jesse shyly as he shuffled.

"What's your name?" Jesse asked the boy.

"Madrone," the boy answered, with a lower voice than Jesse thought normal for a kid. The name Madrone didn't surprise Jesse. He'd heard all the groovy names possible. It was almost abnormal these days to have a traditional name like Jesse or Lizzie. But he was grateful that his mother hadn't named him after a tree or a bird.

"You playing?" the boy asked, looking up at Jesse.

"I need to get going. I'm gonna do laundry, Liz. Do you have any dirty stuff?"

"Mama did ours," Lizzie said, picking up cards as the boy dealt them.

"Tell Mom I'll come back tomorrow around the same time," Jesse said, standing up. "Don't leave this room until she gets back from visiting Leo, okay?" Jesse ordered, looking at Lizzie and briefly at Madrone.

"Wait!" Lizzie stood up on the bench and reached for Jesse. He scooped her up into a bear hug.

"You actually smell pretty good today, Monkey Girl." He set her back on the bench. "Did Mom take you to the pool for a shower?"

"They have one here!" Lizzie pointed towards the door with the bathroom sign. "You should take one, Jess, you smell like camp."

"I know," Jesse said. "It's these clothes. I gotta do laundry. I'll see you tomorrow. Nice to meet you, Madrone."

"You too…" said Madrone almost inaudibly.

"Don't leave this room." Jesse said, again giving Lizzie a stern look before walking away.

The path from Raya's gate to the front door was lined with small solar lights that lit the way inadequately but cast an inviting glow. Jesse jingled a tangle of bells that hung from a string. The door cracked open and Raya appeared in sweats and a T-shirt, her hair loose around her shoulders. Jesse thought she looked amazing.

"Hey," he said, admiring the deep denim hue of her eyes.

"Come on," she said, pulling him by the arm and closing the door. "My mom just left for yoga, so the place is all ours."

"Sounds good," Jesse wrapped his arms around her and planted a kiss on her neck.

"Did you bring laundry?" she asked, looking towards the door to see if Jesse had left a laundry bag at the entrance.

"Yeah, it's here." He pulled his pack off of his back. "Can I put this in too?" he asked, giving his jacket a sniff. "Everything smells like smoke."

"Do you want to wash your pants and shirt too?" Raya asked with a smirk.

Jesse laughed, "I could, but then what would I wear?"

"Guess you'd have to walk around in your underwear… or you can borrow some of my clothes." Raya walked over to the wall heater. "I'll turn this up so you don't get cold."

Jesse looked at the front door, worried that Raya's mom might appear at any moment.

"Don't worry," Raya said, noticing Jesse's concern.

"You're more outgoing at home than at school," Jesse said, unbuttoning his jeans and pulling them off. Raya looked surprised, as if she hadn't expected him to call her bluff.

"I'll get a basket," she said, and walked quickly into the kitchen. Jesse followed her. In the corner there was a round table covered with papers and books. Jesse pulled the rest of his dirty clothes out of his pack and set them in a heap on the floor.

"What about your shirt?" Raya asked, coming back from a side room cradling a laundry basket.

"You don't mess around! I just got here and you've already got me almost naked," Jesse teased.

"You said you wanted to do laundry." Raya sounded suddenly embarrassed.

"Here you go," Jesse said, pulling his T-shirt off and tossing it into the basket.

Raya flushed and quickly scooped the dirty clothes into the basket. "Okay, I'll go start the wash." She walked back to the laundry room. "You can spread out your homework on the table," Raya said from the other room.

"Okay." Jesse sat down in his boxers. He got out his math book and looked through the pages of problems he'd missed during the week. He knew how to do most of the stuff, but he hated the idea of wasting time doing all of the assigned problems.

"Here," Raya said, coming back into the kitchen and tossing him a T-shirt. "Put this on or we're not gonna get any homework done."

"Really? Maybe I should leave it off." He leaned back in his chair and raised an eyebrow at Raya.

"Okay, now you're sounding creepy. Put the shirt on." Raya sat down opposite Jesse and started reading her biology book. Jesse slipped the green T-shirt over his head. It was too small, so he flexed his arms, Popeye style, making Raya laugh. They sat for a few long minutes before Jesse let out a long sigh. Raya looked at him and smiled. "You bored already?"

"Nah, it's just busy work. I don't see the point."

"Well, some of us have to practice the problems in order to remember how to do them on the test. You seem to be able to just go in and take a test cold turkey."

"I look at the examples in the book,'" Jesse said, "but doing twenty of the same problem seems like a waste of time."

"Hey," Raya said, putting down her book. "I haven't shown you my room."

Jesse forgot that on top of the cozy kitchen and the living room and even a laundry room Raya would also have her very own bedroom. "Let's see it," he said, standing up and following Raya to a small door off the kitchen that led to a narrow flight of stairs.

"My mom hates these stairs, so I get the whole loft to myself." They climbed the dark stairwell and Raya flicked on a light switch at the top of the stairs, revealing a large open room with three dormer windows and a couple of skylights.

"Wow," Jesse said, taking in the size of the room and the bed against the far wall. "This is amazing." He was thinking that a room this size would be plenty big for him and his mom and Lizzie to live in for the rest of their lives. "It must be nice knowing you have this to come home to every day."

"I guess." Raya giggled. "It's just an attic really, but the skylights are cool. I'm glad you like it. Sit," she said, patting the end of the bed with her hand. Jesse ducked to avoid the low eaves between the dormers and sat down next to her. He bounced up and down a little.

"Nice mattress," he said, falling onto his back and looking up at the posters on the ceiling. She had movie posters from films Jesse had never seen. He recognized photos of John Lennon and Elton John, but most of the other posters were just faces of people he couldn't name. Raya leaned back and stared at the photo-plastered ceiling with him. She reached for his hand and laced her fingers through his. It was so comfortable and warm on the bed that Jesse let his eyes close and his mind drift. He could think of lots of things he'd like to do with Raya in this room, on this bed, but feeling the warmth of the room and holding her hand almost felt like enough. A dream was starting to form in his mind, nudging away Raya's room and everything else.

He was in the mountains somewhere by a deep lake. He thought he saw a fish swimming near the surface, so he plunged into the water, hoping to catch it with his hands. He was diving deeper and deeper into the depths of the lake, swimming after the fish. Then he had it, slippery and firm in his hands. Jesse's body twisted and he darted toward the air. At the surface, he looked for the fish but it was gone, and there was Raya, treading water next to him, smiling.

He woke to the gentle touch of her lips kissing his cheek. "Oh man, I had the strangest dream. I think you were a fish and then you were you," Jesse said, turning onto his side to face her.

"That is strange," she said, stroking his arm with one tentative finger. "You're really beautiful," Raya said, studying him. She sounded almost sad. Jesse pulled her towards him and kissed her gently and shyly at first. Then he was leaning over her, kissing her neck and chest. His hands pulled at her T-shirt and she let him pull it up and over her head. She looked like a goddess of some kind lying there with her dyed red hair sprawled out all over the pillow and her breasts rising and falling beneath the constraints of a purple bra.

"Talk about beautiful," he said, running his finger along the outline of the bra.

"You can take it off... if you want..." Raya said, in a breathy whisper.

Jesse slowly pulled one of the narrow straps off of Raya's shoulder and leaned down to kiss her where the strap had been.

"Bang!" the front door slammed downstairs, and they could hear Raya's mom walking into the kitchen. "I'm home early!" she called up the stairs to the loft.

Chapter 7

PLEASE remove the bedding from the cot and place it in the tub by the door." The gray-haired church lady walked between the beds giving her morning lecture. "None of your personal belongings can be stored here during the day. We re-open at five o'clock tonight. Have a nice day." Jesse and Lizzie were always the first ones to strip their cots and wait at the door. Carla inevitably had to return to her bed to collect some left-behind item. The temperature had dropped again, so Jesse had been sleeping at the church with his mom and Lizzie for almost a week. They weren't allowed to bring personal bedding into the shelter, so almost everything they owned was stashed under a tarp at camp. For once Jesse wished his camp weren't a secret, then maybe he'd take Raya to the forest and explore more than just the tall trees and fern-lined swales. He spent way too much time thinking about what he hoped would happen the next time he was alone with Raya in her room. But Raya's mom had been at the house every time he visited lately.

Ben had forbidden Jesse to check on him for several days, but Jesse had spotted his old friend around town with the dogs. He thought Ben still looked shaken—a smaller version of himself—like an air mattress that had only been inflated halfway. When Jesse had offered to come by at night, Ben had been almost gruff. "I need my space, kid, and you've got homework to do."

The end of the semester was approaching. Jesse had papers to write for history and English, plus he had labs to make up for biology after school. His family had settled into a routine at the shelter. He'd get Lizzie to school in the morning, already fed and showered. He felt like a proud mom dropping her off all clean and shiny instead of delivering her with redwood needles tangled in her hair and duff-covered clothes smelling of urine. Carla had been picking Lizzie up after school, so Jesse could spend the afternoons making up his missed bio labs. At dusk he'd jog to Raya's house, where they'd spread homework on the kitchen table and drink cups of black tea to stay awake. It was easier doing homework with Raya's mom, Janet, puttering around the kitchen. He tried to imagine his mother plopped into a house with sinks, laundry, showers, and wall heaters. He couldn't really picture it. He didn't think she'd know what to do with all that convenience.

Sometimes Raya would slam a book closed and say, "Wanna go upstairs and listen to music? I downloaded a new song I want you to hear." This was code for "Let's go make out on my bed now!" But as per Janet's new rules they left the door open at the bottom of the stairs, and Jesse wasn't allowed to visit unless Janet was home. He didn't push things too far if he could hear Raya's mom doing dishes or putting in a load of laundry. He didn't want a repeat of the embarrassing moment when Janet had marched up the stairs after her yoga class and found Raya quickly pulling a shirt over the purple bra that he'd been about to remove. His pants had been in the washer, so all he'd been able to do was wrap a blanket awkwardly around his waist to hide his underwear and the humiliating bulge.

Thanksgiving at the shelter had been like any other that Jesse had spent eating from a church kitchen staffed by a bunch of volunteers eager to do good and serve food to the less fortunate. When Jesse reached the food line, he noticed Marie, the food-bag girl, serving up big helpings of stuffing and mashed potatoes. They made eye contact briefly and then both looked at Jesse's plate. Marie tried to give him extra stuffing, but he pulled his plate away quickly and moved down the line. He felt bad for acting ungrateful, even a little bit mean, to such a nice person, but when he saw her all he could think about was how she had the power to unravel his social life in an instant. Jesse had the feeling Marie hated their encounters as much as he did. He guessed he was lucky that she was the only volunteer he knew. He should be grateful there wasn't a whole pack of helpful high school girls serving up goodness all over town.

Christmas was looming and Jesse was already dreading all of the fuss people would make at the shelter. It was like suddenly the homeless became visible and in need. Then, as soon as the holidays were over they were invisible again or, at the very least, an eyesore. People like Marie had year-round compassion instead of the more common holiday variety. But Lizzie loved all of the Christmas charity. She'd say yes to anything that was offered to her, whether it was a pink stuffed bear or a toothbrush. Jesse always had to "lose" things because they couldn't haul it all around.

Jesse was using a Swiss Army knife to whittle and carve a piece of driftwood he'd found at the beach. He sat outside on the curb outside the church attempting to scrape free a recognizable shape.

"It's kinda like a salamander!" Lizzie pointed at the diamond-shaped head and the tail curling in on itself like a snail shell.

"You got it." Jesse smiled, hoping Raya would be as perceptive as his sister when he presented the salamander carving to her at Christmas. He had another two weeks to get it shaped, smoothed, and sanded into a salamander like the one he'd shown Raya in the tree.

"Where's Mom?" Jesse asked, looking up at Lizzie and then resuming his methodical shaving of the salamander's belly. He wanted the whole thing to be smooth and perfect, almost slimy-looking, if that kind of sheen was possible to achieve in driftwood.

"She said she had to go to the Occupy," Lizzie answered, as she mindlessly opened and closed the locket that still hung around her neck. "Is Leo leaving?" she asked, sounding concerned, like she might actually miss him if he did take off for warmer Occupies elsewhere.

"I think he's just going back East to spend the holiday with family. He'll be back in a month or so."

Lizzie snapped and unsnapped the locket, occasionally peering down to check on the tiny photos of Grandpa and Heart. "You're gonna wear that thing out, Liz. You ought to just give it a break. Maybe do some of your finger knitting or something."

Lizzie shoved her hands in the pockets of her pink jacket like it was a punishment. "Mama seems sad," she said. She lifted a hand upward toward her neck and then caught herself and stuffed it back into her pocket.

Jesse stopped whittling and looked at her. "She's just worried about missing Leo while he's gone. She'll be okay." Jesse was secretly worried too. His mom had become dependent on Leo for everything from sleeping bags to toothpaste. The guy had a good heart and really seemed to love Carla. He wanted to help out with Lizzie and even Jesse, if Jesse would let him. Everything had been less of a struggle since Leo showed up. If they were low on cash or food, Leo somehow always found what they needed at the Occupy. Jesse wondered if Leo had money in a bank somewhere. He had a family back East and enough money to fly home for Christmas. Maybe the whole homeless thing was just something Leo was trying out, like a temporary experiment.

"Is that for me?" Lizzie asked, pointing at the partially formed salamander.

"I'm gonna give this to Raya for Christmas. But I've got something in mind for you, too."

"Hey, would you guys like a bag of food?" Jesse and Lizzie turned around, startled by the unexpected voice. Marie must have come from the back of the church, because she seemed to materialize out of nowhere. Jesse tucked the salamander into his jacket and closed his pocketknife. He wasn't sure why he didn't want her to see the salamander. This girl always made him feel like he was standing buck-naked in a classroom full of teenagers.

"We're fine." Jesse barely glanced at Marie. Lizzie looked longingly at the bag of food, which had a crispy baguette pointing out of the sack. She went back to flicking her locket opened and closed: *snap click, snap click.*

"We could eat the bread and give the dog food to Ben," Lizzie said, smiling at Marie as she *snap click snap clicked* the locket.

"Oh, wow!" Marie set down the food bag and reached for the necklace brushing her fingers over the etched surface. "Where'd you get this?" she asked, her voice strained.

"I found it…" Lizzie said, taking a step back. "It's mine now." She flicked the heart open, revealing the small faded photos. "That's Grandpa and this is my dog, Heart." She tapped the photo of the yellow dog with her finger.

Jesse looked at Marie, whose eyes brimmed with tears.

"Are you okay?" Jesse asked. "Is that your neckl…?"

"No," Marie interrupted, "It's hers. I like the name of your dog… Heart." Marie smiled at Lizzie, her eyes still glassy. "I better go," she said, turning quickly and walking away. "Thanks," Lizzie called after her, pulling the baguette out of the bag and tearing off a piece.

"Liz," Jesse said, taking the chunk of baguette she was offering. "That locket is hers." Lizzie stopped chewing and reached for her neck.

"She said it was mine. And it's true. It really is mine." Lizzie caressed the locket protectively.

"I just want you to know it was probably her necklace before you found it."

It was strange seeing Marie like that, all teary and out of sorts. Jesse thought it made her seem more human, like maybe she'd lost things in her life too. Not just lockets; important things like people and dogs. Things that mattered.

***

On Saturday, Jesse headed to the forest to find Ben and unload the dog food from Marie that he'd been hauling around all week. It was still early; there was thick frost on the park lawn. A raven cawed and flew from a branch of a redwood to the grey bars of the swing set. Otherwise, the park was still and quiet with a bank of low clouds and little promise of sun.

When Jesse reached their empty camp, he took a cursory look behind the stump and under the tarp that concealed their belongings. It was mostly bedding, the tent, kitchen supplies, and a few articles of clothing. In a way, it was nice to have the stuff stashed. It made Jesse realize how little they actually needed from day to day. He had his schoolbooks with him, a notebook with his observations and drawings of the salamander, two shirts, a pair of pants, and his toothbrush. Everything fit neatly in his pack. He thought about rifling through the clothes under the tarp and swapping out a couple of shirts for the two he'd been wearing all week.

"I'll do that on my way out of here," he said to himself, not wanting to put off getting to Ben's place. Thick fog crept between the branches of the trees and took up residence there, hovering, making the forest look mystical. At Ben's stump he saw no sign of the dogs. That meant Ben was still in town, walking the streets, bumming change for his morning coffee. Jesse turned to go back down the trail but remembered the plastic bag of dog food that had been weighing down his pack all week. He knelt in the damp padding of redwood needles and dug through his pack for the food. He considered just tossing the bag through the hole in the stump for Ben to find later. But Ben kept a tidy camp, and Jesse wanted to put the food with the other stash in a metal tin, and maybe leave a note, so Ben wouldn't think he'd been intruded upon by some dog-food-giving stranger.

Crouching low, Jesse pushed through the hole into the dank stump. There was only dim shadowy light leaking in through the smoke hole. A slow, steady *thump, thump, thump* sound that Jesse couldn't place was beating like a woodpecker at a tree hole. Then Jesse felt a wet dog nose snuffling his face.

"Toby... what the... I didn't hear you guys in here." Jesse crawled the rest of the way into the stump. He sat scratching Toby's soft ears and letting his eyes adjust to the faint light. Jesse remembered Ben talking about being a canine officer in the army. He'd mentioned that the training came in handy with Toby and Emma during the camp cleanups. Just like in the army, Ben had trained the dogs to keep quiet and not give away their location.

"Whatcha doing in here, Tob? Where's Emma and Ben?" Toby's tail thwapped the dirt floor, and Jesse opened the bag of dog food and folded the sides down, creating a makeshift bowl. Toby scarfed-up the food. "What the hell happened, bud? Why are you here alone?"

Enough time passed for Jesse's eyes to adjust to the shadowy darkness of the stump. He rummaged through his pack for his headlamp and turned it on. The place was a mess, which was out of the ordinary for Ben. It smelled rank, and Jesse wondered if Toby had taken a dump somewhere. There was shredded garbage scattered around the floor. It looked like Toby had been digging through Ben's food. Jesse scanned the rest of the stump, shining the headlamp around in a three-hundred-sixty-degree motion like a lighthouse beam.

Ben's blankets and clothes were in a messy heap against the stump wall instead of the neat piles he'd adopted in the military.

"What the hell!" Jesse said aloud, wondering what could have caused Ben to leave the place in such disarray—and to abandon Toby. He couldn't think of a time when he'd seen the dogs apart. Why would he only take Emma? Jesse's stomach sank as he realized the possibility that Ben might have gotten sick again. Maybe he'd been taken to the hospital this time. Maybe Emma had refused to stay; maybe she'd followed Ben.

"I'll have to take you with me, Tob," he said, scratching the dog under the chin. "I'll see if Ellen can watch you while I figure out where Ben is."

Jesse thought of Ellen's dead dog and how she might not mind having Toby around for a few days. Jesse scanned the stump for the rope that Ben used to leash the dogs. He started scrounging through the messy pile of clothes and blankets, feeling for the rough texture of the rope. The smell was strong by the clothes, and Jesse worried he was going to inadvertently stick his hand into a pile of dog crap. He reached more gingerly through the pile and breathed through his mouth to avoid the stench.

Then he felt something that wasn't the squishy texture of dog shit. It was the short, coarse hair of an animal. Jesse pulled his hand away quickly and scooted back from the pile like the thing he'd touched might spring to life and attack. Then he thought of Emma and how he'd never seen Toby without her. He strapped the headlamp onto his forehead so he'd have both hands free to investigate the source of the hair. The beam from the headlamp revealed a grey-black patch of hair that matched Emma's wiry coat.

Carefully, Jesse pulled away articles of clothing and pieces of blanket shrouding what he was certain was Emma's body. One of Ben's coats covered Emma's face. When he lifted the fabric, he was surprised how perfect she still looked. Jesse leaned down and put his ear next to her mouth to listen for breath. He lifted a blanket off of her abdomen so he could check if she was breathing. And there, wrapped around her torso like a hairy banner, was an arm.

"Gahhh!" Jesse jumped to his feet and screeched. "Shit, shit, shit..." he shouted, grabbing at his hair with his hands. Toby looked up at him and whined in sympathy as if to say, "Now you know."

Jesse inhaled deeply, trying to gather courage to look again at the arm slung over the dead dog. It had to be Ben. But was he dead, like the cold dog, or alive? The thought of Ben alive under the pile of stinking blankets and clothes gave Jesse the courage to kneel back down and pull away the remaining coverings. First the rest of the arm was revealed, and finally Ben's body, curled like a crescent around Emma.

Jesse reached out tentatively and touched Ben's grey cheek. The skin was waxy, cold and lifeless. Jesse stared at Ben and Emma in disbelief. He could feel himself collapsing, but before he broke down and became immobile he needed to run, to get out of this place. Quickly, he crawled through the stump opening.

"Toby, come!" he said, and reluctantly the dog followed. Jesse leaned over, hands on his knees, and breathed hard, wanting to get the scent and taste of death out of his lungs. He started running down the maze of paths until he reached the creek. Toby followed him to the water and drank, standing belly-deep in the stream. Jesse vomited violently into a mass of fern fronds. He squatted, put his arms into the cool water, and watched it rush over his hands, distorting their outline. He rubbed his hands furiously, trying to wash off the stench. But the water didn't seem capable of washing anything away. He splashed his face to see more clearly. But his eyes just blurred and he let go...

He woke up at dusk, by the creek, cold and disoriented.

Toby was curled up next to him, sleeping. The sight of the sleeping dog reminded him of Ben and Emma; he closed his eyes again, hoping to forget.

***

The grave was in a secluded spot off the trail. Ben wouldn't want anyone knowing where he was, certainly not any government officials. He'd simply want to disappear; Jesse was sure of that. It was a climb getting to the grave, and the extra weight made it a struggle. To stay balanced, Jesse used the toes of his shoes to grip the soft dirt. Toby had been trailing Jesse all day. He'd watched while Jesse used Ben's old shovel to dig the deep pit. The dog even climbed in a couple of times to scratch at the powdery dirt.

It had been awkward pulling the stiff body out of the stump. Ben's frail frame felt surprisingly light wrapped in the tarp from camp. Jesse had refused offers of help from two of the homeless guys when it came to carrying the corpse. He'd spent half a day digging the hole. He'd probably made it deeper than necessary, but he didn't want to risk the smell attracting animals.

When Jesse arrived at the grave with Ben in his arms, he was surprised to see a half dozen people gathered around. Alder, one of the young guys who hung out in the park, had carried Emma to the spot earlier in the day. Jesse had warned Alder that Ben would want it quiet, but Alder had obviously gone down to the park and talked. Even without cell phones, word spread fast. Jesse didn't look at the people who'd gathered around; instead, he walked to the edge of the hole and laid Ben down before jumping into the dark pit. He was breathing harder now. It didn't feel like exertion, but something else pounding and flying around inside of him.

The hole was as deep as Jesse was tall, about six feet. Toby leaned over the edge, looking like he wanted to dive in and offer assistance.

"Stay, Toby." Jesse put up a hand to stop the dog. He saw someone kneel and hold onto Toby's collar. Jesse looked up and saw that it was Marie. *Shit,* he thought to himself, *this girl knows everything!*

"Okay," Jesse said, looking toward Alder and the guys from the park. "Can you lower Ben to me?" Alder and two other guys with dreads and ratty clothes lifted the tarp at either end and slowly lowered Ben until Jesse had the tarp in his arms like a bride at a different sort of threshold. Jesse swallowed hard and awkwardly set Ben down, trying desperately not to step on the crinkly tarp. With his legs straddling the body, he ordered, "Now Emma." Alder picked up the bundle of army blanket that contained Emma and gently handed her down. Jesse felt the tarp for Ben's head. He wanted to be sure to put Emma next to Ben's chest where Jesse had found her in the stump. He took his time placing her and arranging the blanket and tarp, until he was satisfied that Ben and Emma were covered and in good order.

"Do you want a hand up?" Alder asked, squatting at the edge of the grave. Jesse looked down and placed his palm on his tarp-shrouded friend and said a silent farewell before reaching for Alder's outstretched hand.

Jesse didn't know what to do next. He'd planned on doing this alone; instead, Ben's buddies were looking at him expectantly. The forest was silent except for the knocking sound of a woodpecker's beak against a nearby stump.

"Ben always shared whatever he had," said one of the homeless guys, whose name Jesse couldn't remember.

"Man, the dude was awesome," Alder chimed in. "His stories about Nam… epic…"

"He hated Nam," another guy piped up.

"Yeah, but his stories… man…" Alder repeated.

It got quiet, and Jesse worried that it was up to him again to keep the ceremony, or whatever this was, going. For once he actually wished his mom were there. She would have called in the grandmothers or said something groovy that these guys would have liked.

"I loved Ben's smile," Marie said, quietly, "and Emma's happy tail." Jesse looked at Marie and realized he was grateful she was there. Compared to the rest of the crowd, he felt like he actually knew her, even though her presence usually made him feel paranoid. He was starting to think she would always be around, and that maybe he should just accept it.

"He told the truth," Jesse said, surprising himself with the sound of his own voice. "And he was always there for us." Jesse could feel himself buckling so he reached for the shovel and started to dig at the pile of fresh dirt, filling in the big hole. Everyone helped, throwing in handfuls of dirt or kicking at piles with their feet. At some point Jesse stopped shoveling because his vision had blurred so completely with tears. He squatted next to the hole and let himself cry into the dirt. There was a tentative hand on his shoulder, light like a feather but enough to tether him there, keep him from running or leaping into the grave with Ben and Emma. Then there were soft arms around his neck and a head leaning on his back and a steady stream of tears joining his as Marie held him and cried.

***

He didn't know what to say to Lizzie about Ben. He would have to tell her eventually, but he needed time to let it sink in and feel real. Raya wanted to know why he hadn't told her anything about it until afterwards. She thought he'd just blown her off by not coming to her house all weekend.

He tried to explain that it had all happened really fast and that they hadn't had time to plan a real memorial or he'd have invited her. He couldn't tell her about finding Ben in the stump or burying him in the woods with the help of Alder and a bunch of Ben's friends. He could tell that Raya was hurt that she hadn't been included and that he hadn't called to tell her what was going on. He could feel a rift forming and the gap between them getting wider every time he told Raya a lie. "It was just family," he lied, thinking of Marie's embrace and her tears on the back of his neck.

When Jesse told his mom about Ben, she didn't seem surprised. "He's been on his way out for a while," Carla said, taking a drag on a cigarette she'd bummed from a guy at the shelter.

"Well, I don't know how to break it to Lizzie," he said. "She's so attached to him and to Emma."

"Just tell her, or I will. She's adaptable."

"I guess she doesn't have a choice. Why are you smoking?" Jesse asked his mom. "Leo's gonna be back soon and he'll be pissed that you're smoking again."

"I'll stop when he comes back," she said, smashing the cigarette against the curb.

"But you won't quit for us." Jesse walked to where Lizzie was drawing with chalk on the sidewalk. "Hey, Chipmunk," he said, sitting down cross-legged next to her.

She looked at Jesse and smiled. He saw a trace of strawberry jam from lunch at the corner of her mouth.

"I need to talk to you about Ben and Emma," he said. "Something's happened."

"I know," she said, without looking at him.

"You know what?" he asked, curious to hear what she would say.

"I know that Ben and Emma are with Grandpa and Heart now."

"Wait, you do? Did Mom talk to you?"

"No." Lizzie continued shading in the orange butterfly she was drawing on the sidewalk. "It was that girl with the food bags. She came by yesterday and told me. She said it would be hard for you to talk about." Lizzie's eyes started to well up and she wiped her cheeks with her chalky hands.

"Marie? Really? Hey, we can visit Toby sometime," Jesse offered.

"We can?" Lizzie asked, her face brightening.

"He's gonna live with Ellen at least for now, maybe forever. She hasn't decided."

"Let's go now!"

"We gotta wait until sometime when Mom's not around, but I promise we'll go see him soon."

"Yay!" Lizzie leaned across her butterfly art and wrapped her small arms around Jesse's neck.

***

A week later the recruiters were back on campus. Jesse couldn't help thinking of Ben and how he'd promised to shoot Jesse in the foot if he joined the military. Now everything reminded Jesse of Ben—dogs, coffee, the park, gray-haired men, military recruiters—it seemed there wasn't anything that didn't link back, in some way, to Ben and his glaring absence.

"Take a pamphlet," one of the recruiters said, shoving the glossy handout at Jesse.

It would be easy now to step up to the table and sign the paper attached to the metal clipboard. There was really no one stopping him, except maybe Raya, who would be disappointed. His mom certainly wouldn't care. She might even think it was a good idea. She and Lizzie could use his paycheck to get an apartment, or at least a room in a house. Leo would try to talk him out of it, but Leo was out of town for who knew how long. Jesse rubbed his thumb over the surface of the silky pamphlet, but kept walking towards the cafeteria.

Raya was alone at a table with her back to Jesse. He was late for lunch and the cafeteria was nearly empty. Raya's hair looked reddish in the strange fluorescent light, like the color of redwood bark.

"Hey," he said, leaning down and nuzzling her neck.

She jumped a little at his touch, then smiled. "Where've you been?"

He held up the military pamphlet. "Just looking at this," he said, sitting next to her.

"Oh God! Not that again. I thought your uncle Ben had you..." Raya suddenly realized she'd brought up Jesse's dead uncle. "Sorry, Jess. I wasn't thinking. It's just I know you said he was totally opposed to you joining up."

Jesse inhaled through his teeth. He didn't want to think about Ben and how he wasn't there to follow through on his threats to shoot Jesse if he enlisted, but Raya was right. Ben didn't want Jesse to turn out like him, suffering from PTSD.

"You're right," Jesse said, tearing the pamphlet in half and letting the pieces fall onto the table. "I'll think of something else, another way out."

"Jesse, you can go to school. Is it that you want to leave Humboldt? Because there are lots of schools out there. You could go to a community college just about anywhere. They don't cost that much."

"I don't really want to leave. I'm just complaining." Jesse had forgotten, as he often did, that Raya didn't know the truth about him. She didn't know that, more than anything, he wanted stability—a place to go home to each night, a place with food and a bed. It was easier if he just didn't discuss his life at all. When he did, he ended up having to talk his way around some big piece of himself that he couldn't tell her about.

"I missed you," he said, kissing her neck and smelling her mango-scented hair. She sighed and let him continue his exploration of her neck.

"I wish you had let me come to the memorial," she said softly. "I'm pretty good at being helpful and supportive."

He sat up and noticed Raya's tray of untouched food: Alma's casserole swimming in red sauce and melted cheese. He could smell the warm gooey mixture. He knew he should address the memorial or lack thereof, but what he really wanted was to get some food before Alma shut down the kitchen. Or better yet, just eat Raya's food that sat untouched and beckoning.

"It happened really fast. There wasn't time to invite people, or I would have." Jesse sounded defensive. He hated telling Raya another half-lie. "I'm going to get some lunch." He stood up and walked over to get a tray knowing that he'd said the wrong thing. But he didn't want to talk about Ben's memorial, and he didn't want to tell Raya any more lies.

Chapter 8

A N icy wind whipped at Jesse's thin jacket as he straddled
the crown of a redwood. It had been weeks since he'd
climbed. He didn't bother taking notes or making observations;
he'd moved quickly toward the narrow crown where the branches
were frequent and spindly. The tree arched in the brittle wind.
Jesse wrapped his legs tightly around the narrow trunk and
released his hands. He wanted to feel the air whipping around
and the swaying of the tree. He wanted the clouds and the first
drops of rain to engulf him and block out everything else in
his crazy life. *I'm not that different from my mom*, he thought, as he
leaned into the swing of the tree.

***

Christmas had come and gone, which was a relief. Jesse hated
the holiday. It meant more people paying attention to him and
his family, noticing what they lacked in their lives. He'd had some

nice talks with Marie at the shelter. She'd actually sat down and eaten Christmas dinner with him and Lizzie.

"Why aren't you at home with your family?" he asked, thinking it was a little extreme that she was missing her own holiday dinner.

"We celebrate Solstice and Hanukkah, so we've already had our feast and burned our wishes with the Yule Log," she told him casually, like Christmas was no big deal.

"So you're a hippie?" He raised an eyebrow and smiled at her.

"No, just raised by hippies. Jewish hippies, I guess. But I don't like to pigeonhole my parents—or anyone, really."

"It'd be hard not to pigeonhole my family," Jesse said, stabbing a fork at his over-cooked slice of turkey.

"Why do you say that?" Marie asked. Her brow was furrowed, making her look almost stern.

"Well you know… because we're homeless. So we're lumped into everybody's brain that way… those homeless people."

"I don't think of you that way," Marie said, cutting a pattern into her mashed potatoes with a fork.

"Then what do you think when you see me?" He paused. "I know you think about food. You're thinking, 'He needs food!'"

She laughed a little. "I do like giving people food but, I don't know, I think of you as yourself, as Jesse. And that you're a teenager like me only you have, you know, far less stuff."

Jesse rubbed his chin. "I wish I could read your mind so I could see if that's really what you think."

"It is," she said, and stared at him with such sincerity he had to turn away and feign a cough.

***

Lizzie had accumulated too many Christmas toys for them to haul around. People didn't think about the logistics of homeless people storing big stuffed animals or dollhouses. Jesse didn't want to take the new toys away from her, but he couldn't imagine what they'd do with them. Lizzie had presented the idea of storing them in Ben's stump. Jesse was startled at first, not having been back to the stump since he'd hauled Ben's stiff body out of the rank-smelling hideout.

"I don't know, Liz, it might be weird. And I'm sure someone lives there by now."

"Let's just look, Jess, it's perfect for my dollhouse and Oscar." She pointed at the big stuffed hippo she'd been hauling around by the neck. "We could make it pretty with a rug and flowers." Jesse smiled at the thought of Ben's rustic camp transformed into a fairy playroom for Lizzie. He knew Ben would approve, but he also suspected the stump was already overrun with guys from the park.

"I guess we could walk up there and take a look."

***

Jesse had been right about people taking over the stump, but it was just Alder and another guy inhabiting the place. They had cleaned the whole thing out and divvied Ben's useable belongings between them.

"She can keep her toys here," Alder insisted. "Ben would want that. We're not here that often, only in the evenings." Alder swept his arm through the air as if to illustrate how much extra room there was in the stump. "Jesse, you should have this," Alder added, pulling a horn-handled knife out of a leather sheath on his belt. "Ben would have given this to you, I'm sure."

Jesse turned the knife over and inspected the knobby handle, made of some type of antler. "Thanks," Jesse said, tucking the knife into a pocket of his backpack.

***

He felt for Ben's knife in his pocket as he held tightly to the tree with one hand. He hadn't even looked for the yellow salamanders. They would be hibernating in a protected crevice somewhere. It was easier thinking about all this stuff while lurching around in the top of a tree. Thoughts popped into his mind and were just as quickly plucked up and swept away with the battering wind. He should climb down—and fast. It was getting dark, and it wasn't a good idea to be up in a tree at night in a storm. Besides, he was supposed to meet Raya at the library and she got irritated when he was late. He climbed down quickly and carelessly, deeply scratching his side on a branch as he made the final wild leap to the forest floor.

***

The swinging doors to the library made a whoosh as they closed behind Jesse, sealing out the wind and pelting rain. He was out of breath and soaked from running through the forest and down the hill to the campus.

"There you are!"

"Oh, hi," Jesse said, startled. It was the professor, Dr. Pelsinski standing in the lobby of the library. Jesse hadn't been by the professor's office in over a month. There had been too much going on lately to think about salamanders and tree ecology. "Sorry I haven't come by. I've had family issues and..."

"No problem, really. Just come by when you get the chance and bring your notes. When the weather gets better, I'd like you to show me where you've seen the salamanders."

"Sure," Jesse said, nervously running a hand through his wet hair. He pulled a redwood needle out of his hair and stuffed it into the pocket of his jeans.

"Go get warmed up," Pelsinski advised, pointing his chin toward Raya waiting on one of the lobby couches.

"Hi," Jesse held out a tentative hand, not wanting her to feel excluded from the conversation with the professor. Raya walked over and laced her fingers through Jesse's outstretched hand.

"Glad to see you again, Jesse. Get dried off. You look like a wet salamander," Pelsinski said.

Jesse smirked and waved goodbye to the professor before turning to follow Raya upstairs to their third-floor table.

"I have those clothes you left at my house last time. I washed them," Raya said, pulling jeans and a T-shirt out of her pack.

"Wow! That's awesome. I'll go change in the bathroom." He stood up to take the clothes. "Be right back." He leaned down to kiss her on the lips and then, more gently, on the neck.

"We're not going to get anything done," she said, closing her eyes and succumbing to his kisses.

"We're going to get stuff done," he whispered into her neck. "Just not school stuff."

"Go, just go," she said, pushing him away. "Change your clothes. I have to finish this paper before you turn me into a useless pile of mush."

"Thanks again for the clothes!" he said, and sauntered down the aisle of books towards the bathroom.

In the bathroom, Jesse changed out of his wet clothes, thinking how lucky he was to have a girlfriend who did his laundry and didn't ask too many questions. Jesse wondered what Raya thought his house looked like. Did she imagine a bungalow like her own, minus the washer and dryer. He looked in the mirror at his wet hair that was almost to his shoulders. He needed a haircut. Maybe Raya would offer to trim it the next time he was at her house. Although she seemed to like it long. She was always running her fingers through it and comparing him to some Brazilian soccer player who Jesse had never heard of.

"Thanks," he said, when he got back to the table. He sat down across from Raya and tangled his feet with hers. She smiled at him mischievously. It wasn't her normal innocent smile; it was her cat-girl smile, slanted and sultry.

"I've been thinking about your birthday," she said, letting the sentence trail off seductively. Raya had prodded out of him that his birthday was coming up on the fifteenth of January. She had hinted at a New Year's Eve party that she wanted to do something special for him. At the party, they'd been slow-dancing all night, even to the fast songs; he'd kept his hands on her hips, and they'd moved slowly to the rapid beat.

"Let's do something fun for your birthday," she'd whispered in his ear while they'd danced.

"Okay," he'd whispered back, pulling her closer.

She hadn't mentioned his birthday in over a week, but it was only a few days away, and now she seemed intent on making a plan.

"What do you want to do?" she asked, rubbing her foot against his calf under the table.

He could think of lots of things he wanted to do with her but he wasn't going to tell her what they were. He couldn't even replay the fantasies he'd had about her in his mind without blushing and getting an inconvenient hard-on.

"I was thinking about going to… Planned Parenthood," Raya said, looking down at her open English book.

"For my birthday?" Jesse asked, confused.

"No," Raya let out a long embarrassed sigh. "I mean this week, before your birthday."

"Oh, shit, I see," he said, shaking his head at his own slowness. "Wow!" It was sinking in. What she was offering awed and terrified him at the same time. "That would be amazing." He stared across the table at her until she finally looked up and stared back.

**

Carla inhaled sharply on her cigarette. "He's not coming back," she said.

"You don't know that." Jesse tried to sound convincing.

He actually doubted that Leo would be back, at least not any time soon. "Maybe he's a Fair Weather Occupier," Jesse offered. "He'll be back in the spring to take up the cause again."

Carla glared at Jesse and stabbed her cigarette out on the sidewalk. He couldn't joke with his mom; she took everything personally.

He wanted to tell Carla that he was nervous about going to the clinic with Raya because of all the outbursts he'd watched his mom have in the waiting room over the years. It was crazy that he fantasized about normal conversations with his mother. He knew she would just get defensive and think the whole thing was about her. For once he wanted her to think about how something might impact him or Lizzie.

Carla had always insisted on seeing a nurse practitioner named Alice. She was the only woman who could calm Carla down and talk her through the ordeals she had over the years. The appointments went smoothly as long as Alice was there. But on the occasions that Carla's favorite practitioner was not there, his mom would freak out. And the time they arrived to find that Alice had retired, Carla had thrown a full-blown fit. It was the kind a three-year-old might have in a grocery store, writhing around on the floor like a worm struck by lightning. Jesse was probably thirteen the last time he'd gone with his mom to an appointment. On his hip, he'd held Lizzie, who must have been around two. They watched, stunned silent as the staff tried to calm their squirming mother. He remembered there'd been blood on his mother's pants. They had gone to the clinic because of a miscarriage Carla had been enduring for days in a soggy tent.

***

Jesse and Raya got off the bus in Eureka. As they approached the big grey clinic Jesse could feel a prickly itchy sensation all over his skin, like he was having an allergic reaction. Raya was holding his hand, and he could feel his fingers grow clammy with sweat. At the door, he let her hand go and wiped his damp palms on his jeans.

"I've been here before, with my mom," he said, sounding shaky. "A while ago... I don't think I can go in. It's too much stuff to remember." He was clawing at his face, trying to shake himself out of a state of panic.

"It's okay Jess, don't freak out. You don't have to go in. You can wait for me out here if you want." Raya pointed to a bench in front of the building. "It's cold though." She rubbed her hands together. "You're going to freeze your cute booty off," she said, and smirked.

Jesse didn't care about the cold. He didn't want to go inside that building and relive his mother's breakdowns, or worse, have someone recognize him. They might ask how his mom was or where they were living now. There were a thousand things that could go wrong if he escorted Raya into that building. "What was I thinking?" he asked aloud, wondering why he'd thought he could actually accompany Raya to this appointment.

"If you don't want to do this, we don't have to, at all." Raya sounded almost angry now. "I mean I don't want to force you to do something you don't want to do." She stared at Jesse, waiting for him to respond. He let out a long-whistled sigh, trying to release some of his pent-up stress. He reached out and laced his sweaty fingers with hers.

"It's nothing to do with you, Raya. It's my mom. She had a really hard time here and it's all flooding back. I'm sorry; I wish I could go in. I really do." A light stream of tears was smearing Raya's face. Jesse felt a wave of guilt for not being able to march through those doors and help his girlfriend acquire contraceptives. Any normal guy would be running, itching to do whatever it took.

"It's okay," she said, releasing his hands and turning to go inside. "I'll do it alone," she mumbled as she walked away.

"Shit, shit, shit..." Jesse said aloud, when Raya was out of sight. He thought about how he could climb a hundred-foot redwood but he couldn't walk through the doors of the clinic and follow his girlfriend. He slammed his hand against a concrete pillar in the entryway. He looked at the bench, but he couldn't possibly sit, so he walked.

An hour later, he was standing outside waiting for Raya. He'd spent half of his last five bucks on a hot chocolate for her, something he would never waste money on for himself.

"Thanks," she said, grabbing the cup from him. "These are for you." She shoved a plastic bag into his hand and started walking toward the bus stop at a fast pace.

"How was it?" he asked timidly, as they reached the bus stop. The bench was too puddled with rainwater to sit, so they stood apart at awkward angles to one another.

"I don't really want to talk about it." She stared up at the clouds, which Jesse noticed were moving steadily to the south. The rain had stopped, but a cold wind still whipped past. Raya pulled the collar of her wool coat around her neck. Jesse wanted to reach out and wrap his arms around her but he didn't dare.

The bus pulled up, spraying their legs with rainwater from a street puddle. Jesse followed Raya toward the back where she sat next to a well-dressed young man. The guy looked surprised that someone would sit next to him on the nearly empty bus. Jesse let out a groan and flopped into the seat behind Raya and the guy. The bus rolled north toward the freeway. Jesse looked alternately at the bay to the west and Raya's neck, revealed by the high bob of auburn hair that she had twisted and piled onto her head. He exhaled loudly and saw that his breath moved some of the wispy strands of hair around her neck. He liked the idea that he was making contact even if it was just a shared breeze. He inhaled deeply and blew out a big exhale that caused the man next to Raya to scoot away and lean against the cold window.

Raya turned around, glaring. "What?" she asked.

"I just want to talk about it," he said, looking at her and trying to soften her glare with his pleading eyes.

"What do you want to talk about? That you can't go into a

doctor's office with your girlfriend, not even the waiting room?" She faced forward again, her shoulders like rigid posts. Jesse stared out at the whitecaps on the ragged wind-whipped bay and then noticed Raya's back shuddering as she tried to hold back a sob. He reached out and placed his hands gently on her shoulders.

"I'm so sorry." He massaged her back and rubbed his fingers in small circles on her shoulders and neck.

"Excuse me," the guy sitting next to Raya stood up and moved to an empty seat near the front of the bus.

Raya hardly seemed to notice that the guy had been sitting there listening to their whole conversation. "It's… just…" she was choking out words between sobs. "There were couples in the waiting room holding hands and I felt so stupid and alone."

"I know, I'm sorry," Jesse said. "I just couldn't go in there after what happened with my mom." He didn't mention his fear of running into people who might ask revealing questions if they recognized him.

"What did happen?" Raya turned around, and her eyes dared Jesse to confide in her.

Jesse's throat seized up and he felt like he was being choked. "Never mind," he said quietly. "I should have gone with you." He sat back in his seat and closed his eyes, trying to will away the images of his mom twisting in the bloodstained pants with a waiting room full of gawking onlookers.

***

"Hold still!" Marie said sternly, then smiled and ran her fingers down strands of his hair, making sure the sides were cut evenly. Jesse glanced at his watch, a cheap digital thing he'd gotten as a Christmas present from some stranger at the shelter.

"I said, hold still." Marie peered intently at his head, this time lifting his chin so that he was looking straight ahead at her pale neck. He could see a small vein pulsing on her throat, and he had the urge to reach out and touch the throbbing blue streak. What was he thinking, agreeing to this? She'd been cutting his hair for almost two hours, and he couldn't stand to sit there for another minute feeling her fingers brush and flutter around his head.

"I'm sorry it's taking me so long. I'm kind of a perfectionist." She laughed. "I think it's almost even." She looked back and forth between the two sides, comparing them. It wasn't that he minded Marie touching his hair or his chin or brushing the cut hair from his shoulders. What bothered him was how it made him feel. Horny wasn't the right word; more like consumed. He felt like he was in some kind of vacuum bubble, just him and Marie, with her hands snipping and sculpting. It was so comfortable and easy it made him squirm. *I shouldn't be feeling this way,* he thought. It should be Raya cutting his hair, running her fingers through his locks. But she'd insisted she couldn't cut a straight line through a piece of paper, let alone hair. "Besides," Raya had said, "I like it long."

***

Raya had forgiven him for not going to the appointment. She'd surprised him on his birthday with cupcakes and little glasses of some sugary alcohol she'd siphoned from her mother's liquor cabinet. Her mom was out of town, and Raya was staying at a friend's house for a few days. She and Jesse had ditched school during lunch and used the spare key to get into the house, which felt cold and lifeless without the heater on.

"I have birthday cupcakes!" she said, running down the steep steps from her loft to retrieve the cakes from the fridge. She brought them back to her loft with candles in them and the little glasses of liquor, all on a painted wooden tray that looked foreign and exotic to Jesse.

"Thanks," he'd said, after she sang a timid rendition of "Happy Birthday."

"Do you mind if I take a shower? You know, before we…" He pointed at the bed and the orange floral comforter.

"Sure." She looked deflated and set the cupcake tray down on the bed. As he navigated the steep loft stairs, he thought that maybe he should have eaten the cupcakes before showering. He wasn't good at birthday etiquette. His birthday usually came and went without much notice.

When he got back from his shower, she was in the bed and under the covers, pretending to be asleep. He could tell when someone was really asleep; their eyes didn't twitch nervously like hers were now.

"Thanks for the shower," he whispered as he climbed under the covers next to her. The shower line had been long at the shelter that morning, so he'd gone to school wondering if he smelled rank or sour. He'd even borrowed her toothbrush and scoured his teeth in the privacy of the bathroom.

"Oh, man, you're freezing," he said, wrapping his leg around her torso.

Raya giggled and opened her eyes. "You're warm," she said, letting him snuggle against her. He noticed that she'd kept her bra and panties on while he'd mindlessly jumped into the bed naked. He could feel himself growing firm against her now-warm thigh, and he wondered if she was freaked that his bare penis was resting against her hip. "I hope you brought those condoms," she said, "because my pills don't start working for a couple of weeks."

"I have them," he said quietly, into the warmth of her neck. He thought about how she had this whole loft full of stuff and everything he owned was in his oversized daypack in the corner of her room. Of course he had them. He always had everything with him. "Should I put one on now?" he asked. "I mean, are you ready?"

"I guess so," she said, staring up at the twinkle lights that spanned the blond wooden beams of the ceiling. He kissed her slowly and deeply, hoping she would relax.

***

The sex hadn't been exactly successful, he thought. Raya had screamed as he entered her, and he'd misinterpreted the scream as some sort of primal pleasure, while in fact it had probably been a cry of pain. Being inside Raya had been so overwhelming that he'd come almost instantly and then pulled out quickly when he realized she had her hand over her mouth to muffle her sobs. She cried herself to sleep with Jesse apologizing and stroking the hot tears from her cheeks.

When he woke it was dark out, and only the strand of twinkle lights illuminated the bed. Raya was gone but had left a note on her pillow.

Had to go to my friend's house by five. Can you stay and wash the sheets so my mom doesn't see? The door will lock automatically when you leave.

Thanks,
Raya xox

Jesse stood up and pulled the bloodstained sheets from the bed. He threw a blanket over his shoulder and went down to the laundry room. He put the sheets in the wash along with his own dirty clothes. He wrapped the blanket around him and walked into the kitchen, where he found bread and peanut butter and helped himself to a sandwich and a glass of milk. He went into the living room and perused the bookshelf for something to read while he waited for the laundry. His eyes stopped on the binding of a white book with bold red lettering titled *The Joy of Sex*. He slipped the book off the shelf, noting the titles on either side so he could replace it unnoticed.

***

Images of Raya crying and the bloody sheets kept popping into his head while Marie fussed and perfected his haircut. Marie's hands ruffling his hair felt forbidden. Abruptly he stood up from the chair, and strode away. He mumbled, "Thanks for the haircut," over his shoulder. He knew he was being rude, and if he knew Marie, he guessed he'd hear about it later.

"Wait!" she called after him. "I still have a few spots to fix."

He kept walking out into the parking lot where he stopped and ran his hands through his newly cut hair. "What is wrong with me?" he asked, under his breath. He turned to see if Marie had followed him. There was no sign of her. She was probably sweeping up the scattered bits of hair or returning the chair to the dining area.

He walked mindlessly toward town, catching his reflection in a store window. He looked like a normal teenager with a fresh haircut. Marie had done a professional job, except for the almost two hours it had taken. He couldn't help smiling to himself at the thought of Marie's labored perfection. Then that feeling he got when she was touching his hair crept back into his body and he tried hard to shake it off. That feeling confused the hell out of him. He took off running fast through town, up the hill towards Raya's place.

***

"Mama's sick again, isn't she?" Lizzie asked, looking down at her half-eaten plate of macaroni.

Jesse hesitated. "Chipmunk, you're right. She is kinda sick." Jesse could tell that Carla was using again, and he worried that they might get kicked out of the shelter if it got too obvious. Carla wouldn't give him any of her welfare money and he'd checked her purse at night for cash. Nothing. It didn't look like Leo was coming back, so Carla was hurting. And when his mom hurt, she used. Jesse didn't even want to know what she was taking or how she was getting it. For years he'd monitored her drug intake until he realized it didn't make any difference if he knew what she was using. There was no denying that it was happening again. It was February, and the holiday frenzy of helping people had almost exhausted itself. Jesse needed new shoes; he had for a while, but he hated the idea of asking anyone for help or money. He'd attached the delaminated sole of his right shoe with Krazy Glue from a drawer in the church kitchen. But there were actual holes in the bottoms of both shoes that neither glue nor duct tape could plug. By the end of a rainy day his shoes were soaked through and his feet pruned.

Marie had noticed his deteriorating footwear and insisted they go to The Closet, a center run by the woman who had given Lizzie her pink backpack at the beginning of the year. It was a place for homeless teens to get clothes and shoes for free. Jesse hated the idea of entering a building that pretty much announced he was homeless. But Marie had persisted, talking him and Lizzie into going with her after school one day.

***

Arriving in Marie's car didn't seem very homeless: maybe people thought he was just another volunteer like Marie, or maybe people would think he was her boyfriend, just tagging along. He could flirt a little, he thought, as they walked up the handicapped ramp to the building. He did a running leap over the rail of the ramp, landing in front of Marie and Lizzie, who were walking slowly, holding hands.

"Hey," Marie complained. "No cutting! Come on Lizzie, let's catch him."

Jesse pushed through the door with the girls on his tail. The girls bumped into Jesse as he stopped abruptly inside the building. The room had four long tables with kids quietly working on homework, snacking on crackers and cheese and small cartons of milk.

"I forgot about study hall," Marie whispered from behind

Jesse. She escorted Lizzie past Jesse and motioned for him to follow her around the tables of gawking kids to a door with The Closet posted above it in bold purple letters.

"So it's not a real store," Jesse whispered to Marie. She glared at him and pushed the door open to the room containing the makeshift store. The room smelled of cedar but there were also strong undertones of used clothing smell, a smell that Jesse knew well.

"Come on," she whispered. The room wasn't big, but it had wall-to-wall racks of clothes, one side for girls and the other for boys. "It's all organized by size," Marie offered, leading Lizzie to the little girls section. Jesse looked at the boys' racks and felt instantly overwhelmed. He didn't want anything except shoes, which were piled in marked boxes on the floor.

"What size are you?" Marie asked, after she had Lizzie happily looking through a rack of dresses.

"Probably a twelve." Jesse squatted on the floor and rummaged through the box marked 12.

"I mean your jeans. I think we should find you an outfit!" Marie was perusing the boys' clothes.

"I just need shoes," Jesse protested.

"Try stuff on. It can't hurt."

"What about you?" Jesse raised an eyebrow at Marie. "What are you going to try on?"

Marie hesitated and then walked over to the girls' dresses where Lizzie had made a careful pile.

"I'm with Lizzie; I'm looking for a dress."

Jesse snorted a laugh. "Really? I've never seen you wear anything but pants. Even Christmas dinner, you wore jeans."

Marie glared at Jesse with exaggerated sternness and began clicking through the hangers of dresses. The shoes in Jesse's size were a disappointing bunch of worn skate shoes. But at least there weren't holes in the soles. Jesse picked out a pair of faded blue Vans. They weren't the most practical pair of shoes in the size-twelve box, but nobody was going to associate Vans with being homeless.

The door swung open and a petite, middle-aged woman entered the room. Marie turned from her dress hunt. "Lauren!" she called out, and ran to hug the small woman.

"You brought friends!" Lauren smiled at Jesse and Lizzie. "Hey, I know you," Lizzie said. "You gave me my shoes." Lizzie kicked her heel on the floor to reveal a weak flash of red light emanating from the dirty sole of her shoe.

"That's right." Lauren squatted next to Lizzie. "You're Elizabeth, right?"

"No, Lizzie," Lizzie corrected her.

"Sorry, no one really calls her Elizabeth," Jesse said apologetically.

"Lizzie, then. You guys are welcome to anything you can use. I also have some backpacks left over from the beginning of the year." Lauren looked at Jesse, eyeing his ratty gray pack slumped against the wall in the corner.

"My pack's still good," Jesse said. He looked down at the Vans he had tried on and couldn't help feeling like an imposter in the trendy shoes, even if they were worn. He should probably take her up on a new pack, but Ben had given him the gray one.

"It holds a lot but still looks like a day pack," Ben said, when he'd presented it to Jesse. How could he switch it out for something stiff and shiny with no link to Ben?

"These shoes fit, though, if that's okay?" he asked, looking shyly at Lauren.

"Of course, of course, anything you want. You too, Marie," Lauren added, and smiled. "It's nice to meet Lizzie's big brother." Lauren held out a hand to Jesse.

"Nice to meet you, too." Jesse shook Lauren's hand. He wanted to act aloof but it was hard not to show some appreciation to this woman and all that she was offering.

"You guys have fun trying stuff on. Just stop by my office, next door, before you leave."

"Okay, thanks Lauren." Marie nodded as Lauren ducked out the door. "Isn't she amazing?" Marie said when Lauren was gone. "She does all of this: The Closet, after school study hall, the shoes and backpacks... It blows me away."

"Yeah," Jesse mumbled. He didn't want to talk about what Lauren did because she did it for people like him, and that made him feel anxious and lacking. The whole topic made his stomach turn.

"You've got a pile, Liz! Let's try these on," Marie said. Marie and Lizzie crammed into the little dressing room surrounded by floor-length curtains.

Jesse found a couple of pairs of pants to try on and a Pink Floyd T-Shirt that he thought looked cool.

"Liz, you gonna do a fashion show?" Jesse asked, trying to lighten the mood.

Lizzie came out from behind the curtain. "I need shoes." She darted out of the dressing room wearing a purple floral dress with the zipper still halfway open down her back. She rummaged through a box and pulled out a pair of shoes at least three sizes too big and slipped them on, seeming satisfied with the fit. She stared at herself in the mirror, teetering on the neon yellow heels.

"Let me get your zipper," Marie said, following Lizzie out of the dressing room.

"Wow!" Jesse blurted, without meaning to. There was no ignoring Marie in that dress. It wasn't anything fancy, just a blue dress with tiny white dots all over it. But Jesse had never seen Marie in anything that really showed her shape or revealed much skin. The dress was one of those wrap around deals that tied in the back. He could make out the curve of her butt and hips, and the dress was low enough in the front to see cleavage. Marie had boobs!

"You should keep that dress," Jesse said, staring at Marie's pale back as she knelt to zip up Lizzie.

"Really, Jess?" Lizzie said. "But I like them all! How many can I take?"

Jesse laughed at Lizzie's misunderstanding; Marie turned and gave him a confused look.

"Three, Liz, no more than three."

"But, I love five."

"You should be looking at pants, Liz. They're more practical… in winter." He had almost said, "more practical for outside," but he didn't want to shatter Lizzie's little fantasy of being a real girl with dresses to choose from.

"How about you, Mr. Practical, what about a jacket?" Marie looked through the boys' jackets and pulled down a dark-gray fleece that seemed brand new. "This is nice, Jess. Try it on." Jesse obeyed and shrugged the jacket on. He was having trouble concentrating. Marie was distracting in that dress; he couldn't help imagining what would happen if he pulled on the narrow cord that seemed to hold the dress together. One small tug and the whole thing might fall away…

He stood in front of the mirror and looked at himself in the fleece jacket. It was warmer than his old jacket, which was cotton and useless when it got wet.

"You look handsome and outdoorsy," Marie said, standing behind him and looking into the mirror.

"Well, I am outdoors most of the time," he said. Marie laughed, and he realized he'd made a joke about his life in front of a friend. That was a first. It felt good to be himself and let his guard down.

By the time they got to Lauren's office with their piles of clothes, Jesse had talked Marie into taking the blue dress and talked Lizzie out of at least four entire outfits.

"All right! What great things you found." Lauren pulled an envelope out of her desk drawer and handed it to Jesse. He shied away like she was offering him something offensive. "It's just a coupon, Jesse, for shoes at the mall. I give them to all of the kids at the beginning of the year."

"Thanks, Lauren, I'll make sure he uses it." Marie took the envelope and glared at Jesse.

"Look, Jesse, if you need anything, you can always call." Lauren handed Jesse her card. "I keep things confidential." She looked at Jesse almost sternly. "You can trust me," she added.

She did seem trustworthy, but he couldn't keep from wondering what motivated people like Lauren or Marie to devote so much of themselves to people like him or Lizzie.

"Thanks." Jesse took the card and slipped it into the pocket of his new jeans, which Marie had insisted he wear. He appreciated what Lauren was doing, but he didn't want to tell her his life story. As far as he was concerned, that never panned out.

"Grab a snack in the study hall on your way out," Lauren said to Lizzie.

"Yum!" Lizzie screeched, holding tight to her dresses.

"And these are for you." Lauren handed Lizzie and Jesse each a plastic bag. "You can look at it later. It's just a bag of supplies," Lauren said, looking at Jesse and seeming to notice his current state of goodwill-overload.

Jesse relaxed in Marie's car driving north towards the shelter. "I can give you a ride to the mall sometime," Marie said, "to get shoes with the coupon."

"Yeah, maybe." Jesse thought he had experienced enough charity for one day.

"Goodie! Mermaid undies and new socks!" Lizzie announced from the back seat. She was rifling through the plastic bags from Lauren. "You got 'em too, Jess," she squealed.

"Mermaid undies? Yay!" Jesse crinkled his nose at Lizzie in the rearview mirror.

"No, silly, yours are blue and gray, for big boys."

Jesse could see Marie smiling as she pulled onto the highway. It was a calm, almost balmy day in early February; one of those rare days that felt like it had been carved out of summer and spliced into winter like a piece from a summer jigsaw puzzle.

Jesse's bag of clothes was at his feet. He was going to have to trade out some of his stuff in order to fit these new things into his pack. Or maybe stash some stuff under the tarp at their old camp. A corner of Marie's blue dress was poking out of his bag of new clothes. He'd have to remember to pull it out for her when she dropped them off. It was unnerving that glancing at a patch of fabric could make him obsess all over again about how Marie looked in that dress. Watching the glassy bay whiz by was a welcome distraction. He remembered how choppy the water had been during the bad bus ride with Raya. He thought of the *Joy of Sex* book he'd taken off Raya's shelf and what he'd read about a woman's body and how he wanted to try again, with Raya. He knew he could do things better. This time he would make sure it didn't hurt.

The bay blurred into the background as he watched Marie focus on the road. He couldn't help noticing the curves under her baggy clothes. Now that he'd seen her in the dress, he could easily make out the swell of her breasts under her sweatshirt and the curve of her hips in her loose jeans.

"What?" Marie asked, glancing at him.

"Nothing," he said. "Just checking out the bay." He slumped in the seat and closed his eyes, trying not to think about anything. Not Marie, not Raya, not the dress and certainly not *The Joy of Sex*. He wished he were in the forest climbing a tall tree on this warm winter day. He wanted to climb fast toward the tree crown until his heart was pounding in his chest and he could see the water from up high like a bird or a small plane soaring over the silky surface of the bay.

***

Jesse couldn't count on Carla getting Lizzie to school anymore. His mom had been sleeping in, getting Lizzie to school late and then forgetting about her in the afternoons. There was an after-school program at the shelter and he had been dropping Lizzie there while he met Raya to do homework. But everything at the shelter hinged on Carla's behavior. They had everyone sign a form agreeing not to use any drugs while staying there. It was only a matter of time before they caught on to Carla's use of whatever she could get her hands on. He'd actually broached the subject with his mom one evening while she was outside the shelter having a smoke.

"You're gonna get us kicked out of here during the coldest, wettest part of winter, aren't you? Are you ready to go back to camp when it's like this?" He held his arms out and let the damp drizzle accumulate in little beads on his new grey fleece.

Carla inhaled sharply on her cigarette and stared at Jesse with the blank look that usually meant she was stoned. "Nothing's going to happen. Relax! You're always so uptight." Carla laughed like she'd said something funny. Jesse shook his head and walked back to the shelter to find Lizzie and get her ready for bed. For the past few weeks the role of helping Lizzie brush her teeth, get in line for the shower, and prepare for bed had fallen on Jesse. He'd gotten used to Carla helping out like a real mom while Leo was around. Now, one by one, the responsibilities were falling back on him.

***

Jesse hadn't been able to get to the library to meet Raya until late because of all of his Lizzie duties. He usually ended up sleeping in Ben's stump with Alder and his buddies, due to the ten o'clock curfew at the shelter. By the time he'd walked Raya home and lingered by her gate, kissing her goodnight, it was almost always too late to get back to the shelter before curfew. His crappy watch had an alarm, and he made a point of setting it for five-thirty so he could get to the shelter before Lizzie woke up.

Staying too late at the library might not be an issue anymore, anyway. Raya hadn't talked to him in three days. And it wasn't like he could find her at school and ask what was going on; she hadn't come to school since the incident at the library three nights ago.

He and Raya had been at their favorite table on the third floor playing footsie and generally distracting one another from getting homework done. Jesse was about to confess that he'd read her mom's copy of *Joy of Sex*. He'd wanted to bring up the subject for a couple of weeks.

"Guess what I did at your house after we made love," he was planning to say. But could he call it making love when she'd screamed in pain and then cried herself to sleep? He was thinking of how he might rephrase things when Raya looked up, gasped and leapt out of her chair.

"Oh my God, I never see you anymore," Raya said, in a voice much too loud for library etiquette.

"I know," the girl hugging Raya replied. "We need to get our moms to plan a family dinner." That voice was so familiar, too familiar. Raya and her friend released each other from an embrace just as Jesse turned in his seat to see if the voice belonged to whom he feared it might.

"I want you to meet my boyfriend!" Raya said, taking the girl's hand and leading her to the table where Jesse sat stunned. "Jesse, this is my oldest and best friend, Marie. We grew up together." Jesse and Marie looked at each other for a few long seconds until Marie extended her hand.

"Nice to meet you," she said. Jesse took her hand. It was warm and charged with some kind of electricity that he felt shoot from her hand to his like a secret code. And then it was gone as she abruptly let go and turned her attention back to Raya.

"I have to meet my mom downstairs." Marie gave Raya a tight hug and glanced briefly at Jesse. She said, almost inaudibly, "Nice to meet you," before hurrying down the nearest aisle of books.

"Wow, I haven't seen Marie in months!" Raya sighed. "She goes to the charter high school so we hang out with different kids. I'm so glad you got to meet her!"

All Jesse could feel was a buzzing tension that made him want to run. "I gotta pee so bad," he said. "Be right back."

"Ok." Raya laughed, picked up her pencil, and continued working on her math. Jesse started off walking, but soon broke into an impulsive run through the stacks to the stairwell, taking two steps at a time until he saw Marie on the landing between the first and second floor.

"Marie, wait!" He ran down the remaining steps to her, practically gasping. "What are you doing here?" he asked.

Marie shook her head. "It's a library, Jesse, I come here all the time."

"Right." His breathing was more even now, but his eyes still glowed, looking feverish. "It's just... Raya doesn't know about... me." He sounded angry, like the whole thing might be Marie's fault.

"Don't worry. I'm not going to say anything." Her voice was starting to shake, and Jesse could see her eyes welling with tears. "I know how you are about... all of it," she said, finally. Now she was crying in earnest.

Jesse exhaled loudly. "I believe you. I'm sorry, I just wasn't expecting to see you or that you would know Raya."

"Well, I could have told you a long time ago," Marie stammered. "But you never mentioned her."

"I know, Marie, it's not your fault. I'm not mad at you, I'm just..."

"You seem different." Marie wiped her face with her sleeve. "Embarrassed to know... me." Then her face crumpled and Jesse wrapped his arms around her, horrified that he had made her cry.

"I'm not embarrassed to know you," he whispered quietly into her hair as she cried. "I'm embarrassed to be me." It felt good to hold her. He could feel her sobs subsiding as he rubbed her back. Unconsciously he leaned down and kissed the top of her head, inhaling her already familiar scent. Then he felt it: the undeniable sensation that someone was watching. It was late, and the stairwell had been empty, but he scanned the stairs and there, a flight above them, looking down at them, was Raya.

Chapter 9

SOMETHING had changed. The sharp wind had softened to a cool breeze, and the rain came in tropical downpours instead of the relentless icy deluge that had engulfed the coast for most of February. A new rope was slung across Jesse's chest as he climbed the tall redwood. Pelsinski had given Jesse a rope to attach to the tree in advance of a climb they'd planned for the next day. Jesse remembered watching Redwood Jack use ropes and pulleys, so he had a vague idea of how to hoist the professor up the tree. He figured that if he tied one end off around the tree now, he and Pelsinski could figure out how to use the rope the next day with the aid of some of Pelsinski's old rock-climbing hardware.

The air felt warmer as Jesse reached the upper third of the tree. There was a breeze, but it lacked the sting of a winter wind. Not wanting to damage the rope, Jesse carefully unwound a few feet from the thick coil and began circling the trunk with the loose end. When he'd circled the tree, he tied a bowline, one of the knots Redwood Jack had taught him years ago.

There was no sign of the salamander as he ascended the tree, but Jesse hoped that he'd have something to show Pelsinski tomorrow. He didn't want to hoist the old man up the tree for nothing. It was March and he hadn't been in any tree for over a month. Climbing reminded him of the last time he'd been in the tall redwood. The clouds had been spitting horizontal rain and the tree was arching like a fishing pole sprung low for a big catch. But he hadn't cared about the wind or the rain or the dramatic lurching of the tree as he'd climbed to the exposed tip. By the time he'd reached the crown he couldn't tell where his tears ended and the rain began, or if the howling came from the wind or his own roaring throat. The weather had drowned out his thoughts and numbed his bare nerves, and for that he'd been grateful.

That day, a month ago, had started as a typical weekend morning at camp. He was adding kindling to the previous night's fire to heat water for tea. They'd been back at camp for only a few days and hadn't yet scrounged enough money for fuel for the camp stove. It was drizzling lightly, the prelude to the afternoon deluge that was coming. Lizzie and his mom were still crashed out in the tent when Marie and Raya appeared at camp as if they'd been beamed there noiselessly like Star Trek characters. He hadn't heard a leaf crackle or a stick snap under their feet.

"What the hell!" Was all he could think to say as he knelt by the fire, staring at them. He hadn't seen either of them since the thing in the library almost two weeks before. Raya had stomped off that day at the library and ignored him whenever he saw her at school. Marie just didn't show up at the shelter or anywhere else she might normally frequent.

"I knew you'd be back here, because of the shelter closing, so I..." Marie stuttered.

"So you thought you'd screw things up even more and bring

Raya?" Jesse's voice shook. He regretted the words even as they darted out of his mouth.

"Jesse, I would never have brought her here. I try to keep my word about privacy, but in this case I had to make an exception." Marie looked rigid and her eyes grew dark. "It's actually you who screwed up!"

Tears were streaming down Raya's face, and Jesse wondered if seeing him like this in his soggy camp, attempting to coax a fire, was worthy of such a dramatic display of grief.

"Well, now you know!" Jesse said, looking at Raya. He stood up and kicked dirt on the fire. "Screw it!" he said, loudly, as he doused the fire with another toe-full of wet duff.

Raya was sobbing now, and Marie was attempting to hold her and at the same time glare at Jesse. "This isn't about showing her how you live, Jesse. Something's happened. She needs to tell you."

The blood rushed from Jesse's face and he stared slack-mouthed at Marie, who was rubbing Raya's shuddering back. "Do you want to tell him?" Marie asked Raya in a near whisper. Raya shook her head and let out a gasp before continuing her sobbing. "Ok, I'll do it." Marie stared squarely at Jesse's pale face. "She's pregnant."

Jesse couldn't move, couldn't even think. There was no way that he'd heard her correctly. It wasn't possible. They'd had sex only once, and he'd used a condom because her pill hadn't kicked in yet. Suddenly the idea of Raya seeing him homeless and making a fire didn't matter. His worst fear, the fear of being found out, suddenly didn't faze him. Being homeless had been surpassed by something worse. He'd tell the whole school he was homeless if he could erase those words: "she's pregnant." He was pretty sure that's what Marie had said and it seemed plausible. Why else would the two of them show up like this out of nowhere?

"Shit!" he said. "Are you sure?" Raya stood up from her slumped sobbing; both she and Marie stared at him with such stern disdain that he looked away and mumbled, "You seem pretty sure."

Carla popped out of the tent after having overheard the conversation from the other side of the thin sheet of nylon. She proceeded to act as a go-between/counselor/mother. She had obviously slept off whatever high she'd had in her system the previous night and the drama of the situation seemed to have induced what he thought of as her mothering high. She jumped into action, coaxing the smothered coals into a weak fire and settling the girls on soggy towels next to the limp flames. Then she ordered Jess to bolster the fire, find cups for tea and a pot for oatmeal. Carla didn't seem to care or notice that her sudden urge to entertain wasn't happening in a cozy house around a friendly kitchen table. It was like royalty had shown up unannounced and she was determined to put on a good show. Only, instead of royalty, she was entertaining Jesse's pregnant ex-girlfriend and Marie, who Jesse had been starting to think might be his best friend.

His first inclination was to run as far and as fast as he could from the whole unbelievable mess. But Carla's sudden display of hospitality was so out of the ordinary that he felt he couldn't run off and leave her alone in this tangled drama. He was actually grateful to his mom for having a sudden go at entertaining.

"Tea will help," Carla, said, stirring sugar from little packets they'd snitched from a coffee shop into two cups of black tea. "You shouldn't have much caffeine while you're pregnant, but a little tea now and then won't hurt." Jesse stirred the oatmeal and thought about how ironic it was of Carla to care about things that hurt the body.

Lizzie climbed out of the tent and crawled sleepily into Marie's lap, as if having Marie show up at camp was an every-day event.

"How far along do you think you are, Raya?" Carla asked matter-of-factly.

Raya's voice still harbored residual shudders from her bout of crying. "I think a little over a month," she said, looking down at her tea.

"Jesus," Jesse said, under his breath. It made sense, it was a little over a month since his birthday, the day they'd made awkward, painful love in her cold loft. He tried to imagine the tiny thing in her uterus that would become a child, like Lizzie, a child in need of clothes, food, and shelter.

"Well, that's still early," Carla reassured Raya. "If it's your first, which I assume it is, you have a chance of miscarriage. Or you can consider having an abortion." She said it casually, but with authority, like she was one of the practitioners at the clinic handing out informative tidbits of advice. Carla seemed oblivious to the fact that the girls were receiving advice from a homeless junkie experiencing a rare day of lucidity.

***

But Carla had been right. Marie showed up at camp two weeks later to tell Jesse that Raya had suffered a miscarriage two days before her abortion appointment. Still, he couldn't get the day that Marie had brought Raya to camp out of his head. It was like watching a movie over and over. The only way he'd stopped the image from replaying itself was by climbing the wind-blown tree in the slanting rain, and letting himself roar and cry into the storm.

Now, he was back in that same tree a month later, attaching a rope to haul an old professor up to see a slimy, yellow salamander. He'd stayed clear of Raya at school—or maybe she'd stayed clear of him. He'd sent her the salamander that he'd carved out of driftwood, and a letter, through the tall friend, the one he was pretty sure hated him. The letter just said he was sorry. Sorry for lying about his life, sorry for not knowing how to use a condom safely, sorry for not telling her about his friendship with Marie, sorry about the miscarriage. Actually, he couldn't have been happier about the miscarriage. He almost felt pride for his mom, like she'd predicted the whole thing.

When Marie told him about the miscarriage, he hadn't been able to contain a sigh of relief and the hint of a smile. But he'd turned serious quickly, not wanting to piss her off.

"It's okay," she'd said, not missing the momentary upward curve of his mouth. "Raya's relieved, too. We all are. But it did hurt and you should feel bad about that."

Jesse thought about his mom writhing in pain in the tent when he was little and the blood on her pants at the clinic. He felt a pang of remorse. He wondered if Raya had actually been forced to go through something like that? He'd just assumed a miscarriage in a comfortable house or at a doctor's office would somehow be easier than what he'd witnessed his mom go through years ago.

"Thanks for bringing her here that day, Marie. I know I was mad, but I'm glad you did it."

"Yeah, well, I didn't really have a choice."

He reached out to give Marie a hug, but she was already turning to leave. He ended up giving an awkward wave with his outstretched arms.

"See you around," she said, before walking away. And that was it. He hadn't seen her since. The church shelter was closed now that the weather had improved and she hadn't been to the park to hand out bags of food.

Talking salamanders with Dr. Pelsinski would be a welcome distraction. Jesse let the green-and-blue nylon rope uncoil as he descended the tree, tugging on it occasionally to test its hold on the trunk. Tomorrow he would bring the professor back and somehow lure the elusive yellow amphibian from the mossy crevasses of the redwood tree, so that Pelsinski could see it for himself.

***

"Right there! I think I saw something…" Pelsinski was suspended in the air a third of the way up the tree. "I think I saw it, Jesse: a flash of mustard yellow and some mottled brown markings. I'm going to see if I can swing myself around to the other side."

Jesse was ten feet above Pelsinski with the rope on belay. "Be careful, Dr. Pelsinski. Please don't get scraped up."

"Oh, hell, I don't care. This is the most excitement I've had in years. And call me Henry, really!"

"Okay, Dr.… Henry, but take it easy." Jesse held the rope tight as Pelsinski pushed off the tree with his feet, launching himself to the far side of the trunk. "You okay?" Jesse hollered.

"Fine," Pelsinski called back. "Pull me up a little so I can investigate the armpit of this branch." Jesse pulled on the rope until Pelsinski yelled, "Good, stop!"

"Okay," Jesse called, holding onto the rope. "See anything?" The professor didn't respond, except with "Hmm…" Jesse leaned back against the trunk and let out a slow deep breath.

It was a dazzlingly clear day. Jesse leaned into the tree and listened to the urgent chatter of birds pecking their way through the branches. A prickle of sun warming the skin on his bare arms and neck reminded him of the few times he'd had a warm bath. It was in the middle of this reverie that Jesse heard Pelsinski calling from the other side of the tree.

"Jesse! It's here in this little debris pit. You've got to see it. It's like a nest!"

"Great!" Jesse called back. "Take some photos." Jesse smiled to himself, relieved that Pelsinski had spotted the herp.

After an hour or more of note taking and photo documentation, Pelsinski was finally ready to be lowered down to the needle littered base of the tree.

"My God, this is really something. There's no other salamander like your pale yellow friend up there."

Jesse smiled, enjoying Henry's contagious good cheer. "I'm glad it showed itself today," Jesse said, imagining the disappointment he'd have felt if the herp had not appeared.

"This is going to mean a publication and a naming," Dr. Pelsinski said, raising an eyebrow at Jesse.

"I have no idea how to write a paper like that," Jesse said, shaking his head.

"I don't expect you to write it by yourself, but you could write it with me, be a co-author." Pelsinski looked at Jesse like he was asking a question. Jesse laughed, because it was laughable that this professor wanted him to help write a paper.

"This is serious. This could help with whatever colleges you're looking at. I don't know where you've applied, but this is the kind of thing that could change a university's decision if you're put on a waiting list."

"I don't see why you need my help with the paper. I've shown you everything I know, so it seems like you'll be fine writing it." Jesse pulled on the end of the rope, which was still straddling a low branch of the tree.

Pelsinski let out a long hissing whistle like a teakettle at full boil. He tapped his finger against the climbing harness, still attached to his waist. "Look, it's one thing to go up there," he pointed a finger at the tree, "for one glorious morning and have the good fortune to find what I'm so desperately looking for. It does feel a bit like providence, really." He rubbed his chin and smiled to himself at his own luck. "But you led me to it. You've climbed all over these trees." He swept an arm across the swath of woods that lay before them. "I need your everyday experience and observations to make this paper accurate and to give it the kind of depth it deserves. And this can really do you some good when it comes to choosing a college."

Jesse looked up through the staggered branches of the tree they had just descended. Would colleges really care about climbing trees and hunting salamanders? He wondered. "I only applied to Humboldt, and I don't even know if I'm going to go," Jesse said flatly. He didn't want to explain that he couldn't afford to go to college. In fact, he could barely afford a cup of coffee and a bagel. Lately his mom was using all their money on getting her fix. Jesse and Lizzie were living on school lunches and cans of chili from the food bank.

***

Jesse and Pelsinski had walked right past Carla that morning on the way to the salamander tree. He'd taken a smaller trail that didn't go near camp specifically to avoid seeing his mom. But Carla had crawled away from camp to puke and passed out next to the trail that Jesse was carefully navigating Pelsinski along. Jesse had almost cried out as they came upon his mom. But Pelsinski knelt immediately and felt for Carla's pulse.

"I'm sure she's fine," Jesse said, wanting to get out of there. "I see people passed out in these woods all the time." He wasn't lying. He did see his mom passed out almost daily.

"Her pulse is okay," Pelsinski said. "Help me turn her on her side so she doesn't choke on her vomit."

Jesse sighed, but he wasn't going to deny Dr. Pelsinski's help. He crouched over his mom and gently rolled her onto her side. Then he took off his sweatshirt and folded it into a pillow to elevate her head. With a familiar swipe of his hand he brushed a greasy strand of hair from her mouth. Jesse looked up. Pelsinski stood across from him, staring.

"I think she'll be fine," Jesse said, reassuringly. But he worried that concern for Carla wasn't what Pelsinski's stare was about. "I've seen her before. Her druggie friends say that as long as she's snoring, she's okay." Jesse tipped his head toward Carla as if listening for a signal. "She's snoring, lightly. And we can check her on our way down," Jesse said, and started back up the trail.

***

"Really, you only applied to Humboldt? Well, lucky Humboldt."

"I haven't said yes to them yet. I have to think about some stuff before I decide."

Pelsinski unbuckled the climbing harness from his waist while Jesse wound the rope into a manageable coil.

"Keep me posted. It'd be a shame to lose you to whatever else you're considering doing. Is it travel? Do you want to roam the globe for a year before you put your nose to the grindstone?"

"I don't want to travel," Jesse said, hanging the rope across his chest. "I was thinking more along the lines of getting a job." Jesse couldn't relate to the restless desire kids his age had to travel. Traveling would feel like voluntary homelessness to him. Leaving a stable home for some unknown place didn't make any sense. It seemed like he'd spent most of his life traveling and all he wanted was to get home. Only home didn't exist, so he had to keep moving, traveling endlessly.

"I might have some data entry you could do. Let me think about it," Pelsinski said, as they started down the shadowy, fern-lined trail to the park.

Carla wasn't lying by the trail on their way down. Jesse tried to avoid the topic of their trailside encounter with his mom, but Pelsinski brought it up.

"I hope that woman's okay," he said, looking around like he might find her curled up next to a clump of ferns or leaning against a huckleberry-laden stump.

"I'm sure she's fine."

"But your sweatshirt, she must have taken it."

"I've got another," Jesse said, and quietly continued down the path.

When they reached the campus, Pelsinski shook Jesse's hand. "This is a big day, Jesse. You're going to have to think up a name for your salamander. I want you to consider helping me write that paper, introducing your yellow friend to the masses." Pelsinski chuckled. "And when I say masses, I mean the handful of herpetologists who bother to read these publications."

"Ok," Jesse said, and smiled involuntarily. Suddenly it hit him; he could hardly believe what Pelsinski was offering.

Then he shuddered at the image of Pelsinski kneeling next to his passed-out mother, checking for her pulse. What would Pelsinski think if he knew the truth about him? He'd probably keep his distance like Raya had. But Jesse couldn't help feeling a little cheerful. He longed to share his good news with someone other than his hung-over mother.

He couldn't tell Lizzie, because she'd finally been invited to a sleepover at a girl's house and he wanted that to last as long as possible. He'd made a point of doing all of her laundry the day before with some laundry coupons from Lauren at the Clothing Closet. And he'd taken Lizzie to the community pool for a shower before he dropped her off at the girl's house. He didn't want to risk Lizzie being alienated by the other girls for smelling of urine or campfire smoke.

Jesse had the sudden urge to run to Raya's house and share the salamander news with her. Maybe they could pretend like the whole pregnancy thing never happened. But if she wanted anything to do with him she would have approached him at school, and she hadn't. She had made herself very scarce. Raya was never in the cafeteria anymore; he suspected that she was off campus with her girlfriends for lunch.

More than anyone else, he wanted to share the news of the unnamed salamander with Marie. She would take a real interest in the salamander. She might even ask questions or have an idea for a name. Maybe he could track her down, except he had no idea where she lived and he didn't have the nerve to show up at her charter school. It was such a small campus, there was no way to lurk around without being noticed.

"I'll come by tomorrow after school," Jesse said to Pelsinski. "We have a minimum day."

"Perfect!" Pelsinski shook Jesse's hand again. "We can talk about that job too, if you want?"

"Sounds good," Jesse said, as Pelsinski went into his office. Jesse couldn't think of any reason to walk into town, so he headed slowly through the hillside campus, back toward the forest and Carla.

***

"Good boy, Tob. Look at those adorable paws!" Lizzie sat on Ellen's living room floor giving Toby a thorough rubdown. Toby lay sprawled on his back with his legs in the air and his lips pulled back, either by gravity or sheer joy, Jesse couldn't tell which. Either way the dog looked blissed out.

"Life's rough, huh, Tob?" Jesse sat on the floor next to Lizzie, rubbing one of the dog's silky ears between his fingers.

"He's spoiled rotten," Ellen called from the kitchen. "He has to have wet food on top of his kibble or he just stares at me like I'm forgetting something. And he sneaks on the couch as soon as we go to work, even though I got him that deluxe bed." Ellen pointed to a thick round pad in the corner of the room near the woodstove. Jesse had the urge to crawl over and curl up on the bed himself if Toby wasn't going to claim it.

Things really had turned out well for old Toby. The hound had endured plenty of bad weather and been forced to skip occasional meals when Ben was low on cash, but he'd always been loved. Jesse couldn't help but fantasize that he and Lizzie might be offered the same kind of hospitality someday. Jesse knew that Ellen would take Lizzie in a second, but it would mean cutting all ties with their mother. He wasn't ready to do that, not yet.

"Here's your cocoa," Ellen said, handing a cup to Jesse and another to Lizzie. Jesse wasn't sure what he was more excited about, the warmth of the ceramic mug or the thick chocolaty liquid it contained.

"Thanks. We won't stay long. I don't want to be here when…"

"It's okay, really. He's on a trip and not due back for a couple of days."

Jesse couldn't help but notice Ellen's involuntary glance at the door as if her husband might surprise them and walk in, yelling about having *those kids around again!* "We need to get back for dinner soon. My mom's expecting us."

Ellen looked hopeful. "Oh, that's nice. Is she doing all right?"

"Yeah, she's pretty good," Jesse lied. He wasn't sure why he was lying to Ellen. It wasn't like she didn't know, first hand, what Carla was capable of. "She's probably got dinner started," Jesse added.

"Really? Mama was asleep. Is she making dinner?" Lizzie looked up expectantly from petting the dog.

Jesse winced and Ellen frowned a little. "Yes, I think she's making baked potatoes in the fire; we can pick up some cheese and sour cream to put on top."

"Yum!" Lizzie stood up, ready to leave at the mere mention of sour cream.

"Finish your cocoa first." Ellen smiled. "Jesse, I've been meaning to give you this." Ellen walked to her purse and pulled out her checkbook. "I want to give you an early graduation present in case I don't see you for a while."

"Oh, wow. I don't have a bank account or anything, so I don't really have a way to deal with a check." Jesse pushed his hands awkwardly into his pants pockets.

"That's something we need to remedy before you go to college."

"I doubt I'm going. We can't exactly afford it." Jesse laughed uncomfortably after he said it. Knowing his circumstances, he thought it was crazy that Ellen brought up college at all.

"Jess, I could help a little every month." She put the checkbook back in her purse and pulled some bills from her wallet. "Here's sixty bucks. That's all the cash I have, but I'd like to help you get a bank account sometime soon."

Jesse sighed and looked at the floor. He didn't want to take money from Ellen. He didn't want to end up owing his uncle or aunt anything. Right now he only had two dollars tucked into his pack, and he'd just promised Lizzie a dinner that didn't exist. He couldn't really afford to turn down the sixty dollars.

Lizzie was hugging Toby goodbye, believing that Carla was miraculously making them dinner. It still shocked him when Lizzie trusted that their mother could get it together to cook or do laundry. Maybe it was just that Lizzie thought Jesse would always tell her the truth.

"Thanks, Ellen," he said quietly, as he folded the bills into his pants pocket. Now he could at least make good on the baked potatoes.

"Don't be a complete stranger," Ellen said at the door. "If the truck's not parked out front, then there's a good chance Frank's off on a trip somewhere." Ellen started to cry as she waved goodbye from the porch. "Toby, stay," she said, grabbing his collar with one hand and wiping her wet cheeks with the other.

"Bye, Tob!" Lizzie pressed her fingers together to make the shape of a heart.

***

Carla wasn't at camp when they got there, and Lizzie didn't ask where she was. Instead, she helped Jesse carefully wrap three potatoes in tin foil and place them in the coals that were left from their morning fire.

"Add some wood, Liz, or we won't eat until midnight." Jesse sat on a square of dry tarp material and methodically emptied his backpack. He made piles of clean and dirty clothes and stacked his books on the tarp. When his pack was empty, he slipped forty of the sixty dollars into the bottom lining. When Carla got desperate, she would inevitably go through his things looking for money, but so far she hadn't been thorough enough to find this hiding place. He liked the idea of getting a bank account—that would be the safest place to hide money from his mother. He'd never gotten an account because of all that paperwork and contact information, but if Ellen helped, she could provide all that. A bank account would be more important than ever if he started working for Pelsinski.

***

He'd announced to the professor that he'd come up with a name for the salamander. "I want to call it *Aneides pelsinskii*," Jesse had said and then smiled at the professor. "The common name can be the 'Yellow Canopy Salamander'."

Pelsinski smiled back. "Well, *Aneides* is appropriate for a climbing salamander, but I was expecting you to name it after your girlfriend or maybe your mother, so this is a surprise. Are you sure you don't want to name it after yourself?" Pelsinski was sitting in a swivel chair, mindlessly rotating the seat.

Naming the salamander after Lizzie or even Marie had crossed his mind, but the idea of naming it after Raya or his mom gave him a stomachache. "I'm sure," Jesse said. "If it weren't for you I wouldn't be naming it at all."

"In the paper, you'll get full credit for the original identification. I'm not the kind of academic to steal someone's discovery." Pelsinski's eyes kept flashing toward Jesse's chest, and Jesse glanced down, wondering if he had dirt or a smear of oatmeal on his clothes.

"I see that you retrieved your sweatshirt from that woman," Pelsinski finally said, staring at the faded silhouette of a basketball player shooting into a nonexistent hoop.

"Oh, right." Jesse had found the sweatshirt in the tent and not thought about it when he slipped it on over a clean T-Shirt. "I had another one... just like it," he lied, looking down at the floor.

Pelsinski squinted at Jesse, and then seemed willing to let the subject go. "Let's talk about a job. Are you really interested?"

"Yes, completely interested!" Jesse stood straighter and had the urge to take the sweatshirt off, even though the air was cool in Pelsinski's office.

"Well, some of it will be pretty boring data entry, but I think I can pay you to help with the paper as well."

"That's great! I can work on weekends and most evenings."

"Okay, let's start with a few evenings and see how it goes."

***

Jesse returned his books and the few clean shirts to his pack, confident that his mother wouldn't find the hidden money. He really would need a bank account, he thought, when his paychecks from Pelsinski started rolling in. Lizzie had placed a few pieces of wood in a careful teepee shape over the existing coals that glowed around the aluminum covered potatoes. She sat opposite Jesse on her own patch of tarp. She was hugging one of her stuffed animals and reading a chapter book from school.

"Good work on the fire, Liz. Those potatoes will be done in no time!"

"Yeah," she said, looking up from her book. "I just thought that Mama was going to make them, like you said…"

"I'm sorry. I shouldn't have told you that, I was just… I don't know…" Jesse looked across the fire at his sister. For the first time, he didn't detect the optimism that she usually radiated, regardless of almost anything he said. She just stared at Jesse for a long, uncomfortable moment before looking back at her book. The potatoes sizzled in their aluminum jackets and Jesse watched the smoke from the fire drift into the trees. It felt like something precious was drifting away into the forest shadows. Jesse got up and moved his square of tarp next to Lizzie. He sat close to her and quietly reached for her book.

"Hey, Chipmunk, how about I read that aloud to you?" Lizzie didn't say anything, but she leaned into Jesse's shoulder and let him read.

Chapter 10

PELSINSKI leaned back in his chair and put his hands behind his head. "This is easy for you, isn't it?"

Jesse selected the next column of data and clicked. "Yeah, it's okay."

"You'll take a load off my mind. I've got stacks of notes that need compiling. I can keep you busy for eternity, if you don't die from the monotony." Pelsinski suddenly looked relaxed, like he'd just hired a house cleaner to organize the messiest room in his cluttered mind.

Jesse laughed and thought about how he couldn't afford to get bored, not when he was making money. Pelsinski was paying him minimum wage an hour: a fortune as far as Jesse was concerned. "I don't mind this work. I've used Excel in biology class, so I kinda know the program."

"Good. But you don't have a computer at home, do you, Jesse?" Pelsinski's chair squeaked as he maneuvered into the middle of the room. Jesse stayed hunched over the laptop keyboard.

"No, we don't have one, why?" Jesse looked over his shoulder at the professor. "Do I need to have a…?"

"No, of course not, you can use this computer anytime." It was an older laptop set up on a counter across from Pelsinski's desk.

There was an awkward silence as Jesse continued to roll the mouse around, chipping away at the columns on the screen. He wondered if Pelsinski would stay there watching him or if the professor would use the time to get stuff done. Jesse concentrated on manipulating the long columns of data, hoping Pelsinski would either strike up more conversation or work on his own computer.

"I've been wanting to tell you about something that happened the other day," Pelsinski said, breaking the silence. "I went to get a GPS location for the salamander tree and I…"

Jesse felt his neck stiffen and his shoulders grow rigid. He had the urge to bolt before Pelsinski could finish his thought. The professor sighed. "I came across the woman we saw in the forest. I asked about your sweatshirt and she explained the… the connection." Pelsinski stopped talking, letting the air in the office grow still and cramped with tension.

"Shit," Jesse whispered, leaning his head onto the counter. "What did she say?" He swiveled in his chair and looked at Pelsinski.

"She said the sweatshirt belonged to her son. Then I asked if she was okay, after what I saw the other day."

Jesse sighed and ran his fingers through his damp hair. He'd showered less than an hour ago to keep the smoke smell and camp dirt from giving him away.

"Is she okay, I mean in general?" Pelsinski asked, looking concerned.

"She recovered from that day, but there will be other days." Jesse lowered his eyes, not wanting to see the pity on Pelsinski's face.

The professor let the quiet pile up in the room and then asked, "Where are you living? Are you camping in the forest?"

Jesse could feel all his blood pump into his head and thought he would burst from the pressure. He pushed out of the chair and stood in front of Pelsinski. "What does that have to do with anything? Do you want me to enter data for you or not?"

Pelsinski didn't look scared, just a little jarred by Jesse's outburst. "I'm not judging you, Jesse. I'm just concerned. I can talk to my wife, see about you staying in our shed. It's just sitting there, unused. There's a water heater and a sink, even an outdoor shower and a toilet. My son fixed it up when he came home from college."

Jesse could feel the rage drain from his arms and legs as he realized Pelsinski was trying to help. "But it's more complicated than that," Jesse said, and took a deep breath. "I can't leave my mom. Not yet anyway."

Pelsinski was squinting, as if straining to see what was so complicated about moving out of the damp, cold forest and into a warm, dry shed. "If your mom won't get help, you can't really do anything for her."

"It's not just my mom… " Jesse exhaled as if his breath were a secret he'd been holding too long. "I have a little sister."

Pelsinski's forehead went from smooth to deeply grooved at the mention of Lizzie. "A sister. How old?"

Humiliation swept over Jesse. He was tempted to lie about Lizzie's age just to avoid Pelsinski's reaction. "She's six, but she turns seven next week." It was true about her turning seven and he was glad to be reminded of it. He needed to do something special for Lizzie's birthday. Some of the money from Ellen was still stashed in his pack.

Pelsinski stood up and went to the door. "Let's go. I need to show you this shed." Pelsinski didn't put his computer to sleep or tidy up his desk. "Come on. I'll talk to my wife tonight about you moving in. I can't knowingly leave you out there. It's supposed to rain tonight." Pelsinski shook his head and looked as if he suddenly realized how crazy it sounded to be worried about one night of rain.

Jesse was frozen in front of the computer screen open to the long columns of numbers. He'd rather stay in the office, plugging away at the data. He wanted to forget everything Pelsinski had found out about, his mom, his life, and now Lizzie. It was better when people knew nothing about him. As soon as they knew, they took pity and tried to help—or they got away fast. Jesse wasn't fond of either reaction. He didn't blame people for running. He'd run too if he met himself or his mom. Lizzie, though, she was another story. You couldn't help but want to save her. For that reason alone, Jesse followed Pelsinski out of the door.

***

It wasn't really a shed, not as far as Jesse was concerned. Sure, it could use a wipe-down, but it was a good-sized room with wood floors and a makeshift kitchen. There was a wall of single-paned windows that looked into Pelsinski's backyard. It was dark out, but the porch light illuminated a viney rose bush outside the window, hanging from the eave of the shed. Jesse could see the small tight buds threatening to bloom.

"There'll be hot water once we light the pilot on the heater. And the sink's good-sized." Pelsinski patted the counter affectionately. Jesse could tell that the professor was proud of the place and had probably helped his son convert it from what must have been a shed into a real studio apartment. The shower and toilet were outside, but who cared. Jesse thought the place was a palace.

"This propane burner is all we have for cooking, but I guess you're used to that." Pelsinski looked like he regretted saying the words as soon as they left his mouth.

"This is great!" Jesse was excited. He could imagine bringing Lizzie here after school, making her a snack and doing homework together at the small table.

"There's just the one queen bed." Pelsinski pointed at the futon folded into a couch. "Look, about your mom… We can't have her staying here unless she's clean. I hope you understand that. I'm not trying to be a hard-ass, but it is our home."

"No, no, I get it. I'll talk to her. Maybe my sister could stay some of the time, though?"

"Of course. But God, your sister should be in a foster home. She'd be better off."

"Foster care is a gamble," Jesse interrupted. "It can be great, but it can also end up..." Jesse let the sentence trail off.

"I know," Pelsinski said. "I've heard stories. Look, talk to your mom. If she really thinks she can clean up then she's welcome to stay here with you and your sister. But she can't mess this up, Jesse. One wrong move and I wouldn't hesitate to kick her out."

"I understand; I'll talk to her. It's really nice of you to even give us a chance."

Pelsinski looked around the shed as if he were hunting for a way to change the subject. "The loft is packed with my son's stuff that he's storing. Indefinitely, I guess." Pelsinski seemed to smile a little at the thought of his son.

There was a ladder leading up to what would make a great sleeping loft if it weren't packed tight with boxes and chairs and who knew what else. "But you have to let me pay some rent." Jesse ran a hand through his hair. "I can pay you by working on the data."

Pelsinski looked out the windows into the dark yard. Jesse wondered if the professor was worrying about what his wife would say when he told her that he'd as much as promised their shed to a junkie and her two kids. "I don't want to deprive you of a paycheck; we'll work something out. You could do some gardening, maybe. This yard gets away from me in the spring."

"Anything, really," Jesse said, shaking his head in disbelief. The shed was like a dream home. He couldn't wait to show the place to Lizzie. It was all too good to be real, certainly too good to pass up. He'd bring Lizzie over tomorrow after school, and maybe Carla, if she cleaned up. But when Jesse thought of Carla inhabiting the homey shed, the whole place took on a dank, grey hue, and he felt a cold shiver inch up his neck.

***

Jesse couldn't stand the idea of Lizzie being the one kid whose mom didn't bring a treat to school on her birthday. He wasn't her mom, but at least he could provide a cupcake slathered in chocolate for each classmate. Proof that someone cared about Lizzie.

In the store, hunting for cheap cake mix, Jesse noticed Raya and her friends picking out candy bars. He felt a lump in his throat and his stomach tightened. It was tempting to wave or even walk down the aisle and try to strike up a conversation, but Raya's friends were huddled around her like insulation on a water heater. There was no route past all those teenage girls to get to the one girl he wanted to talk to. And if he had the chance to talk to her, what would he say that he hadn't already said in his letter? Even though he'd said he was sorry, things still felt unfinished. It was like their relationship was a rag hanging on some abandoned laundry line, waiting to get folded up and put away.

Jesse felt nauseous as he walked down the baking aisle. He decided on brownies instead of cake mix. There'd be no need for frosting, and the brownie mix was on sale. At the checkout, Jesse stood looking straight ahead to avoid eye contact with Raya's pack. It was crazy how much discomfort and damage had occurred from having sex one time. Of course he missed the idea of sex with her, but even more than that he missed her company at the library or the luxury of going to her house after school to do homework. If they'd stayed together longer she could have come to the shed to hang out.

It was so hard to believe that he had a place, a home to go to and sleep or shower—anytime he wanted. He got a stabbing sensation in his stomach when he thought of Carla being at the shed, but so far everything was okay. Two nights had passed before Carla showed up begging to stay. She said she'd seen the "alien" and needed a place to hide. Jesse guessed that Ellen and Carla had an encounter somewhere in town.

There was no way Jesse was going to go against Henry's rules and let Carla inside the shed without permission. He went over to the house that same morning to ask if his mom could stay in the shed for a couple of days until she calmed down from the "alien" encounter. Pelsinski's wife, Eve, answered the back door. Jesse felt suddenly unsure of how much information he should divulge about his mom.

"What's going on?" Eve asked, looking across the yard. Carla was sitting on the shed step, with Lizzie's small arms wrapped tightly around her mother like the viney, pink rose that wound up the post next to them.

"It's my mom," Jesse said. "She's... upset and wanting to stay a night or two." Jesse hated asking, but he wasn't surprised that he had to. He'd known that only a few days would pass before Carla tracked them down. He and Lizzie were the only things keeping his mom tethered to any one place; without them she was lost in orbit.

"That's your mom?" Eve asked.

"Yeah. She's upset about running into her sister yesterday. They don't really... get along." Eve was looking across the yard at mother and daughter in their twisted embrace.

"Let me talk to her alone, inside." Eve pointed through the open back door that Jesse imagined led to a warm bright kitchen.

"If you want. She might say some weird stuff. She's kind of—messed up right now."

"I have experience with this, Jesse. I work at the hospital and I've seen all kinds of people."

He wondered what she meant by that; did she mean she'd worked with addicts like Carla? "It's fine with me," Jesse put his hands up. "Whatever works. After she sees her sister she's scared to be alone for a while. She'll be better in a couple of days." It was a half-truth: no matter how much she calmed down after seeing Ellen, she'd still be screwed up.

Eve walked past Jesse to where his mom and Lizzie huddled. She knelt and spoke softly in Carla's ear. Jesse couldn't make out what she was saying, but the soft words sounded like a quiet trickle of water. It was obvious that Eve's soothing voice was having the desired effect on Carla, because she was gently untangling Lizzie from her body and standing up.

"Mama's gonna have a cup of tea." Carla patted Lizzie's head. "You stay with Jess." Carla sounded almost normal, but Jesse could tell the offer of help had triggered something. She was ready to alter, like a chameleon, in whatever way was necessary to appeal to Mrs. Pelsinski.

"Come on, I have hot cocoa inside." Jesse held out a hand to Lizzie, who reluctantly let go of Carla's leg and followed him into the shed.

***

Two hours passed before Carla came back to the shed freshly bathed, wearing clean sweats and a new pair of hand-me-down shoes. Jesse and Lizzie looked up from their game of Crazy Eights.

"She said I can stay," Carla said, sprawling on the futon.

"Yay, Mama!" Lizzie let her cards scatter across the table, face up, and plunged onto the bed with Carla.

Jesse stood and leaned against the counter. "What did you tell her? I don't want you to screw this up for us," he said in a stern voice.

Carla laughed. "Stop acting like a bully. Eve likes me; she wants to help." Carla looked around the shed. "This place is great. I love it! We could do so much with it."

Jesse continued to stare at Carla. "So, she said you can be here? Doesn't she have to check with Henry, Dr. Pelsinski, first?"

"He's there now; he knows. He agrees with the terms that Eve and I have written up."

"Written up?" Jesse sounded worried.

"Yeah, we made an agreement. I can stay here as long as I attend Narcotics Anonymous meetings. I have to show her proof in the evenings—you know, a stamp from the group leader."

"You tried this before. You hate those meetings, you said the people are full of shit."

"For God's sake, don't swear like that in front of your sister."

***

In the days since Carla had made her agreement with Eve and moved into the shed, she'd spent her time cleaning, nesting, and sleeping. There were moments when Jesse saw the look in her eye that usually meant she would find something, anything, to swallow that would help her forget her life. But she'd snapped out of her predatory stare each time and dragged herself off to an NA meeting. She'd even promised to get a couple of presents for Lizzie. Jesse's job was to get the brownies made in time to pass out at the end of school. He couldn't bring himself to ask Eve if he could use her oven, so he had arranged to use the community center kitchen for an hour after the senior lunch.

When he arrived, the dining hall was still full of grey-heads conversing over desserts and coffee. Jesse walked around the tables to the kitchen in the back of the room. He pushed the swinging door open to see a crew cleaning up from lunch. It smelled like lasagna, or something equally rich and savory. Jesse felt his stomach rumble. He'd skipped lunch and left school early. At least he'd had a bowl of cereal at the shed in the morning. He stood against the wall to stay out of the way of the kitchen crew. Peggy, the woman he'd asked about using the oven, noticed him and waved.

"We'll be out of your way in a few minutes. Go ahead and

grab a mixing bowl from the dish rack and get started. It's in that next alcove." Peggy pointed a finger down a short hall.

Jesse could hear the clatter of dishes being washed and the light voices of women chatting. He walked into the next room and stopped, recognition sweeping his face. Should he turn quickly and slip out? He couldn't think of anything to say, so he just stood there silently until she turned to see who it was.

"Jesse!" said a voice that sounded, to him, like sunshine and music. Marie dropped her sponge in the soapy water and walked straight to Jesse and gave him a tight hug. He hugged her back and exhaled, not sure how long he'd been holding his breath.

"I've missed you," she said.

***

The cleanup crew was gone, leaving Jessie and Marie alone in the kitchen. The brownies were in the oven, and the savory smell of lasagna had been overtaken by the aroma of chocolate rolling out of the oven like an impending fog.

"There's lots of this left over." Marie gestured at the tray of lasagna she was about to cover with foil. "Let me get you a plate."

"Thanks." Jesse had been hoping she'd offer. He was way too hungry to act polite and turn it down. "What do you do with the leftovers?" he asked, then blushed, thinking it sounded like he was asking for the food. "I'm just curious," he added, quietly.

"They give it to me to distribute to homeless folks. It's kind of an exchange for my helping out with the lunch."

"You're breaking the rules by giving this to me," he said, looking at her with a serious face.

"What, I didn't mean that you..."

Jesse laughed and interrupted, "What I'm saying is... I've

got a place to live now." Jesse went back to eating the lukewarm lasagna, which tasted to him like perfection.

Marie was beaming and blushing simultaneously.

"That's great! Where?"

Jesse described the shed and how Henry had offered it to him. He even told Marie the part about his mom talking to Eve and moving in. He watched Marie closely as he relayed the details about Carla. Marie's eyes narrowed and she bit her lip.

"You don't think it'll work, do you?" Jesse asked. He could tell by her face that she was skeptical.

"I'm sure it'll be fine," Marie turned to scoop more lasagna onto his plate.

***

Jesse didn't know if Lizzie was going to be more excited about the brownies or Marie coming along to help pass them out. At first Marie had just offered him a ride because he was late getting to Lizzie's school, but it wasn't hard talking her into staying.

"Come to our house, please!" Lizzie was holding on to Marie with one hand and clutching her second brownie in the other. Lizzie had yelped at the sight of Marie passing out brownies outside the classroom. It took some explaining before Lizzie realized that Marie and the brownies were there to celebrate her, not some other kid. Once she figured out what was happening, she couldn't stop grinning and grasping a handful of Marie's blue jacket. Lizzie's teacher gave Jesse and Marie a grateful nod, and Jesse thought she looked vaguely teary.

As they walked back to the car, Jesse didn't stop Lizzie from pleading with Marie to come to the shed for dinner. He shared Lizzie's urge to hold on to some part of Marie, now that they'd found her again.

Marie parked the car in front of the Pelsinski's house and turned off the engine. "I'd like to see your place," she said, and smiled. "And I have a whole lasagna in the back I can contribute to the birthday dinner."

"Yay!" Lizzie unbuckled her seatbelt and climbed over the seat into Marie's lap.

Jesse just grinned and said, "I guess someone's happy."

***

"This is a beautiful yard," Marie said, looking around at the Pelsinski's blooming roses and the big pink camellia flowering in front of the kitchen window.

"Yeah, there's a shower and a toilet behind there too." Jesse pointed at the brick path leading past the shed. Carla had the lights on even though it was afternoon; Jesse thought he could make out the shapes of balloons through the afternoon glare obscuring the windows.

"Let's see if Mom has a surprise for you." Lizzie let go of Marie's hand and darted for the shed. She charged through the door and screeched in delight. Marie laughed and followed Lizzie into the shed, trailed by Jesse still carrying the lasagna. He stopped inside the door and stood rigid, taking in the scene. There were two giant bouquets of balloons bumping around the room; the table was covered with snack food and sparkling soda. He looked at Carla, who was holding a glass of what he hoped was soda in her hand. Her eyes were lit up like the votive candles she had burning on the kitchen windowsill.

"Surprise!" Carla shouted, making a sweeping motion around the room with her hand. Jesse noticed that on almost every surface of the room there were packages wrapped in brightly colored paper. He stood behind Marie, still holding the lasagna, trying to count the number of presents. He couldn't tally them up, but he knew there were too many.

It's Lizzie's night, Jesse kept telling himself. He could ask Carla where she got the money for the presents later.

"Mom, you remember Marie, right?" Carla sashayed over to Marie and gave her a hug.

"Of course, you're the girl from the shelter," Carla said.

"Nice to see you again," Marie said. Jesse was relieved that Marie was willing to hug his mom and act like things were normal, at least for tonight. Lizzie had tied one of the balloon bouquets to the back of a chair and was singing happy birthday under her breath.

"We're supposed to sing to you, Lizard," Jesse said, setting the lasagna on the counter. Marie put her purse on the floor and sat awkwardly on the edge of the open futon.

"Let's have cake and sing." Carla pointed to a fancy bakery box on the table. So she'd gotten cake, balloons, and at least a dozen presents. Jesse could feel a crawly sensation traveling up his back like a tick marching to its destination, ready to sink its pinchers and gorge.

"Marie brought a lasagna. We should eat some real food first," Jesse said.

"Let's sing, let's sing," Lizzie chanted, as she pulled the balloon strings, causing them to bob as if she were manipulating marionettes.

"Birthday girls get what they want," Carla said, with a high voice that Jesse thought was too saccharine sweet to be natural. He flopped on the futon where Marie still perched, trying to look relaxed. Jesse let out a long sigh and closed his eyes, wishing that not looking at Carla would somehow make her disappear.

"No sleeping, Jess!" Carla practically screamed. Jesse's eyes popped open and he looked at the ceiling. One stray balloon had slipped out of the bouquet and drifted into the tangle of dusty rafters. Jesse envied the solitary balloon's escape from the inevitable drama unfolding. His eyes were drawn to the loft and the once-tidy stack of boxes that were now tipped over, the contents scattered across the floor.

"Shit," he said, and sat up glaring at Carla, who was singing out of tune as she plunked candles into the expensive-looking cake.

"Jesse!" Carla snapped back, her eyes stabbing him with a hard glare.

"Why are those boxes knocked over?" Jesse pointed an accusing finger at the loft.

Carla was silent for a moment. Even Lizzie seemed to understand that their mother had crossed some forbidden boundary and tampered with something meant to stay out of reach.

"What'd you do, Mama?" Lizzie asked, staring at the overturned boxes and then back at her mother.

Carla shook her head and smoothed her hair. "I was just looking for something to read. I figured a college boy would have some good books."

"Damn it, Carla. That's not our stuff. You weren't even supposed to be here. They're only letting you stay because…"

"You know what," Marie interrupted, grabbing Jesse's arm. "That cake looks so good!" Marie squeezed Jesse's arm and gestured at Lizzie, whose eyes were spilling over with tears.

Jesse exhaled loudly. Marie's steady hold on him was bringing him back to his body. He gathered his rage and swallowed hard, knowing he'd let it all reignite later when he had Carla alone.

"Yeah, let's have cake." Jesse held out a hand to Lizzie and she walked to him slowly. The perfect evening Jesse had imagined was tainted, blotted by each present that Lizzie warily opened. As embarrassing as it was that Marie was witnessing their unraveling, he was grateful she was there to help them salvage something good and memorable from the ruined evening.

***

It was almost midnight by the time he walked Marie to her car. Lizzie and Carla had crashed out on the futon, but Marie had stayed to make tea and help Jesse replace the Pelsinski's son's things into the scattered boxes. Mostly they found class notes and textbooks, but at the back of the loft Marie found an empty guitar case leaning in the corner.

"I've kept you here too long. Are your parents going to freak out?" Jesse looked at his watch with concern.

"They're out of town for two days, but I texted them anyway, so it's fine."

Outside by Marie's car, Jesse said, "I'll go to the pawn shops tomorrow and see if I can find the guitar. I'm sure she sold it. There's no other way she could have bought all that stuff."

"What are you going to do about the Pelsinskis?" Marie asked.

"I'm going to tell them the truth."

Marie looked up at Jesse. It was dark, but he thought that her eyes looked glittery with tears.

"I'm sorry about today being so hard, Jesse."

Jesse winced and looked into the shadowed light of her eyes. "Every day is hard," he said, and tried to laugh, but it came out sounding more like a groan. "Thank you for making it better for me and Lizzie. If you hadn't been there..." He brushed her pale cheek with his rough hand. "Without you, it would have fallen apart."

Marie leaned towards him slightly, or at least Jesse imagined she did. He brushed his lips to hers. Marie let out a nearly inaudible gasp and he felt that sound travel like a tornado from her mouth to his pelvis. She kissed him back. They found themselves in the back seat of her car frantically pulling each other's clothes off, touching each freshly revealed part with awe and surprise.

Jesse started to pull at Marie's panties but she murmured, "We can't."

He fell on top of her and breathed into her neck and hair. She didn't smell of perfume, but like sun-dried laundry and evaporating dew. "I'm sorry," he whispered. "I got carried away."

"Me too." She laughed. "It's not like I'm not into it," she said, into his ear. "I'm just not prepared. I've never... done this."

Jesse leaned on his elbow so he could look at her in the darkness. "I want to do this right, with you," he said. "I don't want to mess things up. We can take things slow, as slow as you want."

"It's okay," she said, running her fingers through his hair. "You didn't mess anything up."

Jesse leaned down and kissed her forehead, then the tip of her nose and then gently and slowly, he kissed her open lips.

Chapter 11

JESSE meandered through a cluster of scratchy branches to
the crown of the tree. He knew he was unlikely to see the
yellow salamander there, but he couldn't fight the urge to reach
the top and look across the expanse of trees to the bay. It was
early Saturday morning, and he'd promised Pelsinski more photos
of the yellow salamander in its habitat. The birds were singing
almost frantically as he moved through the tree. They hopped
from branch to branch nibbling at the bark like it was an all-you-
can-eat breakfast buffet. Ironically, the bird frenzy made Jesse feel
calm. It was good to be back in the one place he could let go of
his worries. Even losing the shed didn't seem important from this
vantage point. The bird chatter, the lush blanket of treetops, and
the windless, glassy bay put a cheery lens on everything, including
his screwed-up life.

They'd been back at camp for two weeks and readapted to
living off the grid. Carla complained that the tent felt moldy
and wet after the luxury of the shed. Jesse almost wished they'd

never stayed in the shed; at least there'd be nothing to miss, and he wouldn't have to hear Carla's whining. Henry insisted that Jesse could sleep at the shed if he needed to, or stop by for a shower. But their son was moving back in a few weeks, and Jesse didn't want to be in anybody's way. He'd have to go to the shed at some point soon to pick up the box of Lizzie's birthday toys.

It took courage, but he'd walked across the yard to the house the morning after Lizzie's party and told them about his mom selling the guitar. Mrs. Pelsinski drove him to the pawnshop where Carla claimed to have gone. Jesse didn't have the two hundred dollars to buy the instrument back, so Mrs. Pelsinski fronted the money, which Jesse was paying back by tackling a long list of garden chores. He'd promised that Lizzie was living with Ellen; he'd even given them Ellen's number—praying that they wouldn't actually call.

***

There was a skittering noise, and Jesse thought he saw a glossy yellow smudge dart across the trunk of the tree. He'd never seen the salamanders up this high, but maybe they too had the urge to summit the conifer to see the variegated treetops leading down to town, and the mirror-sheen of the bay in the distance. Jesse doubted that the salamander would make itself so exposed to the spring convention of birds gathered in the sun-dappled tree. It was safer for the herps to linger in the damp shelter of the lower branches avoiding ending up as prey to some hungry predator. Jesse inhaled deeply, moving down through the shaded limbs, where he hoped to find the salamander and take the photos Pelsinski needed.

***

There hadn't been many opportunities to see Marie since the

night of Lizzie's birthday debacle. They went to different schools, and now that Jesse was back at camp, he felt too awkward to invite her over. She lived fifteen miles north of town, so he couldn't easily stop by her house after school. They had gone to one movie and spent so much of the film in a heated make-out session he couldn't even remember what the movie was about. She had dropped him off at the park after the film and tried to get him to take some of the leftovers she was carting around from the senior lunch.

"No," he'd insisted. "I'm a working man now. I can buy food."

"Yeah, but you don't have an oven, and I have mac and cheese that you can heat up in a pan."

"Actually," Jesse said, caressing her neck with his thumb. "I've been meaning to ask if I can make you dinner... in the shed one night this week." Marie looked a little stunned that he was bringing up the shed.

"The Pelsinskis' son is coming back soon, but before he does, I'd like to make you dinner. They've told me to stop by and use the place anytime. As long as I don't have, you know... my mom."

Marie put her hands on his. "I'd love to have dinner." Then her face turned serious. "But only if you take some mac and cheese."

Jesse laughed. "Deal." A part of him wanted to ask her to come up to camp and have tea or something. But the idea of subjecting Marie to more of Carla made him wary. There was no predicting what condition they'd find his mom in.

"I'd better go." Marie seemed to be reading his mind. "It's late and I have to be at school early tomorrow."

"Okay," he said, both disappointed and relieved. "So, Thursday, I'm making you dinner at the shed at around six?"

"Yes!" she said, "I'll bring..."

"Nothing," Jesse interrupted. "It's going to be my chance to feed you." He reached a hand into her hair and pulled her towards the passenger seat.

***

"Hey, you're here!" Henry was at the door of the shed. He peered in at Jesse, who was washing lettuce for a salad. Jesse jumped a little at his voice.

"Yeah, I had to pick up a box of stuff and you said I could come by before your son…"

"Of course, of course. He won't be here for another week. Make use of the place. Spend the night if you want."

"No, no. I'm just making dinner, and a friend with a car is coming to help me move this last box." Jesse pointed at the box of Lizzie's birthday toys by the door. Jesse couldn't help but wonder if Henry knew the expensive toys had been purchased with money from the guitar. The guitar was safely back in its case and stashed somewhere in the Pelsinski's house.

The Pelsinskis seemed to trust Jesse enough to use the shed, but he guessed they couldn't predict whether Carla might find her way back and sell the guitar all over again. As if he knew what Jesse was thinking, Henry asked, "How's your mom? Is she getting help?"

"Better." Jesse tore the lettuce into a bowl. It wasn't a complete lie. She'd been going to NA meetings since Lizzie's birthday ordeal. So far, things were okay. He could tell she hated that she'd ruined it for all of them.

"And Lizzie?" Pelsinski's eyebrow arched. "She's with your aunt?"

"Yeah, for now." Jesse lied. "Until I get another place."

"Damn, Jesse, I'm sorry this didn't work out. It's just with your mom, and my son returning, we…"

"It's not your fault. You gave us every opportunity, Dr. … Henry. And your son needs this place."

"Well, I'm still sorry. Have a good evening and stay as long as you like tonight, really. I'll see you at my office on Friday… I'll show you the first draft of the paper!"

He welcomed the change of topic from his mom. "Great, I'm excited to read it."

"I don't want you just to read it. I'm counting on you for your expertise, to give the paper a real detailed look with the eyes of a co-author."

"I'll try." Jesse smiled to himself. The idea that Pelsinski trusted him to make recommendations on a professional paper baffled him.

Suddenly, Marie was standing awkwardly behind Pelsinski at the door.

"Marie! Hi." Pelsinski turned and ushered her inside.

"I'd better be going. Please, stay as long as you'd like." He closed the shed door behind him as he left.

Marie giggled. "Sorry, if I interrupted."

"Never." Jesse pulled her into an embrace. "How are you?"

"Good now," Marie whispered into his neck.

"Me too." He'd relaxed as soon as she walked into the shed. Her presence made him feel comfortable and safe. He wondered if this was what it was like to feel truly at home.

Making dinner turned into a group effort, as much as he tried to get her to sit down and watch.

"I want to help," she complained, and appeared at the counter to chop an onion and stir the ravioli. He finally gave in and let her assist. Marie set down the spoon she'd been stirring the ravioli with and wrapped her arms around Jesse's waist.

"Hey, no distracting the chef," Jesse said, and he meant it. The air between them was already so charged with attraction molecules that he wasn't sure he would be able to pull off this dinner thing at all. He'd promised her they'd take things slow, but he needed to remind himself of that constantly. He said it to himself over and over: *go slow, go slow*. It wasn't easy staying focused on the mantra with Marie leaning against his back, her arms wrapped around his torso, caressing his chest.

"I'm seriously losing my concentration here," he said.

"Me too," she said softly.

"Well, if I'm gonna get this done, you're going to have to sit down. If you keep doing what you're doing there will be no dinner." Marie laughed, but it wasn't her normal laugh. She sounded husky and far away, which was kind of how he felt.

"Let's have dinner later, after…" she said, moving her hands lower onto his stomach. He turned off both burners and turned around to face her.

"After what?" he asked, in an equally far-away voice.

"I have a surprise for you," she said, and started to pull his T-shirt up so her warm hands were touching his stomach.

"What kind of surprise?" he asked, and inhaled.

"I went to the clinic last week," she volunteered, "and we're, uh, good to go, if you know what I mean."

He knew what she meant, but he froze at the thought of the clinic and the image of another girl having to go there alone in order to have sex with him.

"You should have told me." He put his hands on her hips. "I would have gone with you."

Marie smiled up at Jesse. "Really?" she asked, shyly. "Raya told me you weren't too into going there."

Jesse shivered involuntarily at the memory of being at the clinic with Raya. Or maybe it was the idea of Raya and Marie comparing notes. Either way, his heightened hormone levels suddenly plummeted. He didn't want to think about what else Raya and Marie had talked about. He had almost let himself forget that they were friends: really, really good friends.

He turned away from Marie and relit the burner under the sauce. He took the ravioli pot to the sink and drained off the water. The ravioli were mushy and over-cooked, but he divided them into two bowls, then watched out of the corner of his eye as Marie took the wooden spoon and stirred the sauce.

"We haven't had some big talk about you if that's what you're thinking. It was when I brought her to you that day at your tent. She told me how stressed you were about going into the clinic. That's all. I just didn't want to put you through that."

Jesse poured red sauce over the ravioli and sprinkled Parmesan cheese from a foil packet he'd picked up at the pizza place. "Really?"

"Really." Marie said, and placed a tentative hand on his back. "I mean, we've had a couple of conversations, and I told her that we are hanging out."

Jesse set the saucepan on the burner. "How did that go over?" he mumbled.

Marie took a fork, stabbed one of the ravioli and held it up to Jesse's mouth. "She kind of likes Eli, a boy we went to elementary school with. It's gonna be awkward for a while, but I think it'll be okay."

"Yeah," Jesse said and exhaled. It was a relief to have Raya out in the open. He hadn't realized how worried he'd been about it. Mostly he didn't want to ruin Marie and Raya's friendship. He opened his mouth and let Marie feed him the over-cooked ravioli. "Thanks," he said, his mouth still full. "For everything."

***

The birds were beginning their morning concert. Dapples of tree-shadow light made designs on the canvas of the sidewalk. It was early and Jesse jogged leisurely towards camp. He smiled as he ran through town towards the forest. *Everything is beautiful,* he thought: *the birds, the shadowy light, the softness of the spring air, and most of all, Marie.*

They'd woken up less than an hour ago in each other's arms. He thought Marie looked gorgeous sprawled on the futon with her disheveled hair and sleep-creased face.

"Is it okay that you stayed over?" he asked, suddenly remembering that she had parents who expected her home at night.

"It's fine," she said, running her fingers over his arm. "I texted my mom last night and told her I was staying at a friend's house. She lets me do that pretty often... to avoid the drive."

"I'm glad," he said, pulling her on top of him, thinking maybe they had time to reenact the evening all over again before school. Then he remembered that he needed to get to camp early so he could get his sister to school on time.

***

It was blissful jogging through town, letting the memories of making love to Marie replay in his mind. He'd taken it slow and used some of the techniques he'd read about in the book at Raya's house. Marie had even said she was excited to make love again soon. She said she'd heard it only got better after the first time. She seemed happy to let him caress and kiss her ankles, knees and the soft roundness of her hips. It may not have been perfect, but he'd done something right.

He admired rhododendrons and their blooms, in vibrant shades of pink and fuchsia, but they were no competition for the images of Marie's pale skin spread across the futon sheets. There were bloodstains that he'd have to wash out of the sheet he'd borrowed from a box in the shed. It didn't matter; he knew how to get blood out of fabric. Carla often ended up with blood on her clothing from falling. Pouring cheap peroxide from the Dollar Store on red stains before doing the laundry had become a habit.

Suddenly, he remembered Lizzie's box of toys that still sat waiting at the shed. He needed to go back there later and tidy up anyway. It would be easy enough to carry the box up to Ben's stump and store the toys there until Lizzie got bored with the things she had at camp.

A warm feeling wrapped around him as he thought about where he and Marie might make love next. The shed would be unavailable, but Jesse imagined a nest of blankets in a secret part of the forest where no one would come across them or hear their soft moans.

He reached the park with no recollection of having run up the tree-lined road from the edge of town. *This love thing is powerful,* he thought, as he started up the narrow trail to the woods. It was like living in a cloud hovering a few feet above the ground. He smiled, remembering Marie's smooth skin and luminous eyes. He knew she'd felt some pain, but he could tell there was something she'd enjoyed beyond the intimacy of their lovemaking, something purely physical.

A lone jay squawked in the high branches of a nearby tree; otherwise it was quiet when he reached camp. Lizzie and his mom were still asleep in the tent. It was early enough that he had time to start a small fire for tea and oatmeal. He gathered some thin, dry branches and was leaning over the fire pit, blowing lightly to coax the flame with his breath, when he heard Lizzie call from the tent.

"Jess?"

"Yeah, Lizard, I'm making a fire. Be right there." He added a few more dry sticks to the small blaze. "Do you need clean clothes from under the tarp?" Jesse unzipped the tent and leaned his head in. Lizzie was curled in the curve of their mother's body with Carla's arm flung over her. Jesse had a sudden flash of Ben's arm slung over Emma. He shook his head to flick the image away.

"Come on, Liz, we gotta get you dressed and go," he whispered. Getting Lizzie ready in the morning was easier without Carla's help. He was hoping his mom would just roll over and stay asleep.

"I'm cold, Jess," Lizzie complained, crawling out from under Carla's arm. "Mama's cold." Carla's arm fell to the tent floor with a thud. Jesse glanced at his mother, searching for an explanation for the odd noise and awkward position of her body.

"Cold." Jesse said aloud. He pushed his way into the tent and knelt over Carla.

"But your shoes, Jess!" Lizzie said.

"Go add some sticks to the fire," he snapped.

"You shoulda taken off your shoes," Lizzie whispered loudly as she crawled out. Jesse put a hand on Carla's wrist and let out an involuntary hiss at the rubbery sensation of her skin. She wasn't exactly cold but she wasn't warm either. He pushed the hair out of her face and saw that the color of her skin was wrong.

"Shit, Mom!" he said aloud. "What the hell have you done?" He put two fingers on her neck feeling for a pulse, but her cool clammy skin showed no sign of life. Deep down he knew that he was too late. He put his hands on her stiffening shoulders and shook her lightly like there was some chance of waking her.

"Damn it, Mom!" he cried out.

"What, Jess?" Lizzie was climbing back into the tent, wearing her shoes. Jesse looked at his sister as she stared at their mother's grey face and slack open mouth. Jesse could tell that Lizzie saw something had gone very wrong.

"Is Mama sick?" Lizzie asked. Her shaky voice was more grown-up than Jesse had ever heard.

"No, Liz," Jesse wrapped his sister in his arms, wishing he could whisk her away from this soggy tent and any memory of waking up in her dead mother's arms. "She's not ever going to get sick again."

***

Ellen tried to hand Jesse a cup of tea, but he shook his head.

"Take it," Ellen ordered. He reached reluctantly for the warm cup. He couldn't help but wonder if putting the cup in his mother's cold hands could somehow revive her as well. Lizzie was next to him on Ellen's couch, sleeping. When Lizzie realized that Carla was dead, she had collapsed sobbing on top of her mother, pleading with her to "Wake up!" Jesse couldn't leave Lizzie alone at camp while he went for help, so he had carried his sister kicking and screaming to Ellen's house. There, Lizzie collapsed into a shuddering sleep. Jesse hadn't even cared when he saw that his uncle's rig was parked in front of the house. Lizzie's screams were enough to get the whole neighborhood to open their doors. Jesse's uncle was on the front porch when they reached the house.

"Get inside," Frank said. He seemed to want to avoid making a scene in front of all the neighbors. "What the hell's going on?" he asked when they were inside.

"Where's Ellen?" Jesse yelled over Lizzie's sobbing.

"She's at work," Frank yelled back. "What's wrong with Lizzie?" Frank actually looked concerned now, like Lizzie might be sick.

Jesse could feel the prickle of unwanted tears as they seeped from his eyes. "My mom," he said, and let out a guttural sob. He hadn't cried in the tent, but now he felt a big lump of pain inside his chest that was going to spill out of him whether he wanted it to or not. Frank reached for Lizzie, whose sobs were retreating as she fell back into shocked sleep. Frank laid her on the couch, propping a pillow under her head and draping a blanket over her small body.

"Sit down." Frank pointed at the space next to Lizzie on the couch.

"I can't," Jesse sobbed, putting his hands on his knees to hold himself up. Frank surprised Jesse by pulling him up into an embrace.

"It's okay, tell me what's going on with your mom."

Another low moan leaked out of Jesse. "She's gone… dead," Jesse said, letting Frank hold him up as he cried.

Ellen arrived half an hour later, looking stunned, but ready to take charge. Frank had called the police and was headed up to the park to lead them to Carla. Jesse argued that they could just bury her in the forest, but Frank said Jesse needed to draw a map revealing the location of camp and leave the other details to him and Ellen.

"Drink the tea, it'll help," Ellen insisted.

His throat was swollen and raw from crying. But crying was better than the image of Carla's dead body flashing in and out of his mind. The rush of love and warmth he'd experienced on his way to camp that morning was like a faraway dream. That warm feeling had been completely stamped out by the dread he felt when he looked at Lizzie sleeping next to him. Jesse didn't want her to wake up and have to face their mother's death all over again. It was his fault, he was sure of that. He should never have left Carla alone; if he'd been there he would have noticed her taking something. He could have stopped her.

"Jesse," Ellen interrupted his thoughts. "I don't want you taking this all on yourself." She knelt on the floor next to him. She must have seen that his mind was far away. She put her hands on his knees as if to bring him back from the edge of some cliff he was planning to plunge off.

"It's not your fault," she said sternly, looking into his eyes.

He exhaled and the big pain built inside him again. It would overflow soon and there was nothing he could do about it.

Chapter 12

W E'RE almost there," Marie said. Jesse followed Marie and
Ellen up a narrow dirt path that wound around one of the
tall sea stacks dotting the shoreline. Lizzie had been on his back
since they reached the first big hill. She'd broken down crying,
saying she wanted Mama. It had been like that all week. Ellen
contacted the school and had arranged for Jesse and Lizzie to
be on independent study for the last month of the school year.
Ellen didn't think Lizzie was stable enough to go to school.
Jesse thought school would be a good distraction for him, but
he sensed that Lizzie needed him around to adjust to their life
without Carla.

The path was bordered on either side by huckleberry bushes
and what Jesse recognized as low stalks of poison oak. As the
trail became steeper, they had to navigate over and around small
boulders in the path.

"This is it!" Marie said, encouraging them with a wave.
Lizzie had been quiet for a while and the weight of her body on

his back had changed from shifting and restless to slack. Jesse suspected that she'd fallen asleep, and he hated to stop and wake her. During the past week he'd seen her wake up happy and comfortable in the bed at Ellen's house. Then, slowly, creases would form on the soft skin of her forehead, and he could see her remembering that Carla was gone. Jesse, too, woke up disoriented every day, confused to be in a warm dry bed with the smell of coffee and toast drifting in from the kitchen.

It was crazy that he missed Carla. He should be relieved, glad even, that the burden had been lifted. Instead, he kept imagining scenarios where things turned out differently, and Carla was alive. Most of the scenarios included him coming back to camp early and making Lizzie and Carla hot dogs or some other favorite meal. That last afternoon, he had warned his mom that he'd be home late. Carla had made the effort to stand up and reach out to him for a hug. He had hesitated at first, not wanting to inhale the sour smell of her skin or give in to her roller-coaster need for attention. He was grateful now that something in him had buckled momentarily as he allowed her to wrap her arms around him tightly, almost manically, for the last time. He had never intended to spend the night in the shed. Waking up with his body intertwined with Marie's had been a happy surprise. It wasn't that he regretted making love to Marie, but he wished it had happened some other time: a time when Carla didn't have the means to kill herself.

Jesse climbed up the last boulder on the trail and stood between Marie and Ellen with Lizzie still slumped on his back. They had popped out of thick shrubs to an open outcrop, dropping off on two sides to tumbling waves sweeping in and bouncing off the nearly vertical cliff.

"It feels like the edge of the world," Ellen said.

There was a lone wooden bench bolted to the rocky vista with stones and mortar. The backrest was carved with intricately whittled flowers curling in and around a woman's name. *This is the place people come to say goodbye,* Jesse thought. Gently, he pulled

Lizzie off his back and laid her on the bench. Marie took her sweatshirt from around her waist and tucked it under Lizzie's small head. Lizzie's eyes blinked open and then shut quickly; she opted for the comfort of sleep rather than the sound of wind and the battering slap of waves.

A solitary pelican flew overhead and then dropped, revealing its pterodactyl-like silhouette. Ellen took off her backpack and pulled out a flower-patterned cardboard tube.

"She liked violets when we were kids," Ellen said, as if she needed to defend the décor she'd chosen for her sister's ashes.

"She still does... or did," Jesse said, remembering a rare, lucid walk in the woods with Carla. She'd pointed out a patch of wild violets growing in the damp shade of a hollowed-out stump.

"How should we do this?" Jesse asked, suddenly unsure of releasing what was left of his mother's body.

"Let's just reach into the tube, take a handful, and let it go in the wind," Ellen said. Jesse hesitated, so Ellen reached into the tube for the first handful. It surprised him to see the ash lift and spread into a sail-like pattern when Ellen let it go. He had pictured the white dust falling uneventfully down past the cliff to the chaotic waves. Jesse tried not to think about the ash being his mother's body as he reached into the tube. But when he threw the ash out to the wind and it caught the air like sea spray hanging momentarily suspended, he found he couldn't help feeling that some piece of Carla, some essence of her, was nearby.

He was crying now, and it felt right; his sobs matched the rhythm of the waves slamming against the cliff. Lizzie was waking up and Marie sat next to her, smoothing Lizzie's hair.

"Where's Mama?" Lizzie asked, through her sleep haze. It had become her standard question upon waking. It took her at least fifteen minutes to sort it out each time she woke up. And once she put the pieces together she would start with a fresh bout of tears.

"Come here, Liz." Jesse held out a hand, and Lizzie walked

sluggishly to him, leaning against his hip. "Take a handful," he said, tipping the violet tube toward her. Lizzie reached in with her small fist and then Jesse followed, taking another handful of the crumbly ash. "Now throw it over the cliff." Jesse swung his arm hard and Lizzie mimicked him, waving her arm in an arc before releasing the ash.

"They look like fans," Lizzie blurted with delight. Ellen laughed, her eyes filling with tears.

"You're right, Liz, like fans," Jesse said.

"Fans made of lace," she added, watching the spray of ash dissipate as it dispersed into the air and ultimately joined the churning water below.

Jesse took Lizzie's hand and said, "That's where Mama is, she's right there where you saw the lace; she's free now, getting a fresh start out here."

"She's not sick anymore." Lizzie said, still looking at the place in the air where the ash had hovered.

***

"Lizzie and I are going clothes shopping. I wish you'd come with us and pick out a few things." Ellen was standing at the front door with Lizzie.

"Nah, I'm fine." Jesse and Marie were sitting on the couch doing homework. The independent study work was easy; he could finish a whole day's work in a couple of hours.

"Well, I'm going to get you new underwear and socks," Ellen insisted, taking her keys from the hook by the door.

"Have fun, Lizard," Jesse said, "and don't be greedy!"

"Ellen says I get one toy…" Lizzie looked concerned. "That's not greedy, is it?"

"That's fine, but say 'thank you'."

"Enough etiquette from your brother, let's go." Ellen and Lizzie shuffled out the door.

Jesse swung around, lying on the couch with his head in

Marie's lap. Marie laughed and rested the book she'd been review-ing for English on top of his face. Jesse turned on his side so his face was nuzzling her stomach.

"How're you doing there, Buddy," Marie asked, setting her book on the floor.

"Couldn't be better," Jesse said, snuggling into Marie's warm lap.

"I mean really. How are you holding up? I know you prob-ably keep wondering how you could have changed things. I feel bad too, you know, that we fell asleep in the shed that night."

Jesse let out a long sigh, "Yeah, I run through scenarios, but it doesn't seem to change anything."

"I just want you to know that I understand if you're feeling bad about what we did. It feels selfish now, that we were making love while your mom…"

"Stop, really. I've gone over this dozens of times in the past couple of weeks. My mom could have died any night. She could have overdosed with me in the tent right next to her. I don't think I could have stopped this from happening." He almost laughed, as he heard himself lecture Marie. He was repeating what Ellen and Frank had been saying to him every day since Carla's death.

Marie ran her fingers through Jesse's clean hair. Jesse guessed that there probably wasn't a trace of the campfire smell that had lingered there in the past. Ellen had washed all of their clothes, and Jesse took showers, sometimes twice a day, just because he could.

"Look," he said, stroking her bare arm. "We both have a bad association with that night. I think we need to make a new memory, one with no guilt or anything to do with my mom." He rolled onto his back, and stared up at Marie.

"No one's here," Marie said.

"Nope," Jesse grinned. "No one's here."

＊＊＊

A knock on the front door woke Jesse from a heavy sleep. Marie was snuggled against him on the bed. The window revealed that the bright cloudless day had turned damp and grey. Toby was barking, working himself into a frenzy.

The knocking persisted. "Be right there!" Jesse stood up and was glad to find that his pants, though unzipped, were still on. He and Marie had made love, but it was quick and urgent with their clothes half-on. He wasn't sure if their urgency was because of the stress of potentially being walked in on or because of the two-week hiatus since they'd made love in the shed. Jesse motioned for Marie to go back to sleep and he pulled a T-shirt on as he walked to the door.

"Hey, I tracked you down." Henry stood on the porch, his forehead creased with concern.

"Come in." Jesse ushered him into the living room. Toby sniffed at Henry's pant legs and, finding nothing of interest, padded back to his bed by the wood stove. "Would you like something to drink? Tea? Juice? My uncle might have a beer in the fridge." Jesse felt odd offering Ellen and Frank's beverages, but he knew he'd get a lecture from his aunt if she came home to an unattended guest.

"No, I'm fine. So, this is your aunt's place?" Henry asked, looking around the small living room. Jesse guessed that through Henry's eyes it wasn't anything grand, but Jesse thought the house was pretty spectacular.

"Yeah." Jesse looked around nervously. "Sorry I haven't been able to come to work."

"No apologies. I got your message. I'm really sorry about your mom. Take as long as you need. Come back this summer sometime. You know the routine; you have the key to the office." Henry sat on the couch and Jesse sat in the chair across from him.

"I really just wanted to check in on you and to give you this." Henry handed Jesse a manila folder. "It's a copy of the paper." A small smile crept across the professor's face.

Jesse looked at Henry and slid the paper out of the envelope. It wasn't very thick, but then again, how much could you say about the little yellow critters?

"Check out the authors," Pelsinski said, impatiently. Jesse looked at the cover page, and there below the title were the names Henry Pelsinski, PhD, and Jesse Glen: coauthors.

"Wow!" Jesse leafed through the thin pages of the paper. There was a big section called Behavior and Natural History, which included a paragraph reading:

They are also distinguished by their naso-labial grooves, vertical slits between the nostrils and upper lip that are lined with glands used in chemoreception.

Jesse wasn't sure he could have pulled off something like this and he cringed a little that his name was on the paper.

"Look, this paper couldn't have been written without you." Pelsinski seemed to guess what he was thinking. "I don't know how long it might have been before someone found that salamander. You deserve this title. Really."

"Well thanks, Henry. I'm flattered."

"And there's something else I want to talk to you about. I put your name in for a scholarship at the university." Pelsinski locked eyes with Jesse. "We had our faculty meeting and reviewed the applicants for our annual biology scholarship. We usually give just one big scholarship a year, but this time we decided to give out two. I know you didn't officially apply, but if you'll accept the scholarship, we'd like to have you at the school in the biology department this fall."

Jesse hadn't decided if he was going to college. When his mom was still alive, he'd been planning to find a full-time job. "I haven't thought about it. But thank you, that's an amazing offer."

"It's a full ride, Jesse. This is the whole package, tuition, dorm, books, meals, and of course you can keep working for me when you have time."

Jesse couldn't quite believe what he was hearing. He'd gone from being homeless to having a room in Ellen's house and the offer of a free ride to college. "Can I talk to my aunt and uncle about it?" he asked. He didn't really know what there was to talk about. He knew he'd be crazy to turn this down. Still, talking things over with Ellen and Frank sounded like the right thing to do. It was what a normal kid would do with his parents. He at least wanted to talk to Ellen about it. He still felt like Frank thought of him as an extension of Carla, as if Jesse might suddenly transform into the teenage boy version of his mother.

"Of course," Henry said, standing up. "Take a few days to think it over. But I want you to know that we're offering this to you because we think you deserve it." Henry put his hand on Jesse's shoulder. "You're an exceptional young man. This isn't some pity offer."

Jesse walked Henry to the door. The professor turned to Jesse before leaving. "I didn't know your mom that well, but even with her limitations, I think she would have encouraged you to take this offer."

It didn't seem fair for Henry to be bringing up his mom, but the professor was probably right about her. She may have been selfish and vexed by addiction, but she'd cared about him and Lizzie. She just hadn't had the ability to show it.

***

"Congratulations." Marie was standing in the doorway to his bedroom. She'd put her pants back on but her shirt was still unbuttoned to her navel, and Jesse wasn't sure she had noticed. He smiled and walked over to her.

"Thanks," he said, buttoning her shirt. "I don't want you getting caught with your shirt open," he said.

"And I don't want you getting caught with your fly down," she said.

"Did I just have that whole conversation with Pelsinski with my fly down?" Jesse asked, looking down, mortified.

"No, I'm messing with you, Mr. Scholarship."

"You scared me!" he said, pulling her to him.

"But that's huge, what he just offered you. I hope you realize that."

Jesse nodded. "I just haven't been thinking along those lines. I was planning on getting a job and saving up for an apartment."

"Well, rethink things. Lizzie is great here with Ellen and Frank. Pelsinski is offering you tuition, a dorm, the whole college experience."

"And you?" Jesse said. "You're going to Bard for sure?"

"Yeah, I guess. It's a lot of money that my parents don't have, but I love the idea. I've wanted to go there forever. The campus looks beautiful online, and it's got a good public health program."

"And the students?" Jesse asked, "Are they cool like you?"

Marie laughed. "I haven't actually been able to visit in person. We don't have enough money for me to jet back and forth. But I think I'll like the school and the kids."

"When do you go? I've been afraid to ask…"

"I'm supposed to leave at the beginning of July. I'm working at my cousin's deli this summer in New York to earn some money."

"So you leave in a month," he said, pulling her closer.

"Yeah," she laid her head on his shoulder. "I can't quite believe it, but I guess so."

Chapter 13

THE tree limbs squeaked as they rubbed against one another; sounding like high-pitched voices. Jesse closed his eyes and imagined it was his mom or Ben trying to talk to him from somewhere beyond the forest. He had laid a tarp on the ground in the vicinity of their old camp. It was his last day before moving into the dorm, and he'd explained to Ellen that he needed a night in the forest. He hadn't expected to sleep where their camp used to be, but when he came down the trail from climbing the big tree, he naturally headed to their old place.

It was dark now as he lay in his sleeping bag. He'd made a small fire and roasted a hot dog before climbing into his bag. It wasn't the same without Lizzie or his mom. It seemed crazy to be missing Carla, but he found he couldn't help but filter out the bad stuff about his mom, even though there was a lot of it. The brain was a funny organ: hell-bent on seeing the bright side of even the most screwed-up situation.

The branches continued to converse and creak overhead as

he thought about his ascent up the big tree earlier in the evening. He had climbed quickly to the top as he always did, wanting to see the view and the sun setting into the thick bank of fog.

Jesse had carried the last of Carla's ashes with him to the top of the tree. As the sun dropped into the fog and turned the sky the color of apricots, Jesse threw out the last handful of his mother's ash into the fruit-tinted night. He wished Lizzie were with him to see how the colored fan of ash stretched out like a hologram before dispersing into the tree canopy below.

***

Jesse's roommate had already tacked photos and posters onto the wall; Jesse's own wall looked naked in comparison. He'd never had a place to post things in a semi-permanent way. He thought about bringing in one of the eight-by-ten photos of the yellow salamander Pelsinski had offered him. He'd get someone to take a picture of him with Lizzie and Marie as soon as Marie came home for the winter break. He wondered if anyone had ever taken a picture of him with his mom. Maybe during the holidays at one of the church shelters, someone might have taken a picture of them standing next to the Christmas tree.

"These beds suck," the roommate said, rolling over, trying to get comfortable. Jesse thought about Lizzie asleep in her bed at Ellen's house.

"It's too soft," the roommate complained.

Jesse had slept in lots of places that were too hard, but he'd never thought about a bed being too soft. "Mine's perfect," Jesse said, and closed his eyes.

He let himself drift, imagining a canopy of tree limbs clustered for easy climbing. He went up, up, all the way to the narrow, spindly crown, where he could see over the green swath of trees to the ocean, across the world, and beyond.

Acknowledgments

Heartfelt thanks to Kyle Morgan, Amanda Alster, Sarah Godlin, Cheryl Conner, Maximilian Heirich and the team at Humboldt University Press for their enthusiasm, patience, and support, and to Sarah Whorf for literally carving out a beautiful cover for *Far Less*.

Writing opens the door to a community of writers. Thanks to James Hall and everyone who took his class at the Mendocino Writer's Conference in 2016; to authors Julia Park Tracey and Peter Brown Hoffmeister for giving me an invaluable infusion of feedback and enthusiasm; and special thanks to Nora Keker.

I look forward to my bi-monthly writer's group the way I look forward to tea in the morning—I can't get enough of either. Without the insight, edits, backpack full of commas, deadlines, and unending support, there would be no *Far Less*. Love and gratitude to Amy Barnes, Dave Holper, Kristin Kirby, our beloved Darlene Marlow, Lelia Moskowitz, Julie Sylvia, Janine Volkmar, and Janine Woolfson. The Janines proofread and edited the final drafts. I have to add an extra heap of special thanks to Lelia Moskowitz, my longest and most treasured writing companion.

This story is set in a landscape I know intimately, in both its beauty and its tribulations. I have drawn on both as resources.

Many of the situations in the story are inspired by circumstances I observed when accompanying my daughter Elena to volunteer with Maureen Chase, who works with the homeless in a variety of capacities. The remarkable champion of this urgent cause in our community is Betty Chinn of the Betty Kwan Chinn Homeless Foundation.

Jeremy Pelsinski, a local herpetologist, invented a salamander that would plausibly exist in the redwood forest but that had not yet been discovered. David Fix introduced me to a plethora of birds that I could legitimately use to decorate the forest in *Far Less*.

Far Less is also about family. How could I question magic when the two most fantastic and mythical characters I know are my very own children, Larkin and Elena O'Shea? Watching them climb trees, make campfires, love dogs, summit mountains barefoot, help people, and generally shine love wherever they go is all the inspiration anyone could ask for. They will always be my favorite characters. Particular thanks to Danny O'Shea for helping to create these enchanting individuals.

Thanks to Jackie Wollenberg for the unconditional love only a mama can provide, and to Art Morley for supporting and loving Jackie. Everyone should have an Uncle Chuck (Charles Wollenberg). Thanks Chuck, for being there for the long haul.

Many people read the manuscript and offered valuable editorial input, insights and feedback: Mike Wollenberg was one of the readers who frightened me the most and whose opinions of books I truly respect; Steve Wollenberg brought his integrity and calm demeanor to bear; declaring herself a fan of *Far Less* from its earliest version, my sister-in-law, Jenny Bloomfield, gave me confidence that the story needed to be heard; my niece, Leah Wollenberg, and Isaac Mirzadegan, my nephew "one lake removed," worked together to transform my query letters and offered thoughtful, poignant, thorough edits of the manuscript. I am also grateful to my sister-in-law, Susan Wollenberg, and my niece, Mira Wollenberg, for kitchen table therapy, and to dear cousin Jan Waldman Brown for prodding me along in all aspects of my life. A heaping harvest of gratitude to Kelly Valentine for her uncanny insight and enthusiasm, and to Mary Shea for her undeterred love and support.

My tribe of girlfriends, like a pack of unrelated sisters and daughters, give me unconditional love, constant support, and companionship. Thank you Madelin Amir, Holly and Hana Busse, Patty and Indigo Davis, Kat Fashinell, Dana Ferguson, Cory and Eva Fisher, Susan (Buddy!), Kayla, and Dani Gloisten, Denise Javet, Angelina Kavanaugh, Sarah Knox, Teresa Kostiew, Carolyn and Maggie Lyman, Kathleen and Lotus Nunley Monahan, Lisa Murphy, Stacy, Jordi, and Ellie Howard Oliver, Carole and Emily Ontiveros, Keta Paulson, Darcy Robins, Colleen Runyan, Amy and Emma Valentine.

Thanks to all the other friends and family who took the time to read *Far Less* and make valuable suggestions: Jasper Amir, Bella Anderson, Russell Bartley, Sylvia Bartley, Betsy Bogue, Tim Breed, Cynthia Frank, Margaret Grosse, Carol and Mike Hodge, Suren Holbek (for acting on his dreams), Ron Joliffe, Alicia and Maria Kerlee, Marjie and Dick Kiselhorst, Gin Kremen, Cedar Lay, Grant Lay, Eve Lubowe, Toni Lyman, Celia McCormick, Pete Monahan, Julian Monahan, Sachi and Stewart Moskowitz, Tom Pexton, Mark Safron, Carol Wollenberg, Keith Wollenberg, and anyone I've forgotten!

And finally, boundless love to Myla, Wolly, and all of the ghost dogs for leading me through forest trails and up mountain ridges. Adventures with these rascal hounds never cease to fortify.

Made in the USA
Las Vegas, NV
04 March 2023

68527504R10132